END OF THE LINE

A GOTHIKA NOVEL

TONY FUENTES & C.S. KADING

SANDDANCER PUBLICATIONS

Edited by Finley Hislop

Book Cover by Etheric Tales

Illustrations by Etheric Tales

First edition 2024

For anyone who was told you that you "Can't" or "Shouldn't"
be yourself...
Be more of your true self and never look back.

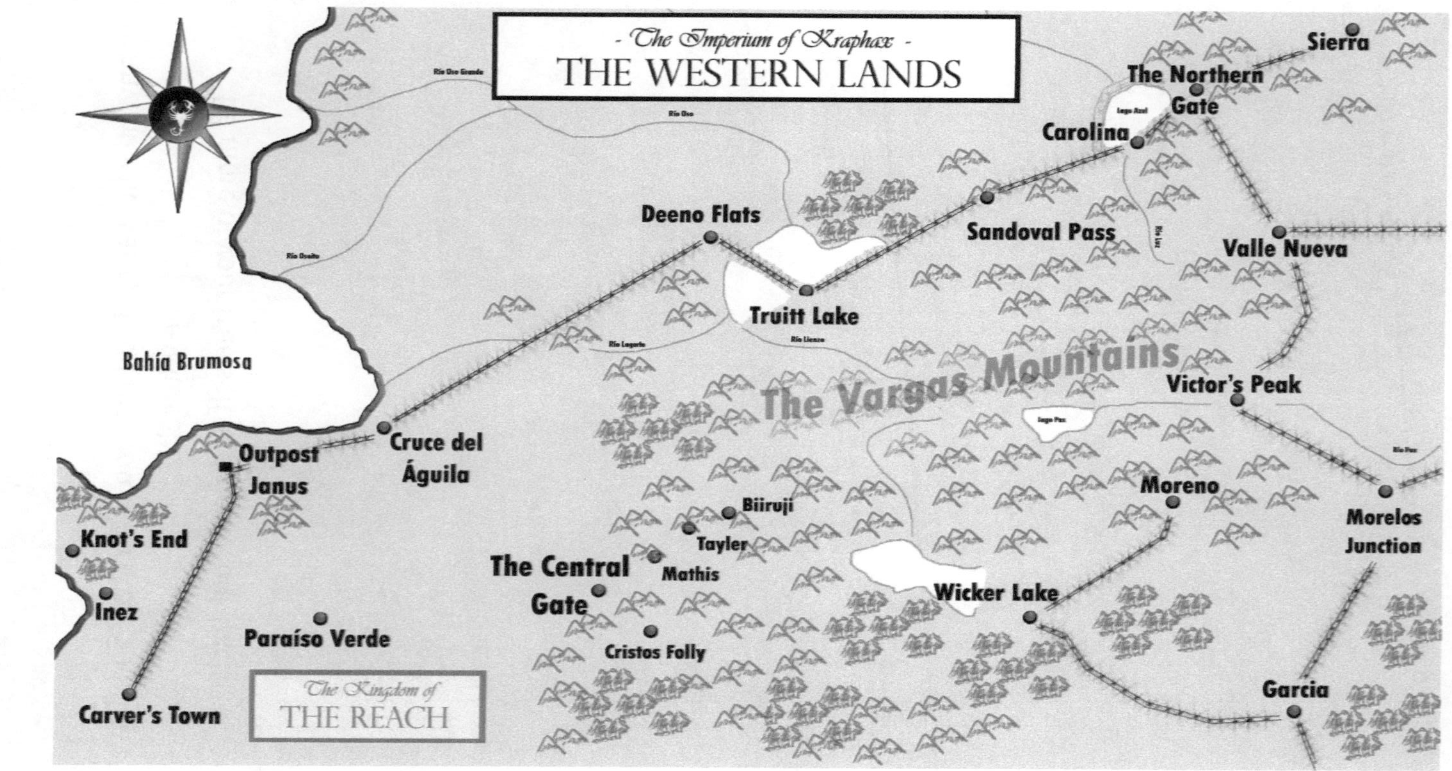
- The Imperium of Kraphax -
THE WESTERN LANDS
The Kingdom of THE REACH
Bahía Brumosa
Río Oso Grande
Río Oso
Río Osaita
Río Lagarto
Río Lienzo
Río Luz
Río Paz
Lago Azul
Lago Paz
The Vargas Mountains
Sierra
The Northern Gate
Carolina
Deeno Flats
Sandoval Pass
Valle Nueva
Truitt Lake
Victor's Peak
Cruce del Águila
Outpost
Janus
Biiruji
Moreno
Morelos Junction
Knot's End
Tayler
The Central Gate
Mathis
Wicker Lake
Inez
Paraíso Verde
Cristos Folly
Carver's Town
Garcia

CONTENTS

KIDNAPPED

"**G**od's breath, Emilio, I can't hold it much longer!" she yelled.

The creature convulsed violently, attempting to shake Marisol off. She clenched her teeth and clung tighter to one of its impossibly long limbs, cloaked within a swirling vortex of palpable darkness. The creature had shed all remnants of its once-human appearance. If Marisol's heart still pulsed with the warmth of life, it would have quickened at the horrific sight unfolding before her.

This tainted soul bore an unsettling resemblance to spectres that had eternally invoked forgotten fears, the kind that haunted every child's nightmares. It embodied a profound, primordial dread—a darkness that defied understanding.

Fantasma, a specter of unfathomable malevolence classified by Emilio as *El Cucuy*.

They had to contain it.

"Hang on, Mari!" Emilio's voice echoed through the eerie stillness as he meticulously drove white oak stakes deep into the tainted earth. His skilled hands etched intricate glyphs onto the natural canvas below. A vile green slime cloaked the ground beneath him and seemed to seep into his skin. He worked with a sense of urgency, aware that Marisol was desperately struggling to prevent the *Fantasma's* escape.

A sudden cry of surprise pierced the air behind him. Whirling around, Emilio watched in dread as *El Cucuy* took hold of Marisol's leg. Marisol swore sharply, though it was abruptly cut short as the creature flung her violently into the wall. The impact left her gasping for breath.

But Marisol was no longer counted among the living. The limitations of the physical world should not affect Marisol. She was an unfettered spirit, the ghost of the late Queen Marisol Failla. Emilio had rescued her from being bound to a questionable fate and a doppelgänger that had stolen her likeness. She was no longer part of the material world. If she could be slammed into the wall, it could only mean that the building was now an extension of the Fantasma!

Recoiling in shock, Emilio watched as the entity struck her again, hurtling Marisol through the open front door.

"Marisol!" he cried as she disappeared outside. Turning back, he could feel his heart pounding as malevolent yellow eyes locked onto him from the abyssal darkness. In that fleeting moment, a tense silence hung in the air as he tried to hold his ground against the sinister Fantasma.

He caught a flicker of movement at the edge of his vision too late.

Swiftly shifting his gaze to the left, Emilio could only brace himself for the Fantasma's writhing limb as it descended upon him with brutal force. The impact struck his chest like a battering ram, expelling every ounce of air from his lungs in a painful rush. The sheer force of the strike sent him hurtling back through the doorway and crashing into the unforgiving earth beyond.

For a breathless moment, Emilio lay sprawled on the ground, his chest throbbing with agony. A rib or two had likely been cracked, but he had no time to dwell on his injuries. Their mission remained paramount, and the relentless darkness awaited.

Marisol! Where was Mari?!

Emilio jerked awake with a gasp, his head reeling.

His heartbeat raged behind his skull, each pump seared and pounded as though his bones were rending asunder.

Waves of discomfort washed over him, accompanied by a heavy, sickening lurch in his gut.

"For the love of Styx," he tried to mutter but instead, an iron gag silenced him. He slowly deduced that the swimming sensation was the result of head trauma.

I've been concussed and kidnapped.

As he fought to regain his bearings, the world around him swam in murky shadows of pain and confusion. With each attempt to move, the bonds that held him tightened their grip. As his senses slowly coalesced amidst the haze of agony, Emilio realized the true nature of his plight. A pair of iron gloves affixed to his hands prevented him from even the smallest magical gestures. El Nudo...The Knot, bound him. The Sovereign of the Reach had bound him in similar constraints two months ago. Things were not faring well.

No, Kane, you're not kidnapped, he thought to himself. *You're in custody. They know who you are,* he realized with a sinking heart.

Beneath the haze of pain, Emilio's mind churned with frustration and resignation. Society's perceptions of him as a practitioner of the dark arts were a burden he bore with grim acceptance. It was a label branded upon him by superstition and the ignorant.

They would never understand.

Emilio desperately strained against his bonds. But the irons that bound him were wrought with magic he could not counter and stifled his connection to the divine essence of Styx, leaving him adrift in a sea of suspicion.

He had to escape.

Emilio realized the first step in reclaiming his freedom was determining where he was. He attempted to draw a deep breath to clear the fog that clouded his mind, only to be met with the constriction of a band across his chest, binding him to an unfamiliar chair. A burlap sack obscured his vision, casting the world into shadow and uncertainty.

His inner voice screamed in protest at the absurdity of his predicament. Bound, gagged, and trapped on a chair with naught but darkness to accompany him, what manner of labyrinth had he stumbled into? He stilled the inner workings of his mind in an attempt to listen to his surroundings. If he could not see anything, he could at least listen.

Clickita-Clackita-Clickita-Clackita-Clickita-Clackita-Clickita-Clackita

There was a pattern of sound. It was rhythmic and almost soothing—metal on metal. The simple cadence was reminiscent of a heartbeat.

With it, there was a gentle, equally rhythmic rocking motion. It threatened to lull him to sleep again, but he had to stay awake. This was... a train? Why was he on a train?

He was moving. But where to?

"Good grief, Kane," he muttered to himself, his words muffled by the gag. "What on earth have you gotten yourself into?"

Something hard slammed into his forehead. A torrent of white-hot pain filled his vision and stole his breath. His head swam as he struggled to outlast the agony.

Then, a woman's voice, tinged with defiance, pierced the veil of sounds and pain. An ally? Perhaps.

"Did you even bother to read the orders?" the woman protested. Her words were a beacon of hope in the darkness. "Ascertain his whereabouts and then escort him back. There is no mention of binding and gagging him! We were gone for only half an hour, and you have trussed him up to be ready for market!"

But her plea fell upon deaf ears, drowned out by the cold indifference of a man whose voice dripped with the venom of authority.

"You read Escritor Tomas' report. This man deals with the dead and cannot be trusted," he intoned, his words a chilling reminder of the dangers that lurked in the shadows.

Escritor is a title within the Inquisition of Hil.

He was in more danger than he thought.

"The man is Certified through the Imperial Fugue Academy as a Necromist," the woman continued. "He also has a formal Writ of Agency from Lykos Eskill, the King of the Reach, to operate within the Kingdom as The Reach's official Necromist."

"Give me those," the man's voice grumbled.

"I understand that a healthy dose of preventative action and precaution is warranted most of the time, but the man has both a King's and the Imperator's seal on his dossier!"

"Forgeries," the man spat.

"Perhaps you should allow the Escritora to make that determination, Manos?" another woman's voice spoke. It was softer than the first and carried a sense of calm, spiked with a stern authority. "Your job is to execute the tasks put before us; it is hers to understand, guide, and record. So be silent and let her do *her* job."

An Inquisitorial retinue? Styx help him! What did they think he was guilty of?

"Thank you, Voca," the first woman replied. "I trust you to do your job, Inquisitor. Trust me to do mine."

A silence fell over the group, filled only by the *clickita-clackita* sound once more.

The band around Emilio's chest loosened. He could breathe! Suddenly, the burlap sack vanished from his head. Light flooded his eyes, blinding him. He blinked and squinted, trying to gauge his surroundings.

They appeared to be in a small office or apartment of some kind. The walls and ceiling were polished tongue-in-groove slats, save for one corner. Metal plates were affixed to the floor, walls, and ceiling there. Sitting in that corner was a simple pot-belly stove. Across from the stove was a red leather couch, well worn and patched with care. A woman sat on the couch. Her faded saffron-colored robes, with embroidered sun emblems, marked her for who she was in this tapestry.

A Voca. The Voice of Hil. One called to the service of the Bringer of Light just as he had been called to serve Styx.

She watched him intently, her honey-colored eyes probing his very essence. With a polite inclination of her head, she conveyed a silent acknowledgment.

Emilio moved to incline his head in return when he felt someone pull back on the leather thong that secured the gag in his mouth, jerking his head away roughly. His head and belly wobbled with pain.

"One wrong whisper from you, and I will send you where you belong, cabrón." The Inquisitor growled against Emilio's ear. He smelled of sweat, leather, and machine oil. This had to be the Manos - The Hand of the Inquisition.

Emilio nodded slowly.

There was no love lost between Hil's most Faithful Inquisition and Emilio Kane. The remnants of the Corpse Wars, armies of wandering dead, ensured that those who bore the mark of Styx earned no trust within the Imperium. Many of Her chosen found themselves imprisoned at best, or executed at worse.

All the writs in the world would not save him from their fanaticism.

With another rough movement, the gag was freed from his mouth. Emilio stretched his lips and ran his tongue over his teeth. *Nothing chipped or broken.* He did not taste blood.

Small miracles.

He began to speak:

"I am not sure what is going on, and I fully acknowledge that I'm in your custody, so no fight from me," he said as he felt his hands and arms come free. "I have two questions: are we on a train, and where are we going?"

The Voca looked toward Emilio's left. Following her gaze, he saw a younger woman, smartly dressed in greens and golds of an Imperial Scribe. Her dark red hair was pulled back into a sensible bun. A few wispy curls had escaped their prison and teased gently around her heart-shaped face. The red tattoo of the Escritora, the Historians for the Inquisition, marked the side of her long neck. At her hips, she wore a pair of holsters that nestled a brace of pistols. She was not a simple record-keeper.

In her hands, she held a sheaf of papers. At her feet sat his black medical bag. Emilio's eyes fixed on the bag for a moment. They had clearly opened it. The contents no doubt rifled through. He dreaded how many items might no longer be of use because of untrained hands. There wasn't anything inherently illegal in that bag. Potions, alchemical tools, bandages, and other medical paraphernalia one might expect to find in the bag of a practicing physician. A craftier mind, one educated in the Ars Necromatia, would be able to determine what the contents of that bag could honestly do.

"Hello, Doctor Kane. I am Escritora Wax. I'm sorry for *my teammate's* response to your person," she said, green eyes fixed on the Inquisitor who stood behind Emilio and neatly cleaned his nails with a small knife.

He flashed a predatory smile at Emilio.

The Escritora frowned at the Inquisitor and returned her focus to Emilio. "That is Inquisitor Cortez." She nodded her head in the Inquisitor's direction.

Motioning to the woman on the couch, she said, "Our Voca, Inquisitor Boyorquez, and to answer your first question, yes, you are on a train."

REVELATIONS

Emilio nodded at the confirmation, "Very well." He took a measured breath and focused back on Lyric. "You mentioned you had orders to escort me?" he asked.

"We do," she replied with careful neutrality.

"May I inquire about the nature of the orders?" Emilio asked. He knew he must be mindful of his actions and words lest they be misconstrued.

"No," the Inquisitor replied curtly.

The Inquisitor moved to lean on a desk pressed against the wall. Despite the elegance of the court finery he wore, Emilio could find nothing appealing about Cortez. He wore the regalia of his office: a crisp, high-collared white shirt adorned with a black vest embroidered with subtle gold suns. Decorative medals adorned his chest, testaments to his rank and accomplishments within the order. A silver pauldron, a silent sentinel of authority, rested upon his left shoulder. His wild tangle of black hair was pulled back and secured with a simple green ribbon at the nape of his neck. Scars of battle and years of service marred his weathered face, lending him an air of seasoned resilience. Despite appearing to be in his late twenties, his eyes betrayed the weight of experience, and bore the burden of centuries.

He raised a scarred and calloused hand to smooth his black mustache. The scars hinted at other injuries that no doubt riddled the body hidden beneath the uniform. Emilio's eyes fixed on a mechanized weapon strapped to the Inquisitor's forearm. A short, silvered blade nestled within a marvel of engineering designed for swift and deadly combat.

He was clearly skilled in the performance of his duties.

The red-haired young woman frowned at Cortez, her expression a silent rebuke amidst the tension that enveloped them.

"Inquisitor Cortez is...," she began.

"Cautious," Emilio finished. He forced a pained smile and then shifted slowly in his seat. He looked over at the man who had been trained to end people like himself. "The Inquisitor is being cautious," he continued. "He does not know me, and even if he did, the history of the Imperium and those with my abilities is dark and terrible." He locked eyes with Jalin Cortez. "One that I, too, am appalled at and seek to ensure never happens again."

Jalin scoffed at the remark and pushed off the edge of the desk. He walked past Emilio's chair and toward the couch where the Voca sat. He glanced down at the saffron-robed woman who had not taken her eyes off Emilio.

"He speaks the truth," she responded without taking her eyes off him.

The Inquisitor frowned at the remark, his visage becoming more sour. He turned then and assumed a position facing the front of the caboose. Leaning against the rear door, he glared at the Necromist.

"Apologies, Mister Kane..." the Voca offered.

"Doctor," Emilio corrected.

Jalin twitched at the correction.

Emilio held his hands up in silent apology. "I am a physician first and foremost. I apprenticed and trained for most of my life. My induction and education at Fugue was secondary to my primary calling as a healer."

It was true. Those so gifted, or cursed, with the blessing of Styx were rarely seen in the open within the Imperium. If a child had the mark of Styx, they were swiftly sent to the Fugue Academy to be trained in the proper use of their Gifts. Emilio's parents had been medical practitioners. Well respected and wealthy. He had learned the art of healing and medicine before anything else. But even they had to submit to the will of the Imperium when it became apparent their son had been so marked.

Necromancer, the word was whispered. He grew accustomed to the whispers and accusations that trailed in his wake. He carried the burden of being seen as a practitioner of dark arts by society, a label rooted in ignorance and superstition.

Esperanza nodded in acceptance of the explanation.

"Apologies ...Doctor... Kane," she offered. "We rarely encounter those of your calling outside of Fugue and Festival."

"No, I don't suppose you do," Emilio replied.

"And our training demands a critical eye on those so ...gifted." She continued.

Of course, it does, Emilio thought. But he remained silent and offered no comment.

"As the Escritora said, you are *not* under arrest or suspected of a crime. We have simply been tasked with escorting you from one location to the next and ensuring your safe arrival."

"Of course," Emilio replied, folding his hands in his lap. "With that understanding, may I ask again, where am I being escorted to?"

"Our ultimate destination is the Fugue Academy," Lyric answered. "We departed Carver's Town while you were... incapacitated." She glanced at the Inquisitor leaning against the rear doorframe.

Emilio's unnaturally green eyes glanced toward Cortez and then back to Lyric. He inclined his head ever-so-slightly toward the man in silent inquiry to the young woman. Lyric's shoulders rose and fell almost imperceptively as they concluded their silent exchange. She dropped her gaze to shuffle through a sheaf of papers and recovered a small map.

Lyric continued, "Our current destination lies at the Northern Gate, where we'll switch to ground transportation and head to the Academy."

Emilio looked down and picked at a non-existent thread on his pants. "The High Lecturer does not like to be ignored." He glanced back up to Lyric and mused with a faint smile, "Guess I shouldn't have turned down that professorship." His attempt at mirth wilted under the room's oppressive atmosphere. "Right, so that brings me to my next question. How did I come to be in Carver's Town to begin with? The last thing I remember I was outside Inez...."

Esperanza shifted on the couch, and answered, "We found you in a clearing, unconscious, surrounded by splintered trees. There were no injuries on your person or indication of what happened."

Emilio frowned, "I was simply... laying in the middle of the forest?"

"In a clearing," Esperanza corrected, "by a fire."

"And you found me how?" Emilio asked.

Esperanza smoothed her robes, "The locals of Knot's End advised us that you had been tasked by King Eskill to deal with an issue in a fishing village."

"Mmm, yes, which I did."

Esperanza gestured to Lyric, who pulled out a rough sketch and handed it to Emilio. It appeared to be a strange sigil.

"You were laying in the middle of this sigil that was scorched into the earth."

Emilio's eyebrows knotted together. He studied the crude drawing cautiously. It seemed familiar, but he could not place it. "That seems to be a binding circle," he turned the sigil around and frowned once more. He reached toward his vest pocket.

Jalin stood upright at the movement.

Emilio held out his hands. "Just glasses, Inquisitor," he continued. He recovered a pair reading glasses out and settled them gently on the bridge of his nose. He examined the symbol Lyric displayed. "Definitely a binding... of a sort." His brow furrowed. He tilted his head to the side, "Typically, one would use salt to confine a hostile spirit. But salt should not have caused that area to burn..." He narrowed his eyes and looked closer.

It's off. Something's missing. Or added?

His head swam and his eyes hurt from concentration.

"What were you doing in the forest, Kane?" Jalin demanded.

Sweet Styx's embrace must why must you be so loud?

"I don't remember," Emilio shrugged finally. "After banishing the Fantasma, I was heading back to Inez to reassure them all that it was safe. I wanted the children to sleep without fear."

"Fighting the boogeyman, were you?" Jalin scoffed.

"Yes, actually," Emilio replied flatly.

Jalin narrowed his eyes, but before he could speak, Esperanza interjected with curiosity. "A Fantasma? Truly? How severe was it?"

The Voca's interest in the spirit was to be expected. The Voice of Hil was charged with the exorcism of the undead. Their ways tended to be far more brutal than his own.

Emilio took a deep breath and tried to pull the memory from his broken mind. Fragments. That was all he had.

"The entire area surrounding the home seemed warped... by fear. Everything had been impacted: trees, grass, rocks... everything. I expected to deal with a Screamer, or possibly a Howler, not a Fantasma. Banishing it required considerable effort, but I managed the Misericordia."

Esperanza's face displayed a mix of shock and curiosity at his actions. "The Banishment of Mercy? For a Fantasma? Surely, if it was so dangerous, one should use the Exorcismo?"

The Voca's concern was just. In the whispering corridors between life and oblivion, some spirits curdled into Screamers. Reflections, whose final earthly screams, like souring milk, became wretched things that echoed their own demise. But the Fantasmas, weren't mere echoes. They were death throes given flesh, the last lingering breaths sculpted by the darkest emotion a soul could carry. A Screamer might evoke fear, a chill skittering down the spine. But a Fantasma became fear itself, a walking monument to terror.

El Cucuy. A monstrosity. Something that Hil's Faithful believed should be extinguished the moment it took shape.

"Destroy it entirely?" Emilio shook his head. "That's not my approach, Voca," he said, his voice steady but tinged with a sense of weary resignation.

"Of course not," Jalin scoffed. "You might need it later."

Emilio paused. He had no interest in enslaving the tormented souls of this world. That was not his calling. And it was not the spirit's fault that it had become what it had become. It deserved a chance at redemption. For peace. But now was not the place for this philosophical argument. It would be both futile and potentially hazardous.

"Regardless, the creature was vanquished... ." He looked briefly to Cortez and then back to Esperanza, "Then... I was here."

"Bullshit," Jalin said simply. "I will tell you what happened." Jalin moved forward and leaned on the side of the couch. "He tried to contain this so-called boogeyman, but it was too much for him. He got sloppy and his binding circle blew up in his face! I've seen it before with would-be Necromancers, and he is not any different, just another freak among the fold. Look at him... I bet that thing's power was so great that it knocked him senseless and took a portion of the forest with it! Don't bother denying, I've examined your bag,

Kane. You aren't fooling anyone! Medical paraphernalia, my ass! I know ritual components when I see them. It's obvious he was experimenting with powers beyond his grasp, and now he's worried he's been caught," he added with a smug look. "Admit it Doctor, you fucked up."

There were many things that Emilio Kane was willing to tolerate. He was used to being bullied and tormented by others for the sake of what he was. Avoidance, threats, and even physical injury were all part of the life that had been assigned to the Fugue Academy. Such a life made many of his kind angry and bitter, often turning them into the very things they were accused of being.

It made Emilio careful. Careful and precise. He knew what he was capable of, and dedicated his life to the safety of others because of that. He attended Fugue Academy and endured years of service and training through the Imperium's regimented course of scholarly teaching. He learned the histories of The Reach and the Imperium. He wrote his thesis on the horrors of the Corpse Wars and the spells the Necromantic Generals used to command their armies. He even went so far as to create spells that allowed one to accomplish many of the same effects without having to take innocent life.

He was a researcher and a physician.

A healer and a guardian of the lost.

What he was not was a fuckup.

He sighed deeply and stared at his hands. "Does the prejudice of your Order impact your ability to think critically, Inquisitor?" Emilio said. "I'm honestly curious."

Jalin's face darkened. "What did you just say to me?"

"The Order would not send a -competent- Manos and his... entire retinue... to escort a single man. Even he is a Necromist." Emilio's tone was careful, measured, and cold. He continued, "By the admission of your Scribe, my files show I am neither an essential officer of the Court nor a known threat to the Realm. And yet, a Manos, Voca, and Escritora were sent to bring me back to the Academy." His eyes shifted and locked on Jalin's. "Not to the Capital. Not under arrest. Not in custody. The Academy. The place of education for the Imperium."

Jalin ground his teeth and seethed.

"Do you know what that tells me?" Emilio continued. "It tells me your Order assigned a Voca and an Escritora to reign... you... in. I'm not the dangerous and unpredictable one here; you are." He gestured to Lyric and Esperanza, "These... competent... members of Hil's Faithful have been assigned to watch over *you* because you must be incapable of completing a simple escort job without injury to the person you have been assigned to! So demean me... I'm used to it. Tie me up. Punch me in the face. Kick me in the gut. You won't be the first... or last. Demean my work; it's typical of the short-sighted and superstitious. But I assure you there is only one fuck-up here, and I'm looking right at him... Manos."

Esperanza was not quick enough to stop Jalin as he surged forward. The Manos moved with the speed of a cat and was instantly on his feet. Far quicker than Emilio had accounted for. With a flick of his wrist, the mechanical device on his arm activated, and with a *click*, the blade swung free.

A gut-wrenching -*thunk*- stopped Jalin mid-stride, his arm restrained. As he looked down, he found the blade embedded in the wall. There was not enough room for the weapon to swing freely. It held fast. Not only had the blade jammed, but also the gears had locked up because of the sudden halt. Angrily, he unclasped the straps on his arm and drew his knife on Emilio.

As Jalin closed the distance between himself and Emilio, the room burst into light.

With her hand in the air, Esperanza held a beautiful gold and red flame in her palm.

"You will STAND DOWN CORTEZ," she said. Her words carried an undeniable power that Jalin could not resist. He dropped to one knee.

"Witch!" Jalin growled through gritted teeth but made no move forward.

Disregarding Jalin's remark, Esperanza shifted her focus to Emilio. One might have anticipated a smug expression on the Necromist's face. Yet, Kane sat as he had, poised and focused on the Voca as if patiently waiting in line. "Have you lost your mind, Doctor?" she inquired, her tone carrying a blend of concern and intrigue.

Emilio carefully folded his hands in his lap. "Voca, I have been kidnapped, bound, gagged, assaulted, and threatened." His eyes glanced toward the window and quickly noted the sunlight outside, "All before lunchtime." He looked back at Esperanza. "If this man had his way," he said and motioned to Jalin, "I'd be dead." His shoulders rose and fell slightly. "I am fully aware of my situation. I am simply tired of being abused. If I am going to die, I prefer to do it on my feet rather than in fear."

"I'm unsure which of you is the most stubborn," Lyric said quietly.

Jalin shot Lyric a scathing look, still unable to break free of Esperanza's magic.

Emilio chuckled a little. "Whichever of us is older, I would presume," he offered. He sighed and looked over at the young Escritora. "Forgive me, Ms. Wax. You seem to be a polite and learned young woman. I have spent my life in fear of the Order for a simple matter of divine fate. A fear carefully curated by the Temple and their Scribes. " He nodded in her direction. "By you. So please forgive me if the yoke of fear I have been saddled with chafes, and I tire of wearing it."

Lyric's shock was apparent, but she remained quiet and shifted her focus to Esperanza and Jalin.

Esperanza watched Jalin, the Inquisitor she had been assigned to. A silent exchange passed between them. He closed his eyes and lowered his head in an unspoken resignation. She lowered her hand. The light faded and returned to normal.

As the room fell into a heavy silence, interrupted only by the rhythmic churn of the train wheels, Cortez slowly rose. Sheathing his knife, he shot Esperanza a chill glare, but her expression remained unmoved. Turning around, he pulled his scoring blade from the wall. With a few practiced repairs, the blade relocked. Ignoring them all, he made for the back door of the railcar.

"Jalin ...," Lyric whispered and reached for his elbow.

"Don't," came the reply. He glanced at the young woman and reached for the handle on the back door of the caboose. It did not budge. Cursing, he attempted to wrench it free, to no avail. With a growl of frustration, he turned on his heel and strode to the opposite door. It refused to open, eliciting another string of curses. He pounded on the door and stared through the small window there.

"What's wrong?" Lyric inquired.

"The doors are jammed! Those idiots must have locked us in when they added the extra cars!" Jalin spat. Pressing his face to the glass window, he peered out only to recoil in horror. With a swift strike from the butt of his knife, he shattered the glass. A foul stench filled the car, a sickening blend of decay, blood, and the moans of dying animals. It was a scent all too familiar to all of them.

Jalin quickly pulled a kerchief from his vest and covered his nose.

Lyric blanched, setting her papers aside, and pulled her scarf over her mouth and nose.

"Ough!" Emilio gagged and buried his nose into the curve of his elbow.

Esperanza's eyes widened as the odor reached her. She exchanged a knowing glance with Emilio. They both stood and turned their attention to the door.

"Is... is that what I think it is?" Lyric coughed.

Emilio nodded grimly. "Ghoul Rot... the cattle cars must have ghouls inside."

SHUNTED

"We need to stop this train!" Esperanza shouted. She looked around the caboose cabin for the emergency pull. A rope-like cord ran along the top edge of the windows from the front of the car to the tail. Pulling the cord would alert the Engineer at the head of the train to an emergency in the tail.

"We have to alert the Engineer!" She reached for the cord and pulled. There was tension on the cord, and then... *SNAP.*

It broke free in her hand.

She stared at the useless item as it lay limply in her hand and draped across the length of the caboose.

"Sabotage...," Lyric whispered.

"We need to get out of here and find a way to stop this train," Esperanza replied. She dropped the cord and started examining the car.

"I'll check this side," Emilio said as he joined her. While they may have been opponents philosophically, the occupants of the cattle car made them compatriots of fate at the moment.

Jalin gestured to Lyric. "Open the windows. If they don't open, break the glass before we all suffocate from rot!"

Lyric nodded quickly and started on the windows on her side of the train. None of them opened. "Glued or sealed shut!" she shouted.

Jalin scowled, discovering the same on his side. "Wax, wrap your hand and use the butt of your dagger to break the glass...."

The sound of broken glass answered his instructions as Lyric broke open one of the windows. "Already ahead of you, Cortez," she said and moved to the next window.

Jalin nodded with a hint of appreciation as he watched the Scribe work. Then he looked at Emilio. "Someone wants you dead, Kane," he commented and moved to re-examine the rear door and window there.

"Just like every other day of my life...," Emilio quipped. "I have nothing on this side. No other call cord to the head of the train or brake lever."

"Same on this side," Esperanza confirmed. She met Emilio in the middle of the car while Lyric finished busting open the windows. The air was still rank with death and rot, but at least it was moving now.

Jalin pressed his face against the rear door window. His eyebrows rose, and his lips curled into a smile. "There's a brake wheel on the rear platform!" He stepped back and examined the doorframe. The door had a single window embedded in it. Two smaller windows flanked the doorframe on either side. Hanging next to the door was a long metal stick. One end sported a flat end, and the other a heavy axe-shaped hook.

The brake stick.

Jalin grinned and reached for the item.

"You'll be useful," he said. He hefted the stick to gauge its weight and the distance in the car, then swung it deftly into the window. Glass shattered and flew out the rear of the caboose, littering the tracks behind them. Nodding, he quickly broke the remaining glass free from the frame.

"Wax, grab my long coat and get over here," he ordered.

Doing as commanded, Lyric grabbed Jalin's long, faded leather coat and brought it to him. He took it from her, draping it over the bottom of the open and now empty window frame, covering as much of it as possible.

Jalin took a knee and knotted his hands together. "Out you go," he said, boosting Lyric up to clear the door's window. She winced as her hands found remnants of glass, and she climbed outside.

The wind blew past her as she stood on the platform, her hair ripping free of its secure knot and whipping wildly around her face. She scrambled to secure it as the landscape dashed by on either side. Kneeling, she examined the lock on the door. The metal there had warped and melted. She frowned.

"Get the door, Wax," Jalin shouted against the wind.

"I can't, the lock's broken!" Pivoting, she turned her attention to the brake wheel. She gripped the wheel and tried to turn it, but it would not budge.

"PUT YOUR BACK INTO IT!" Jalin shouted at her.

"I AM! IT'S JAMMED AS WELL!" She shouted back to him.

Jalin stretched his neck in irritation and looked up. A brace bar ran along the top of the car. Gritting his teeth, the Inquisitor leaped up, wrapping his hands around the bar, then lifted his legs and swung out the narrow window. He landed soundly on the platform next to Lyric.

"Lend me a hand," he said. Without awaiting a reply, he advanced to the wheel. Lyric stepped up, and together, they attempted to move the round brake wheel to no avail.

Esperanza approached the rear window and watched the pair struggling with the wheel. She scowled and looked out the window and down at the lock.

"Melted." She looked across at the wheel. Several teeth on the wheel cogs were deformed.

"Both of you come inside! That's never going to move!" she shouted, her voice disappearing in the wind. She pulled herself back inside.

"Did I hear you say melted?" Emilio asked.

Esperanza nodded. "Mmm. Someone does not want us to interfere with whatever that is," the Voca said as she motioned to the cars ahead of them. "They've been very thorough so far. I am going to guess the other wheel is also damaged. We must find a way past the cattle cars and get to the next set. Hopefully, they have brakes or a communication tube with the Engineer."

Lyric slid back through the window in the rear of the train, a look of frustration on her freckle-kissed face.

Footsteps sounded on the roof of the car above them. Esperanza looked upward.

"What is he doing?" Esperanza asked.

Lyric shrugged and simply stared up as they heard the wood creek under Cortez's footfalls. She recovered his coat from the window. "Trying the other side."

Emilio's eyes tracked the sound of the Inquisitor's footfalls to the head of the caboose.

"He's certainly persistent," he commented.

"Indeed," Esperanza replied.

Jalin's footfalls on the roof ceased, and then there was a heavy *thud* on the front platform of the caboose. Glancing in that direction, they could see the condition of the head brake wheel was the same as the other, as was the condition of the door lock.

Jalin drew his pistols. "Stand away from the door!"

Emilo's eyes widened, "Is he really going to…?"

"Shoot out the lock? Yes, Doctor, now move to the rear of the car. NOW!" Esperanza said, shoving Emilio toward the rear of the caboose. They all ducked into the alcoves beneath the raised cupola just as shots rang out.

With a single hard kick, the door flung open. The metal handle remained nestled into the frame as if it were all one piece. Jalin strode in and holstered his weapons. The trio peered out from their positions then advanced to meet him.

He looked at Esperanza. "Those doors opened and closed easily at our last stop. The Corpse Speaker can't melt metal; otherwise, I would have him dragging behind us by now. Any ideas?"

"Yes, but you won't like it," she said.

"I already don't like today," Jalin replied.

"A Fire Singer could warp metal without a forge," the Voca said.

Jalin's face scrunched up in a scowl.

"More magic…," he muttered.

"Mechanist with a torch?" Emilio offered quietly.

Jalin swung his head around to stare at Emilio. "What was that?"

Emilio balked at the sudden focus on his words. "Oh! I was just saying a member of the Mechanist Guild, a Mechanist, could have sealed them all as well. It wouldn't have had to involve magic."

Jalin narrowed his eyes and focused on Kane.

"And while it is true that anyone using one of their torches could have performed that act... before you begin hurling accusations... I was bound, gagged, and unconscious."

Jalin continued staring at Emilio, "True," he reluctantly admitted.

"And you just said the doors were working at your last stop."

Jalin sucked on a tooth. "Also true."

"The brake wheels couldn't have been done earlier either," Lyric added. Jalin and Emilio looked at her. "They had to use them to stop the car at the station."

Jalin nodded and looked at Lyric. "And the windows?"

She shrugged. "Could have been sealed ahead of time to prevent whoever was in the caboose from opening them and catching a whiff of what they just loaded. Stuck windows are easy enough to explain and would not raise too much concern."

Jalin smoothed his mustache and tugged on this chin beard. "So it happened at the last stop."

Esperanza and Lyric nodded.

"If I may ask..." Emilio began, "When did the cattle cars get added?"

Lyric exchanged glances with Esperanza and then with Jalin. Jalin waved his hand non-committally.

"At the last stop," Lyric answered. She looked at Emilio and said, "They uncoupled us and pulled us onto a shunt rail, then loaded the other cars on." Her eyes darted to Jalin and then back. "We already had you in custody, and Cortez insisted on remaining here."

"History lessons later," Jalin growled and recovered his long coat. He shook it out then and slid it on. The worn and patched leather starkly contrasted the court finery beneath, but the look seemed to better befit him. He patted his pockets and pulled out a tiny spyglass. "Wax, I need your eyes," he said, striding toward the now open door.

Without pause, Lyric followed Jalin out onto the head platform of the caboose. Jalin pulled a black scarf over his mouth and nose and gestured to Lyric to pull hers on. Then he stepped to the edge of the railed platform and looked up along the length of the train.

Nine cars. Between them and the engine, there were nine railcars. He pulled the glass up to his right eye and examined each one carefully. He paused, lowered the glass, and then gestured to Lyric.

"Tell me what you see," he told her and stepped back.

Lyric shifted her weight and carefully lifted the glass to examine what Jalin had already seen.

The two cars immediately ahead of them were cattle cars. The slat board sides were tight, making it impossible to see inside, but the smell of their contents was undeniable. Seven additional railcars made the line-up. At least one of the cars carried passengers, another she assumed was a dining car, the sleeper, baggage, and...

"Is that a water tender car?" she asked, lowering the glass.

Jalin nodded.

"So it's a Mechanist train... running on steam and using generators... ."

"And that car is carrying either coal or oil to heat the water," Jalin surmised. "There is no direct route to the engine and the engineer."

"So, how do we get to the engine?" Lyric asked. She handed the glass back to Jalin.

"The same way we get past these two rolling corpse cars," Jalin replied and nodded at the rear of the cattle car before them. A ladder climbed the back of the railcar to its roof.

Lyric looked inside at Esperanza and Emilio. "They are not going to like this."

Jalin scowled and shoved the glass back into his pocket, "I don't care, " he said and returned inside.

MISSIONS

"**Y**ou are out of your mind!" Emilio exclaimed.

Jalin leaned against the edge of the small desk and regarded the Necromist. The hint of a grin tugged at the corner of his lip as he watched the man's discomfort.

Lyric looked between the two men and sighed. She understood the Inquisitor's distrust for the man who could see and speak with the dead; it was ingrained in the whole of their society. The Corpse Wars ensured it. Who could tell when one of those so "gifted" by Styx might once again attempt to raise an army to attack the Imperium? Caution was the best course of action.

But this was not caution Lyric was witnessing. It was open animosity and bravado. Two things they did not need at the moment.

She glanced over at Doctor Kane, the man they had been sent to escort back to Fugue Academy. He was neither gaunt nor intimidating. Two features they had been taught should be present in a Necromist. No, this man was of average height and build and while he was perhaps thin, he was not skeletal. His clothing was unassuming and threadbare in patches. Evidence of someone who stayed busy and rarely had time to care for their upkeep. His leather medical bag was worn smooth from frequent use, but contained no bits of bone or preserved body parts. Indeed, Esperanza had identified the contents as commonplace items she could pick up for her ritual crafts at the local botanica.

Much to Jalin's vocalized displeasure.

Kane's complexion was the fair color of many in the northern villages of The Reach. While pale, he was not sallow nor sickly looking. It was his hair and eyes that called attention to the Necromist. His shoulder-length locks were a soft snowy white and his eyes a surreal color of green. He had a wide-brimmed flat-topped hat, and dark glasses among his possessions when they found him. He clearly must have been accustomed to hiding his other-worldly nature from passersby, lest he draw attention to himself.

Esperanza commented that she believed the man had been touched by some Divine Hand to be so marked.

Jalin said the man was clearly cursed.

How much truth might there be in that estimation? *How much about you was NOT in that dossier, Doctor Kane?*

"No. Absolutely not," Emilio protested.

Jalin shrugged. "Very well. I'll just tie you up and drag you across the roof then."

Emilio bristled at the suggestion, "Not without a fight, you won't."

Jalin's grin widened, and he pushed off the desk, "Ah. Now you have my attention."

"Gentlemen...," Lyric spoke up. She carefully stepped in between the two men and turned her eyes to Jalin first. "We are under orders, Inquisitor."

Jalin pressed his lips together in a sour expression and sucked on a tooth.

Lyric turned to look at Emilio. "I am sorry, Doctor, but Inquisitor Cortez is correct. It is the only way. If we wish to reach the main body of the train..."

"Who said 'we'?" Jalin interrupted. He straightened his shoulders and looked down at the young woman. "The Voca and I will do this. If the graverobber will not come willingly then you can remain here with the..." he paused, "...Doctor." His voice was cool.

"Like Hells I will," Lyric replied.

Jalin's eyebrows rose in response to the red-haired woman's defiance.

"We have a duty, Cortez," she continued.

Jalin narrowed his eyes. "One I am well aware of, nenita."

Lyric popped her right index finger up and pointed it at Jalin's nose. "No. I am no longer a child, and you will not treat me like one."

The pair stood glaring at each other, neither willing to back down.

Jalin ran his tongue across his teeth in consideration of her words. "Fine. Boyorquez stays."

"No," Esperanza replied simply.

Jalin's head whipped around to where Esperanza sat, hands folded, calmly sitting on the red couch.

"Perdóname?!" he demanded.

Esperanza stood and smoothed her robes, "You are outnumbered on this one, Cortez. We all go. It is the only way."

Emilio raised his hand. "I'm perfectly happy to stay here," he offered.

Three sets of eyes turned to stare at him.

"No? Not happy with the idea of leaving me with a potential army of ghouls to march on the countryside?" Emilio offered a harmless smile. He shook his head. "No, me neither. It's a terrible idea." He looked around the car and began to gather his belongings. "I assure you, I am just as eager as you are to get out of here, though not so eager as to climb on the roof of railcar…," He hefted his medical satchel and adjusted its strap so it could be slung across his back. "Perhaps we can find a way to unhook the railcars on the other end. Might solve one of the several problems we are currently faced with...," he rambled.

Lyric tilted her head to the side as she listened to Emilio. "Doctor?" she asked.

Emilio stopped his random comments and looked over at Lyric. "Hrmm?" He smiled at her as he shoved his hat inside his jacket and buttoned it closed.

She shook her head, "Never mind."

How could anyone consider this man a threat?

Dispatching the staff in the car had been easy.

Choosing the manner of their demise was the greatest challenge. Normally, it would have been a quick bone dagger under the ribs or perhaps a punch stiletto to the base of the skull. Herrera favored the garrote, but they needed the uniforms unmarred. The blue-gray coat with the stylized scorpion button at the collar. They all had to look pristine. The wire strangulation device often sliced through skin and would have ruined the gear he needed.

He preferred working alone—a single man who could slip in, complete the task, and slip back out. He did not have to rely on the skills of others. If things went sideways, he knew who to blame.

But orders were orders, and it was not his place to question the words of El Coro Hueco when they were given.

He knew his place. He knew his duty. He was the quiet voice of death that whispered in the shadows - La Garra.

He glanced briefly at the others in his group. Those also called to serve on this day.

Each was chosen for their aptitude and skill. Their eyes were sharp, and their reflexes were lightning-quick. They would get the job done.

Their point man was named Bonilla. He had the distinction of knowing who their quarry on board was. Herrera and the rest of the team only knew they would be in the first-class car toward the head of the train. Keeping the identity of the target secret ensured none of them could leak the details. If the details *did* leak, they would also know who was responsible.

The plan was simple: Board the Staff Car as the train left the station to avoid detection. Dispatch the staff and take their uniforms. From there, they would move forward to the first-class car. Bonilla would get a visual confirmation of the target, and then they would do their jobs.

It was Herrera's job to ensure Bonilla was silenced if captured. His eyes slid across the cabin to the man and sized him up and down. Did he know his life was also forfeited today? Surely, he must.

Herrera quietly wondered who among their crew had been assigned to ensure his own tongue never wagged. He stretched his fingers. It was unimportant. If they called him, he was ready to die for Ossilaro, the Eater of Bone.

The train slowly lurched to one side as it began taking a long curve around and through the hills. Herrera looked up and out the back window of the car. Something glinted in the light atop the roof of the car behind theirs. Gold and black, and far too familiar.

Herrera spun on his heel. "Bonilla!" he hissed. "There's a damned Inquisitor climbing across the roof of the cattle car!"

Bonilla looked over at Herrera. His right eyebrow twitched slightly.

"Nothing in the reconnaissance report indicated there would be Inquisitors on this run." He stepped smoothly to Herrera's side and glanced out the window.

A figure clad in Inquisitorial colors was slowly making his deliberate way across the roof of the car behind theirs.

"Where there is one, there are more," Bonilla commented. He looked at Herrera and said, "Take Tita and go outside." A woman in a brakeman's uniform stood and joined them at the car's rear.

Bonilla continued, "See if you can uncouple the cars. We are far enough into The Reach that they cannot communicate with anyone immediately." He smiled slyly. "And who knows, maybe the wandering armies of the Corpse Wars will test the dear Inquisitor's faith."

Hererra reached for the door latch. Bonilla leaned over. "If you can't uncouple the cars, dispose of the good Inquisitor however you need to. We don't need a Hand of Hil shedding too much light on things today."

Herrera nodded. "Consider it done."

Bonilla strode toward the front of the car. "We should be hitting the next stop soon. When you are finished, meet me in the Dining Car. Alvarez, you're with me." Bonilla slid open the door and stepped out.

Herrera adjusted the borrowed uniform he wore and patted his left wrist. His bone sling was secure. A simple device made of leather strapping and stretchable animal sinews, it fired poison-laced needle darts at a target. It was Herrera's second favorite weapon after the garrote. Depending on the wind outside, it would either help or negate the weapon's efficiency. Regardless, he would have to deal with the Inquisitor quickly.

They stepped outside onto the platform and pulled the door closed.

Herrera looked around and then turned to Tita. He gestured quickly with his hands. "Do you see the release lever?" he asked her. It was a simple enough language that many of them used when silence was needed or speaking was difficult.

Tita shrugged and looked around.

Gritting his teeth, Herrera leaned over to see the train car coupling. Instead of a traditional latching mechanism, the coupler was like nothing he had ever seen. Two large blocks of steel, inside which were housed equally large balls of shiny metal, were fastened together by some unseen force. Thick black cables ran from each car, terminating at the strange fixture.

Tita shook her head and looked for anything to show them how to uncouple the cars. Her eyes settled on a placard fixed to the rear wall next to the door. She tapped Herrera on the shoulder and pointed. A cogwheel and crossed hammers.

Herrera swore.

They were on a Mechanist Guild train!

"Goddamn Mechanist Guild!" The train they boarded was the latest creation of the Mechanist Guild. Dreamers and Madmen, the Guild specialized in new creations for both leisure and war. Hope and nightmares fueled their creative imaginations, and the train they rode was another testament to their work.

Tita frowned and tapped Herrera on the shoulder once more. He looked over at her.

She gestured with her hands, "I'm going inside. Will look for a switch. Keep an eye on HIM." She pointed toward the roof.

Herrera nodded as Tita returned inside. Readying himself, Herrera lept from the staff car's platform onto the cattle car's ladder. As he grasped hold of the metal rungs, a whiff of something foul hit him in the face. He gagged.

"Ugh! One of the cows must have died."

Shaking it off, he climbed the ladder. He had a job to do.

SOMETHING ROTTEN

Climbing across the top of a cattle car on a moving train was certainly not something that Emilio Kane ever thought he would be doing.

The wind ripped past him as he grasped hold of the wooden planks and crawled slowly along the rooftop. The roof had a narrow, elevated walkway built atop the car. It was designed for brakemen to walk from one car to the next. He was no brakeman. One wrong step and any one of them would be flung from the top of the car to a less-than-desirable fate.

He chanced a glance over the side of the car and immediately regretted doing so. The rich green landscape of The Reach blurred past him as the train surged.

"Doctor! We need you to keep moving!" Esperanza called from behind him.

He nodded and inched forward once more.

At the head of their little retinue stood the Manos, Inquisitor Jalin Cortez. The brake stick in one hand and his long coat flapping in the wind made him look like a picture of rugged heroism. The stalwart Inquisitor sworn to defend the Imperium from the remnants of the Corpse Wars.

If only he weren't such an ass.

Emilio had yet to meet an Inquisitor whose behavior was not that of a schoolyard bully. He wondered if everyone's experience was the same or if it was merely the fact that he was a Necromist that earned him that distinction. There was a cause, of course. When a society fought a war with an army of the dead, it tended to leave them gun-shy when faced with those who could control those same creatures. Nevermind the fact that the Imperium had taken great pains to control those born with these Gifts to ensure that would never happen again. There would always be those who wished for his extermination.

King Lykos of The Reach had wished Emilio's demise. Emilio had only changed his mind by saving the soul of the murdered Queen, Marisol.

A shapechanger had taken the Queen's form, and her soul lingered between the living and dead, unable to move on so long as the creature controlled her actual physical body. The spirit of the Queen had found Emilio and asked for his aid. She was his Queen; how could he refuse?

"Mari...," Emilio whispered. The wind tore at his eyes, causing them to water.

Where was she?

He looked for her when they had exited the caboose and began climbing to the top of the cattle car. He had silently hoped that perhaps the Voca's presence was keeping her away or that perhaps a sigil on the car prevented her from joining him.

But she was not there.

What happened, Mari?

His chest tightened, and his stomach rolled at the thought of losing her.

He needed to know more about where they found him and get another look at the sigil the Voca had sketched. Something had gone terribly wrong somewhere, and until he could be free of this Inquisitorial escort, he would not be able to determine what it was.

He shifted his gaze forward to watch Cortez continue his cautious advance across the top of the car. He used the brake stick to test the wood before stepping on it. A cursory glance proved that the wood was not as solid as one might hope, complicating their ability to traverse the car.

"Rotten wood. Rotten contents...," Emilio mused. Someone wanted whatever was inside to get out.

They had not seen the car's contents, but the stench was unmistakable. In the realm of the undead, nothing smelled as bad as Ghoul Rot. Ghouls were unfortunate creatures born from the desperation of a soul clinging to mortality and refusing to move on. In a final attempt to return to the waking world, these already half-mad souls barged their way into a recently deceased corpse. Determined to remain flesh and blood, they would become bound to their now deceased and rotting prison, able only to pilot the body through force of will. The consumption of living flesh seemed to slow the rot of the body they inhabited.

Many believed that the condition was transmissible through their bite. That was not the case, as the condition was entirely spiritual. However, additional desperate spirits might follow a ghoul, seeking to take advantage of the corpses left in its wake. A single ghoul, allowed to wander through a graveyard and then set loose on a village, could become a terrifying army overnight.

A ghoul's host body could be killed using most normal weapons, but not before they caused irreparable harm to whatever community they were in. Destroying the body would not send the soul where it needed to go. Without the proper care, killing the host only released an angry spirit back into the realm to search for another body to inhabit.

The Corpse Wars had left thousands of unanchored, angry spirits to wander the Imperium. Ghouls were among the most common of the remnants of that war.

Emilio shook his head. "Why?"

He lifted his gaze a moment to look ahead. The Scribe may have some ideas. He would try to speak to her once they were off the top of this ridiculous cattle car.

If he had been paying attention, he would have seen what Cortez was pointing at. He would have known to hang on and await the bridge that the train was crossing. But he wasn't. He had been stuck in his thoughts, wondering why someone would want a car full of ghouls and how they could have loaded them without anyone noticing.

The car suddenly rattled and shook beneath him. It was rhythmic but no less concerning. Emilio's tenuous grip threatened to vibrate free as the cars crossed the bridge over the Lagarto Gorge. He felt himself slipping. He shifted quickly in an attempt to redistribute his weight, but in doing so, slid off the elevated wooden walking platform and onto the roof of the car.

The wood was spongy and soft. There was no time to scramble back to the safety of the center. With a sickening groan the wood gave way.

Oh no.

Lyric clung to the center walkway of the railcar as the train crossed the bridge. She closed her eyes and offered a silent prayer to Hil. Sloughed off the top of a railcar and thrown into a gorge in some distant section of The Reach was not how she wanted to die.

The vibrations of the tracks shook the car and ran through the length of her body. She was suddenly very thankful for her service as a Page and Runner for the Grand Library. All those years running up and down stairways and scaling ladders to deliver books and missives across the Capital had developed strong muscles in her arms and legs. She used those now to hold on.

Esperanza's voice yelled out from behind Lyric.

"HELP!"

Lyric's heart jumped in her throat.

She quickly glanced back behind her.

The blood drained from her face. Behind her, sprawled on her stomach across the roof of the car, lay Esperanza. The Voca had the tip of her right boot wedged into the wooden walkway and was half hanging inside a hole in the car's roof.

Doctor Kane was nowhere in sight.

"Lyric! Help us!" Esperanza yelled once more.

Taking a deep breath, Lyric shifted her weight and turned around. She scrambled toward the Voca as quickly as she could. Biting down her fear, she adjusted her weight and looked over the edge. Esperanza's arms were wrapped around the strap of Kane's medical satchel. Hanging onto the satchel was Emilio.

Beyond the physician, bodies shifted in the darkness of the car below. Empty, hungry eyes stared up at the

Necromist as he dangled just out of the grasp of their gaunt hands. Their mouths opened and closed in soundless words.

Lyric froze. The nightmares of Vargas came crashing down on her. That horrific night in the mountains when she was sure they were all going to die at the hands of creatures that should not exist. Cold sweat beaded on her forearms suddenly. She tasted bile in her mouth.

"Lyric! I need you!"

The Voca's shouts snapped her out of the nightmare's spell.

Esperanza's grip was slipping.

Without hesitation, Lyric quickly removed her belt and fashioned a loop at one end. She wrapped the other end around her wrist and, laying on her stomach, hooked both of her feet into the center brace along the top of the car. She lay flat and stretched out, lowering the looped belt down.

"Doctor, grab hold!"

Kane looked up and reached for the leather loop. "Gladly!" he shouted. He threaded his hand and wrist through the loop.

Lyric looked over at Esperanza.

"Ready?"

Esperanza nodded.

"Pull!"

The two women pulled Emilio up enough for him to scramble out of the hole.

The trio lay atop the rattling rail car for a moment.

"Thank you!" Emilio yelled, his voice lost in the wind.

Lyric nodded and recovered her belt. She glanced up toward the head of the car where Jalin stood. She could feel his seething stare. He lifted the brake stick and pointed at her, then the hole, then Kane, and then gestured off the train. His meaning was clear: *If he endangers you again, I will throw him off this train myself.*

They had tried everything possible to decouple the cars to no avail. Herrera's last peek at the oncoming Inquisitors revealed time was running out. They couldn't let them pass; their mission had to succeed. Taking a deep breath, he nodded to himself. He knew what he had to do.

"Their man in the front has a brake stick. If I act quickly, I'll catch him unaware, grab the break, bring it back, and we may be able to detach the car before the rest can act."

"What about me?" Tita asked.

He chewed on the inside of his cheek and then smiled. "La mentira."

Tita paused and then nodded solemnly. "May bones taste flesh," she said before returning to the staff car.

Herrera rolled up his sleeve, revealing a thick leather bracer. Nestled neatly on one side of the bracer were four metal arrow bolts, their tips covered in wax. Reaching into his pocket, he took out a small vial of violet-colored liquid.

Loosening the cork, he prepped it for quick consumption. He never knew what was in the serum, but he knew the benefit of its effects. No matter the wounds given to him, he would not feel a thing. No man would be able to cut him down. Now was the time to act.

Falling through the slats was not Doctor Kane's fault. They were climbing across an unsafe area at a ridiculous rate of speed. Couple that with the unexpected vibrations from the bridge crossing, it was a miracle that he was the only one who lost his grip.

It could have been any of them.

Lyric tried to reason with Cortez as they climbed down the side of one cattle car and crossed to the second, but the surly Inquisitor would not be moved by her words. He glowered at her and then at Kane as the Doctor bumbled his way down the narrow ladder of the first car.

"We will talk more about this once we reach the staff car on the other side," he said, then turned and clambered up the ladder to the top of the second car.

Lyric sighed. Jalin was an exceptional Inquisitor. Perhaps one of, if not the best monster-hunter they had. He took his duty and his vows to the Temple seriously. A Manos of Hil committed themselves to a rigorous lifestyle. One consumed by battle and tactics. When one's closest allies might succumb to infection or curse at any moment it made them distant and cold. Jalin was no exception.

The Inquisitor's last assignment compelled them to confront Judex Gale Stonebridge. Stonebridge was Jalin's mentor, corrupted by a blood curse and turned into an abomination. *Vampyre* was the name that was whispered between them. It was a name the Order had stricken from her reports, for fear of the consequences of that knowledge. The three of them were the only ones who knew the truth about what happened in Paraíso Verde.

That knowledge weighed heavy on each of them.

Standoffish and rude to begin with, now Jalin was unapproachable and cold.

"One more car to go, eh?" Emilio asked. He tightened the straps of his satchel and readied himself once more. "No possibility that this car is empty I suppose?" he asked.

Lyric knelt on the platform to one of the floor vents. Inside she could see dark figures shuffling in the center.

"Cows?" she asked the Necromist.

Emilio took a knee next to her and peered inside. "Not cows, I am afraid." Standing, he stepped to the side of the platform to allow Esperanza room as she climbed down from the first car. "Thank you for the assist, Voca. I deeply appreciate it."

Esperanza wiped her hands off on her robes. Dirt and grease marred her typically pristine complexion. She reached up to tie a knot in her dark hair.

"I am certain you would do that same, Doctor," the woman replied in an even tone.

"I would! It's true!" Emilio nodded.

Esperanza looked over at Lyric and then toward the top of the car.

"He's already gone up," Lyric replied.

The Voca shook her head and gestured at the ladder.

"One more car."

RIBBONS OF RED

Jalin wasted no time climbing the ladder and reaching the top of the second car. He swung the brake stick back and forth, pausing to test the slats on the roof of the car as he strode from one end to the other. Behind him, the rest of the assembled group began their ascent.

Traversing cars on a moving train was no small feat. Lyric pulled herself onto the top of the car. The wind was too strong for her to stand. She remained on hands and knees and began to crawl across the top of the car. Emilio and Esperanza followed behind her. She glanced ahead to watch Jalin, standing tall and facing the wind. Her heart caught in her throat a moment, watching him. A single misstep could mean his demise. His movement and stride indicated that he did not care to be careful.

Was it anger at the Doctor's endangering the group or something else that prompted his behavior?

She shook her head and focused on crossing the car. Her hand encountered a soft slat. She stopped and shifted her weight, then fished a small piece of charcoal out of her pocket. She marked it with a large "X" and looked back at Kane. She pointed at the slat and waved him off.

He nodded in understanding.

They continued onward.

She followed in Jalin's wake as best as she could. He would test the slats, tapping with the brake stick and gesturing to areas that should be avoided. She would mark the areas to avoid. It seemed a good pattern and they made quick work of the crossing.

As they approached the head of the cattle car, a man in a brakeman's uniform peered over the edge of the car.

Thank the Gods, we have help! She thought. She raised one hand to wave at the man. He raised his own arm and pointed his fist at her. Lyric's eyes widened.

Wrist bow.

She identified the weapon just as something whizzed past her face.

We're being attacked!

The man brought his arm up and aimed at Jalin, firing something toward the Inquisitor. Jalin swung the brake stick out as he whirled around, his leather coat billowing in the wind like a shield. He fell to his knee, Lyric arresting his fall.

"Cortez!" Lyric called. Her eyes fixed on two thin metal rods embedded in his chest. No blood was visible, but a thick, milky, green liquid dribbled down the front of his jerkin.

He glanced down and swore, "Pinche..." Ripping the bandana away from his face, he shouted, "Stay down, Wax! Assassin!"

"Look out!" Lyric yelled as the assassin pulled back on his wrist bow and took aim again.

Jalin's eyes locked on Lyric's for a moment. He took a breath and blew out sharply as he pushed himself up and whirled to face their assailant with a roar. He swung the brake stick like a footman's mace, his coat flapping in the wind around him. Normally he could use the edges of the coat to help deflect projectiles, but the wind denied his advantage.

In order to deal with a ranged weapon, Jalin had to advance.

Herrera offered a wicked smile as he climbed to the top of the car to meet the Inquisitor. He popped the cork on a vial of dark liquid, drank down its contents greedily, cast the vial aside, pulled out a pair of knives and charged.

Jalin's eyes narrowed at Herrera's actions. Years of martial training sprung to the forefront of the Manos' mind. Fighting the dead was one thing, fighting a man took a different set of skills. The contents of the vial the enemy had consumed were unknown, but the Order often issued such potions and concoctions to their Manos to increase their edge in a battle. Jalin had consumed gallons of herbal draughts in his time of service. He had to assume the same was in use now.

Jalin hefted the brake stick in one hand and with a satisfying flick of his arm engaged his scoring blade on the other. His lips lifted over his teeth in an almost feral snarl as he met the enemy head on.

"I am the Hand that swiftly cuts the darkness…," Jalin began. He swung the brake stick low at Herrera's feet, and blocked his incoming attacks with the scoring blade. "I am the Hand that will bear both the Light of Hope and the Fire of Judgement…." He shoved Herrera backward. The assassin staggered and regained his footing, charging Jalin once more, sharp blades at the ready.

He was fast. Faster than Jalin accounted for. "My life is to serve the will of Hil…," Jalin intoned as Herrera came at him in a flurry of blades. Jalin blocked, but he was too slow. Herrera's blades sliced into the arm of his long coat. Jalin hissed as the blade found his flesh. "…to ensure the Light of Providence, and to protect the devout." He pushed Herrera off him. A ribbon of red flew off Jalin into air. He refused to be routed.

"I fear not the denizens of Shadow or their corruptible servants!" Jalin yelled and charged Herrera. Herrera smiled wickedly and met Cortez, blades down and ready to bring them into the Inquisitor's body. Jalin's scoring blade blocked the daggers as they came upward. He pressed the length of the brake stick against Herrera's throat. "As the Light touches the land..." Both men grappled with the other on the top of the moving cattle car. Jalin continued speaking his Oath of the Order as he battled Herrera. He grunted as he pushed and shoved, trying not to lose his own footing and fall off the side of the car. "so too... will Hil's Judgement... befall those... that seek to fester... in the abyss..." Jalin shoved Herrera back. Herrera's blades hooked into the brake stick and yanked it free from Jalin's hand. It clattered on the roof and skidded out of reach.

It was a costly move as Jalin brought the weight of his scoring blade down on Hererra's forearm. He felt bone break and heard a sickening *crunch* as Herrera's left arm sagged downward at an unnatural angle.

Still the man pressed on.

Jalin frowned. *Painfade.* That must have been what his opponent had swallowed. A distillation of poppy, it numbed the pain receptors of the body while preserving the reflexes. It was a last resort for battles one was not expected to survive.

So be it.

Herrera jabbed forward with his good arm, shoving his blade toward Jalin's sternum.

"By fire...," Jalin twisted, catching the blade in his hip. He brought his knee up into Herrera's stomach and shoved him back. He pulled a dagger from his belt, ignoring the slick wetness of blood that trailed down his arm and dropped through the slats of the cattle car onto the occupants below.

Herrera slid back, his arms flailing as he recovered his footing. His eyes fell on the abandoned brake stick. He lunged for it.

"By blade...." Jalin advanced. He turned his dagger around in his gloved hand, took aim, and hurled it at Herrera. It made a *shhthunk* noise as it embedded in his thigh.

Herrera chuckled and pulled the dagger out of his body. Skilled fingers flung it toward Jalin. The Inquisitor turned, trying to shield himself once more with his coat. The blade dug deep into his shoulder. He grunted in pain and slowly turned back around.

Herrera hefted the brake stick in his one good hand. His broken arm swung limply at his side.

Jalin snarled again. He did not want to use his firearm in this position. The wind might deflect the shot unless he was close enough, and he couldn't risk injury to himself or anyone behind him. But he could use it as a club. He reached for his pistol.

"And by my hand...." Scoring blade at the ready and pistol in hand, he braced for Herrera's inevitable charge.

With nihilistic glee, Herrera came at Jalin, swinging the brake stick like a long sword. Jalin ducked low, the brake stick swinging wide.

"My watch is eternal..." Jalin punched up into Herrera's groin. An arc of blood sprayed from the femoral artery.

Herrera grunted and groaned then, rolling away and off Jalin onto the unforgiving wooden slats of the roof. He remained there, on his hands and knees, wheezing as blood gushed from his wounds.

Jalin watched as the slats bloomed with red around the dying assassin. He stood on shaky legs and raised a booted foot. "And the hunt... is unending..." He slammed his boot down into the roof of the cattle car. "This...I...swear."

The roof where Herrera knelt splintered and cracked.

A flash of panic filled Herrera's face as the wood beneath him collapsed and both he and the brake stick tumbled into the hungry horde below.

Jalin's knees buckled, and he collapsed in a heap.

"Cortez!" Lyric shouted and scrambled across the roof to the Inquisitor. Her eyes darted briefly toward the gaping hole in the roof of the car. Months ago, Lyric would have turned away in horror. Instead, she watched as dozens of hands and maws ripped into the man who tried to kill them.

Jalin turned his bloody face toward Lyric and reached out to her.

"Miss Wax, help me off the roof of this damned car."

BARGAINS

The staff car was a charnel house. Five bodies lay sprawled, pin-cushioned by violence. Two were stripped bare, the others in various states of undress. Blood pooled like a nightmare across the floor, a grotesque crimson lake in the cramped confines. The scene was savage and chilling. The killer had been not just brutal, but methodical.

From the carnage, a lone survivor coughed up a gout of blood and reached out a trembling hand. With a grim efficiency that spoke of countless battlefields, Emilio was beside her in an instant, assessing her wounds.

"Let me help you," he whispered gently and set to work.

Jalin's arm draped around Lyric's shoulders as she led him past the dead bodies and into the sitting area onto the couch.

"Take care of him, Ms. Wax," Esperanza said and pulled the door closed between the sitting area and the back of the car.

Jalin slumped down onto the couch's cushioned surface. Blood dripped from his wounds, coloring the soft gray fabric a gruesome maroon. He shifted and grimaced, his body a canvas of fresh wounds, courtesy of the assassin he had dispatched. He grit his teeth and leaned his head back, allowing his eyes to close for a moment.

Lyric's gaze fixed on the metal bolts protruding from his chest. They needed to be removed. She reached out, and Jalin's hand flashed up and clamped on her wrist.

"Arms first," he rasped. "Chest later."

His eyes opened and met hers, holding them for a moment. A torrent of emotions danced in the dark depths of his eyes, but they were without words.

She nodded. He released his grip.

"Unless we can get you out of that coat, we are going to have to cut off its sleeves," she said, examining the injuries.

Jalin nodded and sat up slowly. She helped him shrug the shoulders of the coat off and gently slid his arms free. It had served its purpose, this coat, a shield against a storm of blades. It had probably saved his life. Working quickly, she found a hidden blade - one of many, along with a few items she could not identify - and used it to cut away the sleeves of his blood-soaked shirt.

His arms were a shredded mess. Deep cuts dug into the flesh of his arms. A knife protruded from the shoulder. The blade narrowly missed the heavy leather of the long coat and was buried deep inside him. He needed a medic, not an academic.

She glanced toward the back of the train. Behind the closed door, Emilio and Esperanza were dealing with the lone staff survivor and examining the other bodies they had discovered. Esperanza's magic might be able to help him, but Cortez loathed its use. His beliefs fostered a strong distrust of all magic and those who wielded it. It did not matter that the Gifts she possessed were given to her by Hil Themself and thus Divine in origin.

Emilio was the other option. He was a medical doctor, skilled in the mundane art of healing the body. He would be able to handle this with ease. However, would Jalin even allow the man near him? The Inquisitor would no doubt rather die than allow it. The fear of history and its horrors might cost Jalin his life.

Something had to be done.

"Did they...teach you...triage?" Jalin asked.

Lyric nodded. "Basic instruction only. I..." She stared at his wounds once again. The question of stitching hung heavy in the air. "I was a Librarian, Jalin...not a medic." her green eyes met his, a deep apology for lack of knowledge hanging between them.

Jalin nodded, his eyes closing for a moment, "It's alright... Ms. Wax." His breath came in and out slowly.

"Stay with me, Cortez," Lyric hissed.

"Mmmm" He nodded. "Towels. Pressure. Slow the bleeding."

Lyric nodded and looked around quickly. A fresh stack of towels caught her eye. She grabbed Jalin's hand and pressed it against the worst injury. He nodded and held his hand there as she stood and grabbed the towels. With practiced efficiency, she began tearing them into strips. Bandaging would be needed, and lots of it.

Jalin winced as she tied a strip of cloth around his arm, slowing the flow of blood.

"I'm sorry," she apologized.

Jalin shook his head.

Just as she finished Jalin's right arm, the door slid open from the rear of the car. Emilio entered, a weary smile on his face. "Our lucky survivor," he announced. "Said a stranger boarded at the last stop and quickly went to work with a blade. Nasty business, but I patched her up. Gave her something for the pain, too. Your Voca's keeping her company..." His eyes fell on the bloodied Inquisitor. His eyebrows raised in concern.

Lyric looked up at Emilio. "Doctor..."

"No." Jalin grunted.

Emilio looked from Jalin to Lyric once more and then to Jalin's wounds. "It's an admirable field dressing, but without stitches, you'll bleed out."

Jalin winced and snarled, reaching for his pistol as his bloodied fingers fumbled for the grip.

"...said no...corpse-speaker."

Lyric's fingers found Jalin's and she pulled his hand away from the weapon. "You have to let him help you, Cortez."

"Boyorquez..." he answered.

"Your wounds are deep, Inquisitor..." Emilio eyed the bandages on his arms. They were already soaked again. "Does your Voca have the skill?" It was a simple question.

Jalin stared at the roof and refused to answer.

Lyric answered instead. "No. She doesn't."

Jalin shot Lyric a look of anger and looked away.

The young Scribe reached out and grabbed Jalin's chin and turned his face to meet hers. "There are two cars filled with ghouls back there, Jalin Cortez. Ghouls we are going to have to deal with. Angry spirits just waiting for a new body. Do you want it to be yours? Esperanza's? Mine?"

Jalin's bravado faltered. He stared into Lyric's emerald eyes and then slowly looked away. The anger drained from his face, replaced by a weary resignation.

"Fine."

"Thank the gods," Emilio whispered softly.

Lyric turned to the doctor. "Can we make a deal, Doctor?" she asked. "Explain what you're doing as you go. Every jab, every salve. Let Inquisitor Cortez here know exactly what's happening to him."

"Of course," Kane replied, a hint of his usual cheer returning. "Transparency is paramount. However, I may require some assistance with those... projectile wounds. Once they're extracted, stitches will be necessary, and swift..."

Jalin cut him off with a shake of his head. "Just the knife. The bolts... they didn't pierce."

Shock flickered across Lyric and Emilio's faces. Jalin, with a slow, deliberate movement, unbuttoned his vest. Beneath the blood-soaked fabric lay a revelation, a hidden layer of thin iron plates, meticulously stitched and tied together into a secret suit of mail. Piecemeal as it looked, it had served its purpose. The vest had been a mere facade, a shield against a storm of steel that had saved his life.

Fascination flickered in Emilio's eyes as he plucked the bolt from the fabric. Its head was mangled, alien-looking. He stared at a strange residue clinging to it, and then realization dawned. "Off with the vest and shirt, quickly! And keep them away from his skin! Avoid the areas where the bolts struck entirely."

"What's happening, Doctor?" Lyric asked, already tugging at Jalin's vest.

"Carasin," Emilio muttered, a grim twist to his lips. "The tips were hollowed, filled with the stuff. We need a clear look at his chest, now!"

Lyric sprang into action as Emilio rummaged through his medical bag. Jalin remained silent, a stoic statue as she peeled away the vest and shirt. Blood and sweat mingled on his scar-covered skin, but what truly sent shivers down Lyric's spine were the dark marks where the bolts had struck.

A mixture of relief and worry clouded Emilio's face.

"Ms. Wax," he began, his voice tight, "listen closely. Inquisitor Cortez, the good news is the bolts do not appear to have broken the skin. But the poison still lingers and will seep in unless addressed. I need to..."

"Just get on with it!" Jalin snapped.

Lyric saw it then, a flicker of terror in his eyes. Carasin was derived from the bones of the dead, specifically, those who died of disease or infection. Those whose blood was exposed to Carasin lived a life wracked with pain as their internal organs suffered from necrosis and slowly failed. There was no cure.

The memory of Judex Gale Stonebridge and his confinement to the life support chair jumped to mind. To save himself from his suffering Stonebridge had accepted a dark bargain. Whoever it was that healed the Judex made him into a monster; something even legends said should not have existed.

The scene from that night in Paraíso Verde played in slow motion through Lyric's memories. Had there been something else Stonebridge had said that night? Something about questions and miracles being denied?

Emilio's voice broke her thoughts and pulled her from the memory.

"I need a tightly rolled towel," Emilio said, pulling on a pair of oiled leather gloves. "He'll need something to bite down on, something to hold onto. Once you have it, I'll apply this salve to the wound. It'll neutralize the poison, but it'll feel like his skin's on fire. Agony, pure and simple..."

"DO IT, KANE!" Jalin growled.

Lyric twisted a towel and offered it to Jalin. He clamped down on it with a grimace. Reaching for her hand, he gave her a curt nod. She squeezed back, her grip firm as she watched Emilio prepare the greenish-black salve patches.

With a final nod, Emilio leaned forward and pressed the salve onto the darkening skin. Jalin's body lurched, a guttural scream ripping through the clenched towel. His grip on Lyric's hand was like iron, but she met it head-on. Without flinching, Emilio applied the second salve.

Jalin stomped his foot, the sound echoing in the cramped room. He slammed his other fist against the couch, the knuckles stark white. Slowly, the vice grip on her hand loosened as he faded from consciousness.

"Jalin!" Lyric cried.

Emilio reached a skilled hand out and placed his fingers against Jalin's throat. He was rewarded with the weak beat of a thready pulse. "He's fine, Ms. Wax," Emilio assured. He pulled his hand away and gently squeezed Lyric's shoulder. "Even your stalwart Inquisitor has limitations. He reached his but he will live." Emilio offered, his voice strained.

"We'll need to bandage him tightly. Then, we can remove the knife and stitch him up."

With careful hands, Lyric helped to pull the shredded and bloodied shirt off of the Inquisitor. Jalin, now stripped bare by necessity, seemed a canvas of violence. Scars, old and new, ran like a spiderweb across his chest and arms, each a brutal story left unfinished. Blades, bullets, and claws had marred the Inquisitor's body over his time of service. Tattoos, vibrant displays of his Faith once, now bled into the ravaged flesh. A keen eye could see where they had been retouched when scars marred their once-perfect lines. He lay on the blood-soaked couch, broken but not yet defeated. The sight of his determination sent a fresh wave of hope crashing through her.

Completing the stitch work needed on Jalin's wounds, Emilio stood and stretched, his back sounding in a series of unsettling pops.

Jalin's eyes flickered and opened slowly. He reached for his weapons immediately.

"Jalin, it's all right. You are still on the train." Lyric's voice soothed.

The Inquisitor's bloodshot eyes found hers and focused on them for a moment. He nodded.

Emilio took a breath and addressed Jalin directly.

"You've lost a lot of blood, Inquisitor. From the looks of your scars, you understand what that means. You need fluids and rest. You'll be weak for about twenty-four hours. There is nothing I can do about that, it's simple physiology. An iron-rich diet over the next few weeks will help with the mending." He stretched his neck, "Provided nothing disturbs the ghouls in the rear car they do not pose an immediate threat." He turned his gaze to Lyric. "I assume there is a dining car on this train. If we can manage something back here for him, it will help."

A flicker of relief sparked in Lyric. "Thank you, Doctor."

Jalin grunted a reluctant acknowledgment.

"Alright then, if the two of you would excuse me, I will take care of the bodies in the back and see if I can find something a little less...alarming... to walk around in." He glanced down at his blood-soaked clothing. "I had days working in the Academy's morgue with less viscera..."

His eyes lifted toward the rear of the car and then back to Lyric. " He'll be fine until I return."

Lyric's brow furrowed. "Doctor?"

A ghost of a smile graced the Necromist's face. "As you said, Ms. Wax. Angry spirits, looking for hosts. Can't have that."

"What are you going to do?"

"Only that which is necessary, my dear girl." The Necromist said as he stepped out of the room with grim determination and pulled the door closed behind him.

COMMUNICATION

Esperanza stood in the open sliding door that separated the front half of the care from the sleeping quarters. The sleeves of her saffron-colored robe were rolled up to the elbows. Her face was stained in blood and sweat.

She made her way into the car and sat on the bench opposite the sofa that Cortez was resting on. She watched him carefully for a moment.

"I'm fine," Jalin said, answering the unasked question.

"You are not dead. I will give you that," Esperanza countered.

"Alas, you are saddled with me for yet another day," he retorted. It was difficult to tell if there was a hint of humor in his voice. He lolled his head in her direction and opened his eyes. "Your Gifts?"

Esperanza looked down at her hands and arms. The mortal form was not designed to carry the power of the Divine. Channeling its use too freely carried a hefty toll. For some it was madness. For others, death. It was the price of being touched by the Gods. Esperanza's body remained clear of the telltale marks that would riddle her body should she begin to reach her limits. She folded her hands in her lap and looked back at the Inquisitor.

"Alas, I am not in danger of collapse. You will have to kill me another day."

"MMmm," Jalin mused and closed his eyes.

The Gifts of the Divine would occasionally transfer if a mortal form became infected or possessed. The resulting horror would take enormous resources to dispatch. It was the duty of the Manos, the Hands of Hil, to ensure their Voca never fell to such a fate. Many of the Voca assigned to Inquisitor Jalin Cortez in the past had met their ends in service at his side. Esperanza often wondered if that had been by design.

She shook the thought from her mind. "Have you been able to reach the conductor and appraise them of the situation?"

Jalin shook his head. "Forgive me. I have been busy trying not to die from Carasin poison."

Esperanza's eyebrows shot up. "Carasin?!" she exclaimed. Her eyes darted to Lyric. The young woman nodded.

"The darts did not penetrate the skin. He was very lucky. The Doctor crafted a salve to negate its properties before it infected him," Lyric said.

"Indeed?" Esperanza replied. There was no cure for Carasin, at least not one that the Voca and the Order of Hil could wield. Esperanza's eyes drifted toward the rear door where the Doctor had gone. A conversation best had at another time.

"You said you have not attempted to reach the Conductor or the Engineer?"

Lyric shook her head. "No."

Esperanza nodded and pushed herself up off the bench. She crossed the room to a rickety desk, a faded poster of strange symbols hanging like a forgotten prophecy overhead. A brass contraption, a disembodied yell in metal, jutted from the wall like a skeletal hand. Scanning the poster, Esperanza flipped switches with practiced ease, her brow furrowed in concentration.

"Staff car to engine." Lyric heard Esperanza's voice boom into the horn, the sound echoing through the cramped space like a desperate prayer. "Orange situation!"

Silence. Esperanza repeated the call, her voice laced with a tremor of fear that mimicked Lyric's own. She switched channels, calling out to each car, but only the mocking hiss of static greeted her attempts.

"Not even the First Class car," Esperanza muttered, her frown deepening. "They wouldn't miss the call. Guild protocols...," Her voice trailed off. She turned back to face Jalin and Lyric.

"Sealed in, brake alert compromised, ghouls in tow, an assassin aboard with possibly more, and communications cut off from at least this point... this is intentional. Someone's being targeted."

"By who?" Lyric asked, "And why?"

The Inquisitors and Lyric all shared a sense of unease and looked at the closed door at the rear of the car.

"That is too much effort to try to take out one man," Esperanza said. "The file on Doctor Kane had nothing out of the ordinary. A physician who lives like a pariah due to his curse, no record of open use of the Ars Necromantica. No dark dealings."

"The Cult of Bone and those that follow Styx typically don't get a long," Jalin offered.

"What do those bone-eating zealots have to do with this?" Esperanza asked. She realized the connection as soon as she had said it.

"Carasin tipped bolts," Lyric answered. "Carasin is made from the bones of the dead. They would have the easiest access to it."

Esperanza's normally stoic face broke slightly as she looked back toward the cattle cars. "Carasin isn't exclusive to the Cult of Bone, though I agree they would be the first choice. But a lone assassin?"

"Maybe he was buying time for his accomplices?" Lyric offered.

"Good thinking, Miss Wax. We should anticipate more of them, cultist or not." The Voca nodded.

Lyric chewed her lip, a gnawing unease twisting her gut. "What if all this isn't about him?" she offered, the words tumbling out like stones. "What if the Order...?"

Jalin's eyes flashed open and focused on Esperanza. The Inquisitors exchanged a look, a flicker of disbelief clouding their faces. Jalin, ever the blunt instrument, was the first to react.

"Impossible! You can't be suggesting...." His voice trailed off, a low growl building in his throat.

Esperanza cut him off, her voice laced with a caution bordering on fear. "Blasphemous, yes, but...," she hesitated, "...not entirely beyond the realm of reason."

"Bullshit!" Jalin snapped. "Do you truly believe the Order would...-"

But Lyric cut him off again, two words sharp as a blade.

"Paraíso Verde."

Lyric's words hung in the air, heavy with the weight of a forgotten past. The memory flickered on the Inquisitors' faces, a shared secret etched in lines of worry and a flicker of fear. "Only the three of us," she murmured, the weight of the truth a physical thing in the close confines of the compartment. "No other witness. Silence the three of us, and the only record is buried in my archives... archives the Order now holds."

Jalin bristled. "That's horseshit!" he snapped. "Sure, there's something rotten here, but don't go spinning conspiracy theories like a spider weaving a web of lies. We're on a train, a blasted metal snake rattling its way north. Who else crawls on this iron beast? Where are they headed? Maybe the assassin had eyes for someone else entirely! Our own turning on us? Tu loca, woman! Think!"

Lyric met his anger with a cool stare. "Fine," she conceded, her voice low but steady. "Then explain the mangled brakes? The sudden silence, this car cut off from the rest? And why, in the name of the Gods, are there two damn cars packed with ghouls?!"

"Because it's a bloody Mechanist train, their machines are tied together with spit and dreams!" Jalin spat back, frustration coloring his voice. "Half the time their contraptions break, the other half they blow up in their own faces! Sabotage or stupidity, it's a toss-up. Don't jump to conclusions without proof! I don't know why the ghouls are here, but the answers likely lie in the next cars down the line. We need facts, not accusations! Act with some damned reason!"

"Reason?" Lyric shot back, a bitter edge to her voice. "Where was your reason when you strapped Kane down in Witches Irons? All you needed for proof was the fact he wasn't like you." The words hung in the air, a challenge and a barb, leaving a tense silence in their wake.

"He's a monster, all of his kind are. That's all the proof I will ever need," Jalin said darkly.

As if on cue the rear door slid open and Emilio walked back into the room. His usual garb, stained crimson from Jalin's ministrations, was gone, replaced by baggy brown trousers that stopped above his ankles and a faded grey shirt that hung on his frame like a misplaced sail. He looked like a scarecrow in search of a field.

"Where in the world did you get those from?" Lyric asked.

Emilio flushed slightly. "From contents of one of the lockers."

"I stand corrected," Jalin said, "A monster and a thief."

Emilio looked at the wounded Inquisitor and said, "These looked like they belonged to one of the victims, yes. However, I left some money in their bag, so no. They're not stolen."

Jalin sucked his tooth. "High-minded justifications for looting the dead... pinche graverobber."

Before the situation could escalate further Lyric stepped between them. "Enough," she cut in, her voice firm. "We need a plan, not a pissing contest. We need to figure out how to stop this damn train."

Jalin scoffed. "Or," he drawled, gesturing to the wall with a pointed finger. "We wait ten minutes."

The three of them looked at Jalin in confusion. With irritation, he looked pointedly at Lyric and then motioned to the wall near the couch. "¡Mirar! Use your eyes!"

The map displayed their journey: The Reach, the North Gate, the sprawling Imperium, and finally, Valentina, the northernmost providence. Below it, a list of estimated arrival times for each stop.

A jolt of realization ran through Lyric. Checking the clock, she saw it was nearly half past one. Leaving Cruce del Águila around eleven, their next stop, Deeno Flats, should be coming up in ten minutes.

Jalin watched as Lyric took everything in. He nodded. "When the train stops in Deeno, you and Boyorquez should head to the ticket office and have them shut down the train. Then, we can deal with all of this. That is the plan," he said, leaning back into the couch with an irritated look.

Shame washed over Lyric as she realized she'd been so focused on Jalin, she'd completely missed the information plastered around the room.

Usually, she prided herself on her keen observation skills. Even in the chaos of the crossing and the fight, she managed to glean important details. But here, with Jalin injured, she'd let her focus slip.

Feelings will get you killed, Jalin once told her. She understood the meaning behind those words in this instant.

Instead of dwelling on her mistake, Lyric forced herself to look around the room with fresh eyes. Every scrap of paper, every map, every poster held potential information. Regulations, schedules, and even instructions for the train's communication system – all there for the taking. Knowledge was a weapon, and right now, they were woefully under-armed.

But self-pity wouldn't help. She was the team's scribe, their eyes. When they finally left this train, her job would be clear: observe, analyze, and document. Who disembarked? Who seemed oblivious, who looked on with knowing eyes? At Deeno Flats, she'd scrutinize reactions, quote Imperial regulations to support their actions, and be prepared for resistance.

Ten minutes passed, a lifetime crammed into a single breath. Anticipation hung heavy in the air, thick and suffocating.

And the train did not stop.

TOOLS

Borrowing clothes from the dead staffers had given
Emilio some pause. Ghosts and spirits remained on
this plane of existence because they were bound here. Many
times this was due to unfinished business, but sometimes
it was simply due to duty and obligation. Some served in
death, even as they had in life. A small squad of guards
still patrolled the grounds of the Gran Salon in the Reach,
despite having died decades or more earlier.

Emilio certainly did not want to be accidentally
responsible for binding the souls of these poor people
by nicking their clothing. Stealing from the dead was
one of the ways a person could earn their enmity. How
many legends occupied the Grand Library about some

unfortunate treasure hunter who disturbed a grave, only to be tormented for the rest of their lives by a ghost?

He'd done the needful before searching through their gear. Apologized to any lingering ghosts, neatly unfolded and refolded their clothes, and finally left a handful of silver coins in the pockets of those he had borrowed from. It was a simple thing, respect. But it helped ensure the dead would have fewer reasons to remain.

He briefly considered attempting to escape the company of his escort, but there was no safe way to exit his current predicament. The dime store novels always wrote about the lead character leaping from a train in a heroic escape. The science of the matter made that impossible. He would end up broken in far too many ways for even him to mend.

His eyes had lingered on the rear door and cattle car beyond. So long as nothing disturbed them, and the doors remained closed, the occupants should remain where they were. He worried about the man who fell into the car and to an all too gruesome end. It was possible that his fall into the protected area might have disturbed whatever magics were being used to hold them in place. He watched the service door for a moment and heard only the same metal clacking that had been present to begin with.

He could use the Sight once more to examine the area, but he dare not draw the attention of Cortez, who seemed all to eager to end his existence. The Manos needed little reason to act.

This had been the reason Emilio had simply chosen to rejoin his escort in the sitting area, instead of barricading himself inside the end of the car with the dead. Perhaps he could ascertain more once the train made its next stop.

Damn it, I need to know what's going on!

He sighed deeply and thumbed through the pages of his notebook, hoping to distract himself from his current situation.

Across from him Lyric and Cortez seemed to be arguing. Emilio did not care for how Cortez treated the women in his retinue. He was rough and rude, and everything Emilio hated about the Inquisition. But neither the young Scribe nor the Voca seemed to be cowed by his bully behavior. Perhaps they were all paired for that reason.

He closed his notebook and looked out the window. According to the posted schedule, they should be approaching Deeno Flats.

The train did not feel like it was slowing. He frowned and looked out the window once more. He could see the small village and train depot in the distance. It was quickly approaching.

Emilio had ridden trains before. Operated by The Guild they served as another means of secure transport that group oversaw throughout The Imperium. The Mechanist Guild however, had recently added their new trains to Guild routes. They did not operate the same way that the coal and steam engines of the Guild.

Am I overthinking this? They said it was a Mechanist Train, maybe they slow down differently?

The answer to that question was readily given as their train whizzed past the Deeno Flats platform without so much as a brake squeal.

Oh dear.

Emilio watched as a collection of potential passengers stepped away from the edge of the platform as the train sped past them all.

He turned his attention to Cortez then and watched as the man's pale complexion flushed with anger and frustration.

"Pinche scientists... building mechanical horseshit they cannot control!" he yelled. He winced slightly as he pushed himself up off of the couch.

"Inquisitor, your wounds..." Emilio began.

Cortez turned eyes full of hate on the Doctor. "Do not mother me, demon! I had worse injuries than this before I could shave. I am aware of my limitations. Mind yours."

Emilio held up his hands, and settled back into the bench quietly wondering how much chloroform he had packed and if it would be enough, should the need arise.

Movement to his right caught his eye as the Voca moved to sit beside him. She seemed a pleasant enough woman, and had assisted Emilio in dealing with the both the injured survivor and the deceased staffers in the back. She had offered to assist with the deceased, but Emilio directed her to handle the woman who was yet among the living. Sending the dead to their afterlife, and ensuring they did not linger, was his calling and duty, after all.

Esperanza's eyes watched the injured Inquisitor, as her voice addressed Emilio.

"What are your thoughts, Doctor?" she asked.

Emilio pursed his lips a moment. "Aside from realizing that we need to get to the Engine?"

"Mhmm" she mused.

"And what we might find when we get there?"

"Mmm," she nodded noncommittally.

"How does one actually stop a runaway Mechanist Train?" He said simply. He turned to look at Esperanza. "Who sabotaged the cars and why?"

"Both excellent questions," she agreed.

"I know very little about Mechanist Sciences. My science is not theirs. But I would assume that there is some sort of mechanism at the head of the train, in the Engine that could be... powered down? Perhaps there is a secondary brake mechanism there?" He stared at the ceiling. "I would settle for a means of communicating with one of their people to tell us how to stop this damned thing."

"Possibly also located in the Engine area."

"Back to the original goal, I see."

"Indeed." She glanced across the car to the map on the wall. "Our time, Doctor, is limited." She gestured at the route map that displayed the stops, distances between each and estimated times of arrival and departure.

Emilio squinted and pulled out a pair of wire-rimmed glasses. He set them on the bridge of his nose and examined the map.

The route was non-circuitous. It did not meet up with another set of tracks. It had a clearly defined final stop.

"This route ends in Sierra... the Capital of Valentina." He breathed. He looked back at Esperanza, "So if we don't stop this train..."

"It will crash into the train depot in Sierra. Hundreds of lives will be lost, and the contents of the cattle cars will be let loose in a city that managed to escape the worst of the Corpse Wars. Who would do such a thing?!" Emilio exclaimed.

Esperanza stood and brushed off her robes. "When we discover that, we will have the answer to your second question, I believe."

Emilio watched her stand and quickly tucked the hems of his too-short-pants into the tops of his boots to make them look less ill-fit. He reached for his satchel, slung it over his shoulder and stood.

Not waiting for Emilio, Esperanza walked up to where Lyric and Jalin were examining the map and the routes. Lyric was scribbling down figures and computations while Jalin called out locations and times.

"Have you determined how much time we have?" Esperanza asked.

"Five hours," Lyric replied. She continued to work the math, "Removing the stations stops, that gives us five hours to work."

Jalin scowled. "That does not leave us much time." He sucked on a tooth and looked toward the next car. "Was the Conductor among the bodies you found?" he asked.

Emilio paused and looked at Esperanza. She shook her head. "No, I don't believe so." She answered. "They appeared to be brakemen and porters."

Jalin nodded. "Provided there is a Conductor on this damnable iron beast, finding them should be our next action."

Lyric wiped her forehead with the back of her hand, drawing sweat and charcoal across it. "Because they would be in charge of the staff onboard?"

Jalin glanced over at her and nodded. "Yes. And they will know if anyone else has infiltrated the staff." He glanced toward the tail of the car where the lone survivor rested.

"Has she said anything?"

Esperanza shook her head. "Not much. She only recalled a single assailant. Her head injury is substantial."

Jalin leaned against the small desk and pondered something for a moment. He looked at Emilio. "When you were stealing from the dead, how many uniforms did you see back there?"

Emilio bit his tongue and refused to rise to the bait. "Only one. It appeared to be about the right size for our survivor."

"One uniform and four bodies without uniforms?"

Emilio nodded.

"One dead assailant that fell into the cattle car…," Lyric began.

"Which leaves three uniforms unaccounted for," Emilio stated.

Jalin looked over at Emilio suspiciously and then turned to Esperanza. "How is our survivor? Any hope of getting additional details out of her?"

Esperanza shook her head. "As I said, her head wound was substantial. She is not in any danger but needs to rest. The sedative the Doctor gave her should help."

"Not in any danger?" Jalin scoffed. "She's laying unconscious in the rear of a staff car, with the bodies of her fellows tucked neatly away in a closet. Behind her in the next two cars is a small force of ghouls just waiting for their next meal." He turned to glare at Emilio. "Tell me, graverobber, why are the dead being so well-behaved at this moment?"

Emilio shifted a little uncomfortably and looked at Esperanza then.

"They are being held in place," the Voca answered.

Jalin narrowed his eyes as he stared at Emilio. "By?"

"A warding circle," Esperanza replied. She shifted to interpose herself in between Emilio and Jalin. "He was bound and unconscious, Cortez. Someone else did this."

"More than one of you." Jalin smiled at Emilio. "I can't wait to meet them." His menacing smile faltered as the color drained from his face. His knees buckled slightly.

"Cortez!" Lyric called and reached to brace him, only to find Kane's quick hands already there.

"You've lost too much blood for this bravado, Inquisitor. We need to get some liquids into you." He looked at Lyric. "You said the dining car should be coming up soon?"

Lyric nodded. "Based on the shape of the cars, I think there may be two more ahead of us before then."

Emilio cocked his head to the side. "Are you a fan of the rail, Miss?" he asked.

"My younger brother studied them when we were children. Our home was littered with toy rail cars growing up."

Emilio nodded appreciatively.

Jalin struggled weakly against Emilio. He relinquished the brace of Jalin to the Inquisitor's retinue.

"Inquisitor, I know you couldn't care less what I say, but I am telling you as a doctor - if a fight is coming, you need to take your time and save your strength."

Jalin's response made it clear that he did not appreciate medical advice from a monster. He mumbled something unintelligible before forcing himself to stand on his own feet.

"Voca, take the lead." He nodded at Esperanza.

"Very good," Esperanza replied politely. "Doctor, you will be behind me, then Miss Wax. Cortez, please guard the rear.

We will advance into the next car, check for a functioning means of communication or additional staff, and see if we can locate the Conductor. If this is the Cult of Bone, they will not hesitate to make a second attempt on us. If we are not the targets of this plan, we need to discover who is. Above all else we must do one thing."

"Stop this train."

Tita felt like a fly caught in molasses.

The doctor's medicine dulled the edges of the pain but refused to fully claim her. A lifetime spent flirting with poisons made her well-acquainted with wooziness, a dance she could manage. Strangulations, a messy but necessary tactic to preserve uniforms, now offered a morbid advantage. Mimicking a victim required only a visit to familiar scars, etched from years-old performances.

Herrera had sacrificed himself, but not in vain. She'd learned much: four hostiles with their best fighter down as a result of Herrera's actions. The brake stick remained tantalizingly close in the cattle car. The opposition consisted of a Manos, a Voca, an Escritora, and a white-haired Doctor with strange green eyes, all under the Inquisition's banner.

Tita feigned unconsciousness as their physician went about his gruesome work. They spoke in hushed tones, a charade for "Ms. Reina's" benefit. Serena Reina, a name she borrowed for Eater's business, belonged to her father's long-forgotten mistress. A woman, hopefully still alive, who Tita cursed with every borrowed breath.

The conversation was a maddening stream of half-caught words: tools, the cars behind... then a chilling mention of spirits, some Inquisitorial nonsense no doubt. But the next thing she knew, the doctor was wielding the train's safety axe like a butcher, and cleaving the heads off of the deceased staff members.

A man who could sever heads with such ease couldn't be a simple doctor. Perhaps, in another life, he might have been swayed by the truth of the Bone Eater, but that bridge had long since burned.

Silence from the next car finally settled, lending a balm to her tense muscles. With the stealth of a wraith, she unlocked the door, peering into the empty sitting room. Back to the rear of the car, then to fetch the brake stick from the cattle car and search the forward cars for assistance.

The stench of death, familiar yet strangely different, rolled in as she opened the rear door to the platform. A flicker of hope, maybe Herrera had survived the Manos. With a practiced hop, she landed on the platform and yanked the lock free. The smell intensified, a cloying sweetness that clawed at her throat. Ignoring it, she wrenched open the heavy door.

Gone was the wounded Herrera. In his place, a nightmare. Pale eyes, dozens of them, stared back from emaciated faces. Hands, a writhing mass of them, reached out. The sedative's haze, combined with the horrific scene, rendered her slow. Pain, a searing inferno, erupted as countless mouths tore into her flesh.

In that final, agonizing moment, the Voca's words echoed in her mind, no longer garbled. Not "tools," but "ghouls." What madness had brought them onto this train?

A single, toothy maw filled her vision, the world dissolving into a kaleidoscope of pain as the undead claimed their prize.

DEENO FLATS

T he waiting room thrummed with energy. A man's voice
squealed like a rusty hinge. A woman's outrage echoed
through the cavernous space. Somewhere, a baby wailed,
an omen of warning hidden among the children's laughter
bouncing off the grimy walls.

Christina Olivares, Station Director, hunkered down in her
office. She ignored the primal urge to bellow back at the
yellers... they didn't see the bigger picture scrawled across
her desk in frantic scribbles. A train that wouldn't stop wasn't
just a missed visit to Grandma's; it was a runaway iron beast,
a potential harbinger of doom.

While the rabble outside raged, Christina issued orders
with brisk efficiency. The leather folder, fat with instructions,
felt heavy in her hand. Esteban Marquez, the Guild

Messenger assigned to this dust bowl of a station, scowled at her from the doorway. A shotgun rested in its leather hand-tooled scabbard across his back, a constant companion in this ghoul-infested land.

"Director? Can't you see I'm busy?" He rasped, his voice rough as desert sand.

Christina caught a whiff of something foul, a fleeting but potent odor of decay. It vanished as quickly as it came, leaving her with a prickling unease. "Esteban," she said, urgency lacing her voice, "grab your fastest horse and get this to Sandoval Pass."

Estaban frowned and accepted the folder.

"At its current rate, the train will pass you by the time it hits the stop in Truitt Lake, but you should be able to make up time if you cut through DeMarlo Woods. Your priority is to beat the 505 to the Sandoval Pass."

He flinched at the name of the next station, a place notorious for bandit raids and worse. "You can't be serious, woman! Did you not smell that?"

"It doesn't matter," Christina pressed, shoving the folder into his reluctant hand. "The 505 is a ghost train, Esteban. No brakes, no signal... a two-hundred-twenty ton nightmare barreling down the tracks. We need to warn everyone!"

Marquez's face contorted in a mix of annoyance and grim acceptance. "Why not your fancy telegraph machine?" he spat, bitterness clinging to his words. "They promised it was faster than us Guild Messengers, didn't they?"

Christina swallowed the retort. Now wasn't the time for petty squabbles. "Look, Esteban," she said, her voice low, "we can't take chances. Lives are at stake. I'll get the footmen to scout for ghouls, but those people on the 505 need you to be their guardian angel. Now get moving!"

The defiance in his eyes flickered, replaced by the gleam of duty. "The Guild will do its part," he muttered, snatching the folder and striding out.

Usually, she would have warned the Guildsman for the insult, but now was not the time for admonishments. There were too many lives at stake. Clutching the drawing compass that hung from her belt, she ran her thumb across its frame. She hoped the Mechanists were not to blame as she made a silent prayer to Geekind, the Child God of Creation.

Back inside, she sat at the telegraph, the rhythm of her tapping a counterpoint to the pounding of her heart. The Guildsman was a backup, a redundancy. The telegraph was supposed to be the swift answer. But the 505 had failed to trigger the "handshake," a ten-minute courtesy call from the Mechanists. It worked for their steam engines and their newfangled Railed Gear Cars. When the ever-reliable 505 didn't ping, she sent a footman to investigate. He returned pale-faced, the spotter confirming the train had passed the marker showing no signs of slowing. No way to know if it was the marker or the train itself. Then, silence from the telegraph connector. That's when Christina truly panicked. A simple glitch, or a cascading system failure?

Better safe than sorry. She composed a stark message, fingers flying over the keys.

ST27-TO-ST29_STOP_505-DIRE-MAL_STOP_SIDELINE-ALL-ACTIVE-RAILS_STOP_INFO-IN-ROUTE_STOP

A sliver of fear pricked her heart. No sign of ghoul rot now, but what if...? Sending another message, she prayed it wasn't too late.

ST27-TO-ST29_STOP_505-POSS-G-INFECT_STOP_REC-FULL-SAFE-PCAUTION_STOP

"Who the hell are you and why are you on my train?!" The old man shouted. The name tag on his uniform screamed CONDUCTOR. Lyric was grateful for Esperanza's silver tongue in that moment. Jalin's diplomacy usually involved a well-oiled pistol, but the Voca could talk a troll out of a bridge toll.

The Conductor was all sharp angles and controlled tension. His uniform, though worn, held itself together with an air of quiet pride. It sat on him like a second skin, bespoke for a life spent barking orders and wrangling chaos. An assassin? Maybe. But Lyric's gut sang a different tune. This man's body language spoke of rheumatism and a lifetime spent hauling, not skulking in the shadows.

"Apologies, Conductor," Voca's voice cut through the air. "Voca Esperanza Boyorquez, Inquisition of Hil, at your service. We were... misplaced in your rearmost car."

The Conductor narrowed his eyes. "Impossible. The caboose is for the cattlemen and their beasts. There's no Inquisition on my manifest."

Lyric and Esperanza exchanged a worried glance, but before either could speak, Jalin stepped forward. "Seems there's a lot you don't know, old man. Now move aside before we make you move."

The Conductor's spine stiffened. "I won't be bullied, boy! You lot are going nowhere near the engine car." As if on cue, four porters stood from their seats in the baggage car. They weren't in staffer uniforms – these were utilitarian clothes, built for a purpose. Not assassins, then. But loyal, that much was clear from the way they bristled at the Conductor's command.

Just then, the unmistakable click of a pistol being drawn shattered the tense calm. Lyric whirled around to see Jalin, face thunderous, his gun glinting in the dim light. This wouldn't end well.

"Gods' teeth, Cortez, put that away!" Emilio hissed. "We've got enough trouble without turning this into a shooting gallery."

Jalin sneered. "Shut your trap, Kane."

The Conductor's voice cut through the bickering. "Trouble? What trouble?"

Lyric met his gaze. "We believe the train's been sabotaged."

"And why, pray tell, would you believe that?"

"Because, sir," Lyric began, "we weren't on the manifest. Yet, here we are, writs and vouchers declaring the caboose as our quarters until the Northern Gate. The problem is, the doors were sealed shut from the outside, and the brake lines were limp. We tried to alert the engine car – nothing. Electrovox dead, brake lines useless. Top that off with the fact you're not hauling cattle, but a good score of ghouls, and you've got yourself a situation, wouldn't you say?"

The pistol did little to faze the Conductor or his men. But Lyric's words hung heavy in the air. The Conductor licked his lips, his composure cracking. "Ghouls? Why haven't they attacked, then?"

"Let me answer that," Emilio piped up, stepping forward.

All eyes turned to the disheveled doctor. "And why would you know, sir?" the Conductor rumbled.

"Doctor Emilio Kane, at your service." he bowed, a touch too deeply. "Authorized Necromist for The Reach."

The bravado drained from the porters' faces, replaced by a primal fear. Even the Conductor seemed to shrink a little. Lyric stole a glance at Emilio, who appeared unfazed, as if this little dance of terror was a daily routine.

"They haven't attacked," Emilio continued, "because they are bound. I was able to glance into the cattle cars... they were all standing in a binding circle. Someone knew what they were doing."

Jalin muttered something under his breath about dropping Emilio in for a closer look.

Ignoring him, Lyric pressed on. "We have one of your people in the staff car. Unconscious, but maybe one of your men could fetch her? She might know more about what happened."

A burly porter named Ryan shook his head violently. "No way in hell I'm going near those forsaken things."

The Conductor turned and snapped at the man. "Silence, Ryan! Are you a Guild man or no?"

"Why can't they bring her here?" Ryan shot back, gesturing at the group. "There's enough of you lot."

"Well," Lyric said, her voice dropping to a low murmur, "Inquisitor Cortez here" – she flicked a glance at Jalin, who scowled back – "had a bit of a disagreement with an assassin on the way to the staff car. Seems the fellow decided to take a rather permanent...nap ... courtesy of Jalin's pistol. Our Physician," she nodded toward Emilio, who nodded politely back, "...is needed here to tend to his wounds. Our Voca was able to stabilize your crew member's injuries." She focused her gaze on the Porter, her green eyes hardening, "And more importantly, the four of us just finished climbing across the top of two cattle cars, narrowly avoiding falling through the ceiling of one, battling an assassin, and discovering that this whole train may be compromised. I believe my team has done their fair share of both protection and discovery at this juncture... is it too much to ask you to recover your wounded teammate?"

The Conductor's face had gone the color of a poorly cured ham. He ran a hand over his bald head, sweat beading on his brow. With a sigh that rattled his chest, he said, "Ryan, Marcos, get the emergency gurney from my office. Double-time it back to the staff car and bring that woman here, wounded or not. We may be a Mechanist train, but we are still true Guild men and don't leave our own behind. You lot," he gestured towards Lyric and her companions, his voice tinged with weariness, "come with me. We've got a lot to discuss, and precious little time to do it."

TICKETS PLEASE

There were no windows in the Luggage Car. Gas lamps, perpetually on the verge of sputtering out, cast flickering shadows that danced across mountains of luggage. Unlike the Staff, who sipped lukewarm tea in the previous car, these Guildsmen were bound to their burdens.

They slept on narrow cots wedged between steamer trunks and dented valises, the rhythmic groans of the engine their lullaby and the unseen things that lurked in the tunnels beyond their only companions. It wasn't a life for the faint of heart. The air hung heavy with the metallic tang of sweat and the cloying scent of old leather. Yet, for many, it was also a badge of honor, a testament to their wanderlust.

Some were young, their eyes glittering with the cartographer's dream of etching every twist and turn of the track onto their very souls. Others were weathered veterans, their faces etched with the cynicism of a thousand wrong turns and the ghosts of a thousand forgotten stations. All, however, bore the silver sigil of the Guild, and all answered to the iron fist of the Conductor, a man as imposing as the engine itself.

Lyric had gambled on the presence of the Porters, would the train have them? If so, they would surely be in the next car. But the Conductor... that was a stroke of twisted luck entirely. He would be able to sniff out an imposter in a stolen uniform faster than a starving ghoul could scent fresh carrion. He was also a walking archive of Guild lore, a man who could read a passenger's intent from the scuff of their boots. An invaluable asset, then, but a dangerous one too.

The assassins, cloaked in borrowed skins and borrowed lives, would surely want him silenced for the same reasons.

The Porters, a hulking, unshakable wall of muscle and grime, parted for Lyric and her companions as they followed the Conductor deeper into the cavernous luggage car. Row upon row of trunks and valises lined the walls, each meticulously labeled with faded ribbons. Some bore the muted hues of distant lands, whispers of forgotten journeys... a deep crimson that spoke of the sun-baked deserts of the South, a faded turquoise that hinted at the turquoise waters of the West. A pang of memory stabbed at Lyric's heart, a memory of her mother tying a similar ribbon in her hair before their first train ride, a journey east to visit long-lost kin. The laughter, the excited chatter, felt like a lifetime ago, swallowed whole by the relentless symphony of steel and steam that pulsed through the train.

The Conductor shrugged off his massive coat and hung his garment on a hook with a reverence that bordered on worship. He then settled himself behind a small scarred desk. Stacks of worn ledgers and manifests rose like miniature skyscrapers, held down by paperweights and memories.

"Tickets please," he rasped.

Lyric unslung her bag to fish out their travel vouchers, paper thin and worn at the edges. As she handed them over, the Conductor's gaze sharpened. His eyes flicked across the numbers, a silent language only he could understand.

"Where did you board?" he finally asked.

"Carver's Town," Lyric replied. "We were... issued vouchers by the Order. From there, a brief stop at Outpost Janus, then Cruce, for supplies."

"And your party?" He leaned forward, the lamp casting grotesque shadows across his face.

"Just us four. The Order provided the vouchers, we exchanged them for these tickets."

The Conductor grabbed a book bound in red leather and opened it. He flipped through a manifest, his brow furrowing. "Manifest says a dozen cattlemen. Caboose is usually Staff only, but seems someone bought their way in, hoping for a comfortable ride. Names and ticket numbers here, but...," his eyes slid up to Lyric. "You are certainly no Mateo Hinds." He resumed his examination of the documents. "They boarded in Carver's, livestock added at Cruce de Águilas. Irregular, that's for damn sure."

Esperanza, ever the pragmatist, cut through the tension. "Forgive the interruption, but have we persons of interest aboard? Given our recent... encounter."

Lyric saw the glint in the Voca's eye, the unspoken plea. "Yes, there might be passengers in danger. Potential targets..."

The heavy door at the far end of the car screeched open, shattering the fragile tension. A chorus of hissing shrieks filled the air, a sound that sent chills down Lyric's spine.

Ghouls... the ghouls were coming.

Minutes Earlier

The staff car reeked. Ryan shoved open the door, the stench of blood and decay hitting him like a rusty fist. Everything was covered in crimson.

"Gods," Ryan choked out, bile rising in his throat. "What the hell happened in here?"

Marcos chuckled, a dry, humorless sound. "Maybe the Necromancer's pets felt peckish." He busied himself with the straps on the gurney, the metal groaning in protest.

Ryan made a face at the word.

"Did that eskeleto bother you, sunshine? Come on, these Inquisitors wouldn't know what to do with him if he was the real thing. Probably some scare tactic to keep the sheep in line."

Ryan wasn't convinced. "Necromancers bring death with them, that's what they say. Why would the Inquisition drag a monster around with them? Makes no sense."

"You want answers, kid? From the Inquisition? They deal in pronouncements from Hil on High, not reason," Marcos said flatly. "Laypeople, you can talk to. These lot? Zealots with a taste for blood."

With a grunt, they hoisted the gurney. The old metal groaned. As they reached the sliding door to the sleeping quarters, dread coiled in Ryan's gut. He yanked the door open.

There, bathed in the sickly lamplight, stood a single figure. Humanoid, vaguely, but wrong in all the ways that mattered. It stared at Ryan with dead, milky eyes. The stench of the grave clung to it like a shroud. Before Ryan could even scream, the creature launched itself at him in a monstrous parody of a hug with razor-sharp teeth.

Panic, sharp and hot, flooded Ryan's veins. He tried to shove the thing away, but it was too late. The world blurred as teeth sunk into his neck, the iron tang of blood filling his own mouth. He could have fought a man, fended them off, but this? This was a nightmare made flesh.

Marcos, blessedly quicker on the uptake, bolted back as the monstrous horde swarmed Ryan. The gurney strap, in a cruel twist of fate, held him fast. Using the makeshift shield with desperate strength, he shoved and kicked at the grasping, decaying limbs. The sound of metal on bone echoed in the confined space. He needed to warn the Conductor, the Inquisitors – anyone!

With a final surge of adrenaline, Marcos ripped the strap free, collapsing the gurney into a makeshift weapon. The steel bars became a desperate flail, the sickening crunch of bone on rotten flesh his only solace. He couldn't tell if they felt pain, there was no pause in their relentless advance. His only companion the raw terror that gnawed at his insides.

This fight wouldn't last.

One last swing cleared a path in the writhing mass of bodies. Marcos spun, heart hammering against his ribs, only to find another monstrosity blocking his escape. A hiss, cold and almost reptilian, filled the air as more shambled through the open door.

"H-how..." he croaked, the word ripped from his throat. It was all he could manage before the tide of death engulfed him.

Jalin steadied his pistols on a nearby shelf and fired. He took a breath and reloaded.

"Wax!"

Lyric stepped up to aim. The report of her shot was a thunderclap in the cramped corridor. But they had no other choice. These weren't human things they faced. These weren't bandits or rogue hunters. These were horrors born from nightmares, their rot a palpable stench in the air. She aimed and fired.

"YOU SAID THEY WERE BOUND, KANE!" Jalin shouted. He stood to aim once again as Lyric reloaded.

"THEY WERE!" Emilio shouted back. "SOMETHING MUST HAVE HAPPENED TO THE WARDS! AND NO! IT WAS NOT ME!"

Assessing the situation, Esperanza felt a momentary sense of inspiration. "The trunks!" she yelled, her voice hoarse with frantic urgency. "Throw the steamer trunks! Block their path!"

The two remaining porters blinked at her, their faces slack with shock. They looked to the Conductor, his once-proud bearing now a crumpled mess. "Just do what she says!" he barked, his voice hoarse. Panic had finally cracked the veneer of control he'd held so tightly.

With a surge of unexpected strength, the porters hefted the heavy trunks and hurled them like battering rams at the oncoming tide of horror. The air filled with the twisted harmony of splintering wood and crunching bone, a chorus of gunfire blending with the creature's unearthly screeches. The luggage, once a symbol of journeys and faraway lands, became a makeshift bulwark against the encroaching darkness.

Lyric spun on her heel, her eyes locking with the Conductor's shattered gaze. "We need to stop this train!" she shouted, her voice cutting through the cacophony. The old man stared at her, his world of timetables and polished brass collapsing around him. "We have to get out of this car before we all die!"

A long beat of silence followed, broken only by the rasping breaths and the sickening thuds of bodies colliding. Then, with a tremor in his voice, the Conductor finally spoke.

"Throw that last luggage rack, and then follow me! This way!" He gestured wildly towards a single, battered door, a beacon of uncertain hope on a train hurtling towards hell.

Carlos Monterro, freshly minted Assistant Conductor, perched on a sliver of wood that dared to call itself a desk. His uniform, crisp and new, mirrored the Conductor's sense of order. Six months ago, he'd been a dreamer with a clipboard; now, the weight of the train pressed down on his shoulders. The world was an orderly machine, or so he'd thought. But the rails had buckled, the timetable was crumpled scrap, and the passengers were a flock of startled pigeons.

The train should have stopped at Deeno. A simple, expected pause in the iron beast's predictable rhythm. But Deeno was a ghost now, a forgotten echo in the train's memory. Panic, a cold, insidious thing, wormed its way into Carlos' belly. Protocols, he knew, were the train's bible, but the sacred text little solace in this uncharted territory.

The Mechanist 505 was not expected to ever miss a stop.

He thumbed through the book the Guild provided to the staff. It was something no one ever hoped to have to open.

Orders were clear: the Conductor would contact the Engine while the staff worked downtrain.

Assess the passengers first.

He started with the posh folk in First Class, then the disgruntled din of the Dining Car. Coach passengers were next, their concerns scribbled on his clipboard – a litany of missed connections and misplaced luggage.

Next to Carlos a weary-looking woman in a staffer uniform filled cups with water from a cooling cistern. Ginny Elba's orders were much more straightforward: appease disgruntled passengers with food and beverage where possible. Any questions or complaints would be directed to the Conductor or his Assistant.

The offer of free food and snacks killed off any immediate ire but would not stem the tide of customer dissatisfaction for long.

Neither Carlos nor Ginny anticipated the sudden entrance of the Conductor from the tail end of the car. The old commander of the train had been missing for some time, no doubt handling some issue down train.

Perhaps the missed stop was connected?

Behind the Conductor followed a menacing-looking man with pistols drawn. In their wake trailed a bizarre procession of people.

A robbery? A thief, perhaps?

The mind leaped to the obvious. The missed stop, a wound in the train's rhythm, the silent electrovox - all pointed to a common culprit. But then, a flicker of saffron, a sun-kissed symbol, disrupted the familiar narrative.

Inquisition? What the hell was happening?

"Carlos!" The Conductor grabbed him by the elbow and pulled him aside. "Lead the passengers out of the car... now. No questions. Go through the kitchen and into the dining car."

He turned to Ginny, his voice low and urgent. "Small ones first, mothers with babes."

"Sir," Carlos asked as his eyes were riveted on the man in the stained shirt. Sweat beaded on the man's brow, a stark contrast to the crimson tapestry of its shirt. Illness? No. Injury. A wound, fresh and recent lay beneath his attire. His gaze flickered to the woman in saffron, a beacon in the gathering gloom. Then back to the wounded man.

Inquisitor!

Carlos' eyes darted toward the tail of the car. Two figures, one with hair like spun copper, the other an enigma of white, fought to hold back an unseen horror. Something was coming.

Carlos spun, a puppet jerked by invisible strings. Ginny was already moving among them to alert the most vulnerable. He cleared his throat.

"Ladies, Gentlemen, and fellow Travelers, please excuse the disruption to your journey, but there is a situation in the tail cars which necessitates you moving to the fore..." he began in his most polite tone.

Murmurs, like the low growl of a waking beast, rose from the crowd. The Inquisitor found his voice. "We have no time for this," he growled, a challenge in his tone. The flame haired woman, her face etched with terror, cried out, "They're coming!"

Questions died in Carlos' throat, strangled by the urgency of the moment. He inhaled deeply, a desperate plea for courage, and roared, "Move!"

EXORCISMO

The bar on the door slid into place, a finality in the sound that chilled the blood. Beyond, a tempest raged, in the belly of the train.

Emilio closed his eyes for a moment and offered up a silent prayer. Two young souls, lost to the darkness, echoed in his mind.

"I ask that they be given their Promise and escorted home," he intoned softly.

Grief, a cold and heavy thing, settled in his heart. Innocent lives, extinguished like candles in a gale. All due to the actions of someone who was clearly perverting the Gifts of Styx.

A writhing mass of bodies pressed against the glass of the car behind them. They would break through soon enough.

With hope, perhaps they would fall to their demise between platforms and there would be fewer to deal with.

But what of those that did not perish who fell from the train? What of the angry souls left to wander when these host bodies were destroyed? They would infest the wilds.

Emilio sighed deeply.

"Where are you coming from?" he whispered. Taking a breath he closed his eyes and focused beyond the glass, beyond the platform, into the writhing mass of bodies that defied death.

A maelstrom of energy met him. It swirled in and around the creatures weaving their very beings into one another.

"Doctor?" The Voca's voice pulled him from his visions.

He blinked rapidly and turned to face Esperanza. "Sister." He inclined his head.

"Ms. Wax is taking the Inquisitor and Conductor forward with the rest of the passengers. How long will it hold?" she asked.

Emilio shook his head, "Not long I am afraid." He wiped his hands on his pants. "They seem more focused than what I would typically encounter."

Esperanza nodded. She lowered her gaze and replied in a hushed tone, "We dealt with a ... significant infestation some months back. Those were also more clever." She looked up at Emilio. "As if controlled by another."

Emilio frowned at the thought.

"Tell me, Doctor," Esperanza asked, "What does your Lady's Sight show you?"

The Necromist carefully watched her for a moment. Her invitation could be a trick meant to condemn him. Instead of judgement or prejudice, her honey-colored eyes carried only grim approval.

A single, sharp nod, and he understood. With a muttered word, the power of Styx grew to a cold whisper on his tongue and he swept his hand across his eyes. The world blurred, then sharpened into a horrifying tableau as the luggage car and its familiar clutter was replaced with a churning vortex of madness.

The Sight, a blessing or a curse, revealed the world beyond the veil. His normal abilities allowed him to see the dead, but The Sight gave him full view of the world past El Velo the Veil between realms of the flesh and the dead.

What he saw caused the blood to drain from his face. It wasn't just flesh and bone lumbering towards them, but storms of twisted emotions. Anger, Sorrow, Fear - a cacophony of human misery given monstrous form. They were puppets animated by a darkness that fed on their despair.

A cold dread coiled in his gut.

These were not just mad souls clinging to material world. This was so much worse! This was the horror of La Corrupta.

If these vessels were destroyed, the raw power they held captive would be released. La Corrupta would be free to wander the world. It would be a terrible, hungry thing unleashed and uncontrolled.

Then realization set in... Cortez and Wax had already been firing on them! Were they destroyed or slowed down?! What corrupted soul had they released and where? Panic began to grow as he continued to stare at the mass of madness in front of him. He needed to concentrate... he needed to focus on the tendril of power. Where were they coming from?

A tendril of fear snaked through Emilio as he focused The Sight once more.

There!

Cords. Dark, bloody tethers that stretched from the furthest, monstrosity in the back to the ones swarming across the luggage car. Entwined, warped, and slick with a sheen that made his stomach churn. All of them connected, a writhing network of spiritual hooks that... that led to him?

The blood leeched from his face once more. They were all attached to him. Why? How?

"Doctor?" The Voca's voice, laced with concern, yanked him back. "What did you see?"

He spoke, his voice hoarse. "These... these things are not fresh kills! They have been harvested. Someone harvested dangerous, and terrible souls. They are bound to the walking corpses, and all of them are mad. If we destroy their bodies, what they hold... could become... La Corrupta. All of them. Spirits of Wrath, Sorrow and Fear will run rampant across The Reach!"

He felt Esperanza's gaze on him, searching, dissecting his words. The Sight revealed, but it also burdened. If he turned that gaze to her now, the Voca would be a blazing sun, her divine power burning bright. He couldn't see her face, but her tone spoke volumes –

"What else, Doctor?"

Fear, cold and sharp, echoed in her question. It mirrored his.

He had a choice to make. Attempt a falsehood that might buy him some time, or tell her everything, and let the blade of Hil fall where it may. If he was the tether, the reason these creatures rampaged, her choice would be clear – cut the cord at its source.

He would not blame her, not for this.

Despite it all, a part of Emilio screamed, *This is not my doing! Lie, you fool. Lie!*

He forced his gaze back through the spectral cords, their power pulsing like a sick heartbeat. He followed them, tracing their path until it stretched beyond the maelstrom, disappearing into the swirling chaos. A flicker. A faint, spectral thread in the distance. It solidified, revealing ancient sigils, their meaning a grim revelation.

The Dead never lie.

"A... cord," he rasped. "Their maker's tether. They are not here... not on the train... but there is an anchor, feeding them control. We sever it... they're power crumbles. But..." his voice trailed off, a leaden weight settling in his gut. "Without that control, the bindings might unravel. They might become what they were meant to be. And that... that will be so much worse."

The Voca spoke, her tone no longer laced with alarm, but a steely resolve. "There is an option, Doctor. It is impossible for me to wield while the train is in motion. The power... it would derail us."

He turned, as he met her gaze, the Sight fading. Her face, once an impassive mask, held a grim determination. "El Eterno... The Final Cleansing? You can..."

She simply nodded. "But only once."

The solemn communion was shattered by a clatter above. Scrambling feet, like rats in the walls, and the thunderous percussion of fists against metal heralded their descent.

"They are upon us!" Emilio yelled, his voice a clarion call.

With the urgency and haste, they moved, Emilio and Esperanza a vanguard against the encroaching chaos. The car, a funnel of fear, began to empty its mournful procession of souls. The porters, steadfast as rocks, bridged the chasm between cars, ferrying the terrified to safety.

The dining car loomed ahead, a refuge besieged. The ceiling, a fractured shield, threatened to collapse. Just as the last of the passengers crossed the threshold, the ceiling crashed down in the passenger car, rotting, slavering bodies falling to the floor below.

The closest porter helped Esperanza across the gap to the next platform and reached for Emilio. A shadow passed across his face and then a creature was upon him. He screamed and flailed, falling backward toward the rail.

"No!" Emilio yelled and reached for him. It was too late.

They struggled for a moment, and then were gone. The wind and speed of the train having hurled them over.

The other porter stepped up to the doorway, an iron bar in his hands. He stretched his neck from side to side.

"Get to the other side." he said.

"No, you can't..."

"Guild protects their passengers..."

"Don't do this." Emilio pleaded.

"Go!" he yelled and shoved Emilio toward the other platform.

The porter hefted the bar and swung it at the head of one of the approaching creatures. It popped open like an overripe melon, and the creature collapsed to the ground. Another swarmed forward and launched itself at him. He wrestled with it for a moment and then stepped backward enough to allow it to pass by him. He shoved it off the side of the platform and under the grinding wheels of the train.

"Get inside!" the Porter yelled as two of the creatures fell on him. One of them dug its teeth deeply into his forearm. He yelled in pain.

Esperanza watched as the swarm of creatures began to fill the car they were just in. They were relentless and unstoppable. She took a breath and stepped to the rail of the platform she and Emilio now stood on.

"Hil's Blessed Light Fill me with your Grace," she intoned and threw her arms wide.

Beside him, Emilio felt the surge of energy within Esperanza begin to gather. The Voca's power forced the ghouls to pause as the light burned their rotting skin. Their advance halted, but it did not drive them back.

"My boy, now is the time for you to join us," Emilio said quickly and reached for the young porter who had been battling the ghouls. He pulled the man across the gap.

"Run." Emilio told him.

Without hesitation, and cradling his injured arm, the porter dashed inside, leaving the chosen of Hil and Styx on the platform alone.

Emilio turned to Esperanza, her tan features were spiked with lightning-like scars of light. The barest of the divine light should have been enough to frighten creatures like these away. But they were somehow able to struggle against the power of Hil.

He squinted back into the maelstrom, a fresh detail snagging his gaze. Each rotten neck sported a black leather choker, a sickly green stone embedded in its center.

"Hold them, Voca, a moment longer!"

Emilio lunged forward, grabbing a ghoul's throat. Styx's power surged, a wildfire of power, through him. He'd always been so careful, rationing the goddess's bounty. But the Voca held these abominations back, risking everything. He couldn't skimp on the answers they might hold. A mere hour ago, he'd sworn off the Exorcismo, but the alternative loomed too large.

Forgive me, my Lady.

Drawing upon the words and power, the struggling monstrosity froze in place. He could see the Corrupted soul writhing, yearning for freedom from its mortal tether. As Emilio finished the last incantation, he let the power flow through him. He braced himself for entropy's harsh bite, but a curious coolness washed over him instead. Styx's fury lanced into ghoul and soul, setting them ablaze in eerie greenish-blue flame. The creature crumbled to ash, the spirit dissolving into nothingness. Only the choker and a pile of tattered clothes remained.

He stumbled back, shaken, the exertion leaving him lightheaded. His stomach rolled with nausea.

He snatched the collar before turning back to the Voca. Her lightning scars pulsed brighter than ever, a terrifying portrait of power.

For a horrifying moment, she seemed lost in the ecstatic power coursing through her. This was the price one paid for wielding the Divine. He couldn't let her drown in the power's seductive embrace.

Grabbing her arms, he channeled Styx again, a mere whisper this time. The cool touch snapped Esperanza from her trance. Her eyes, wide with shock, met his.

"WE NEED TO GO NOW, PLEASE!" he pleaded.

Dropping her arms, she fell into Emilio. He quickly pulled her inside and slammed the door shut. The light of Hil had only paused them... what was this madness?

THE LIGHT OF HIL

The wind sang a mournful dirge in Esteban's ears, a contrast to the pounding rhythm of Bonita's hooves. No other horse, not even a warm-blood from the Eastern plains, could take this punishment. They rarely had the chance for such a furious gallop anymore, not since the damned telegraph began spitting their messages across the land, strangling the life out of the open road.

There was a savage joy in the wind whipping at his face, the world blurring into streaks of ochre and brown. But it was a bitter joy, poisoned by urgency. He'd thought Bonita might balk at the pace, but the mare seemed to share his desperate need. Esteban harbored no particular hatred for the Machanist Guild or and their contraptions, though their smug faces often turned his stomach. The true Guild still ran the trains, their hands on the levers, their blood and sweat on the tracks. No infernal machine could take that away, not yet.

Still, a nagging worry gnawed at him. Was it the crew's fault? Were they to be scapegoats for the machine's failure? It didn't matter. He had to eat sixteen miles in under an hour if he was to beat the 505 to Sandoval Pass. So far, luck had smiled, a fickle, capricious thing with razor-sharp teeth. The road around Truitt Lake had been blessedly empty, allowing him to skirt its glassy surface.

Truitt Lake, a vast beast of reflected sky, stretched before him. The station there was a crossroads, a harbor for boats chugging north on the Río Oso or south into the Vargas mountains along the Lienzo. The 505 would have puffed past it by now, forced to take the long, watery route. Even if he made it through the damned woods, they'd still be a third of the way back while he had a clean shot to Sandoval Pass through the high roads.

But the woods... Even as he kicked Bonita onwards, he felt unseen eyes prickling at his back. It was only two and a half miles, but the path twisted and turned like a drunken snake. He kept his hand near the worn grip of his revolver, made sure the leather folder tucked against his chest was blatantly visible. Bandit logic was a simple thing – young ones, bold and stupid, went after Guild Messenger. The smarter ones, the ones who knew their trade, steered well clear unless the pickings were guaranteed fat. Even then, greed had a way of turning the most cautious thief into a fool.

But a wilder thought snaked its way into his mind. What if it wasn't greed? What if these unseen watchers knew the stakes? The Lovers Cartel, La Familia Ortega, or even the shadowy Sombra, all held sway over the criminal underbelly of the Imperium. Perhaps this was their doing, a way to disrupt the flow of information, to sow chaos. It didn't make sense, though. Cartels dealt in coin, tangible wealth. The 505 was just passengers and cargo. There hadn't been any word of high-value shipments, no mention of the Guild taking out extra insurance.

Maybe the truth was more prosaic. Maybe, just maybe, some folks simply didn't want to mess with a Guild Messenger on a demon-possessed horse, barreling down the road like a harbinger of the storm. Esteban allowed himself a grim smile. Maybe that was enough.

Esteban burst from the treeline, blinking against the sudden expanse of sky. One last, desperate glance back offered a glimpse of the lake, a shard of reflected sunlight catching the distant form of the 505. It chugged purposefully across the horizon, a familiar silhouette marred by a strange unease. Was it the light, warped by the lake's shimmering surface? Or did something... shift... on the back cars of the train? A disquieting flicker, like a swarm of tiny, agitated ants crawling across its metal skin. Unease tightened its icy grip around Esteban's heart.

What was happening?

Esperanza and Emilio tumbled through the doorway, the porter slamming the bar shut behind them with a practiced thud. Lyric steadied Jalin, her gaze flicking to the Inquisitor. The bandages held, but his ragged breaths spoke of a well running dry. Still, they couldn't afford to pause.

Jalin snarled at the Necromist, "What do you mean they were coming from the roof?!"

"He speaks truth, Cortez," Esperanza wheezed, her voice strained. "These things..." she gestured vaguely, "are relentless. And worse, empowered. Controlled by some sort of charm." The Voca leaned heavily on the doctor who braced her as best as his slight frame would allow. Exhaustion lined her face.

Lyric caught a glimpse of telltale red streaks peeking from Esperanza's collar – the strain of channeling the divine, leaving its mark like a spiderweb of cracks. Were these creatures truly stronger than those they faced in Mathis, or was Esperanza's connection to Hil frayed beyond repair?

Esperanza met Lyric's gaze with a flicker of understanding, then quickly shook her head, a silent plea for calm. The Voca leaned further into Kane, who held out a simple leather collar with a green stone pulsing like a sickly heart.

"We were able to get this off of one of them," he offered. He held the collar out to Lyric and Jalin.

It reeked of death.

Jalin snatched the collar, his eyes narrowing. "Someone keeping ghouls as pets now?" He flipped it over, scrutinizing the faint markings etched into the leather, then showed them to Esperanza, "Do you recognize these?"

Esperanza shook her head, "It's not something I've seen before, no."

"And the stone?"

"Magic, but none I've seen," she replied.

"You wouldn't have," Emilio offered softly. He gently helped Esperanza to a seat. He knew they would not have much time before they needed to move again, but every moment was a blessing.

Jalin scoffed and glowered at Emilio. "Why am I not surprised to hear you know what this is?" He handed the item to Lyric.

"I've not seen it in person. I've only read about it while at the Academy. It was part of the Corpse Wars history we all had to take," Emilio began. His eyes darted toward the rear of the car. The doors would hold, but for how long?

Following Emilio's gaze, Lyric recognized an opportunity. She ducked past Jalin and headed to the rear of the car.

"Where are you headed?" Jalin demanded.

"Buying us some time. Doctor, keep explaining!" she called back.

Emilio blinked his confusion away for a moment, "Of course," he paused.

Lyric darted toward the tail of the car to look for severed brake cables. With practiced hands, she yanked several yards of the thick cord free and wove it into a makeshift net across the doorway. Sheer force could break glass, but it would take reasoning to get through knots. Her eyes darted toward the door.

Or mass.

She gambled that the unseen hand controlling these horrors couldn't unravel knots with the same ease that shattered doors.

Any delay would buy them time.

Esperanza brought them all back to the conversation, "You were saying?"

"Right!" Emilio said, "The collars are not the main concern, Inquisitor. What's been done to the ghouls is the main concern."

Jalin rubbed his face in exasperation. "Pretend we don't have time for dialog and lecture, and ...get...to...the...point."

Kane picked up the thread, his voice grim. "The souls of these people were not simply harvested and placed in these bodies. The primal emotions at the time of death have been stoked like a blast furnace. If we destroy the bodies, we will release the corrupted soul within. Every time we destroy the body its bound to, we release a Howler or a Screamer into the land to terrorize the people. Whoever is behind this wants someone like you to destroy these shells so they release a wave of terror in their wake. It's part of their plan. It has to be. Someone is playing a deadly game, Inquisitor, and ensuring these dead bring nothing but horror and death."

Jalin ran his tongue over his teeth, "This is why the Imperator killed all of your people at the end of the Corpse Wars, Kane. No one should wield this power."

"I agree," the Necromist replied.

Jalin kept his eyes locked on Emilio, suspicion simmering beneath the surface. "Wax and I," he announced, "we'll clear the roof. Guns will keep them pinned down, or we'll send them tumbling off the damn train. We can follow up on their locations and clear up the stragglers once we stop."

He stretched, reluctance twisting his features. Then, the words he clearly loathed to say, "Voca, unleash Hil's glory. Burn them all. Simple." He pushed himself to his feet, a monument to grim resolve. "Wax, my guns."

Esperanza's voice, barely a whisper, cut through the tension. "I can't."

Jalin froze, body taut. "¿Qué? What do you mean you can't?"

Esperanza slowly stood to address Jalin, "While your idea is sound, it would derail the train, killing us and everyone else on board in the bargain."

Her words gave Jalin pause. Killing men who were in service to evil was one thing. Murdering innocents was something different. He considered her words a moment.

"And La Luz?" he asked.

She shook her head.

Jalin frowned.

"I was wielding La Luz Divinia, the Light of Hil. They should have retreated or been burned to ash in Hil's Holy Light. They held their ground. They burned, but did not care. They were unmoved."

The truth, stark and unwelcome, settled on Jalin's face. He looked at Esperanza, searching for any sign of deceit, but her expression was solemn.

"They stood... before the Light of Hil?" Jalin whispered.

Emilio watched as the two members of Hil's most faithful struggled with the realization that something might be on parr with their own faith. He knew that Styx and Hil were equals, that one was not inherently more powerful than the other. But for the devout followers of Hil, such a notion was heresy, a blasphemy against their vain and jealous god. Part of him wanted to let them drown in their moment of crisis, but this was neither the time nor place for such comeuppance.

He cleared his throat.

"Hil has not failed you, Inquisitors. There is merely a Necromancer at work, who is using circumstance and surroundings in their favor." He touched Esperanza's elbow gently. "Have faith, Sister. The collars are empowering them somehow."

Esperanza turned weary eyes to Emilio and nodded, "Thank you, Doctor."

Lyric's voice broke the tension. "Finished your theological debate? Excellent. That netting won't hold them forever." She jerked a thumb over her shoulder.

Jalin looked back toward the doors and at the netting the Scribe had crafted. He looked back to her and nodded. "Good work."

Unphased, Lyric ducked under Jalin's arm once more and jogged toward the head of the car.

"One of us has to keep working while you three are having a crisis of faith," she said with a dry wit. "If you would excuse me, I have to go shoot some ghouls before they manage to cross from one roof to the other."

"Remember Ms. Wax, cripple them; impede their progress, but don't destroy the vessel," Emilio added.

Jalin nodded and reached for his weapons. "I'll join you."

Lyric shook her head. "Go check on the Conductor. I can handle this."

"Wax..."

Lyric locked gazes with the gruff Inquisitor. A flicker of concern danced in the depths of the Manos' dark eyes. It had been just a month since he and the Voca bore witness to her Verdad, her coming of age. An experience that unfolded in ways none of them had foreseen.

Paraíso Verde.

"You can't protect everyone all the time, Cortez," she answered and looked at Esperanza. "The dining car is made of steel. It will take them longer to get into."

A glimmer of hope flickered in Emilio's eyes. "Or get out of, if we can trap them, perhaps?"

"One can only hope," the Scribe replied, a hint of grim humor in her voice. Then, with a fluid movement, she hauled open the front door and scrambled onto the roof, ready for her grim duty.

THE PROMISE

The dining car of the 505 was a marvel to behold. Divided into two saloons at its head and tail, each adorned with tables and chairs, it catered to the whims of its passengers. One side boasted intimate single tables, while the other hosted communal dining experiences. Through the tempered glass windows, the ever-changing landscape painted a backdrop for their meals.

If the Engine was the heart of the train, then the kitchen was its soul. Nestled between the saloons, it occupied a significant portion of the car, a bustling hub of culinary creativity. One side dedicated to the art of cooking, the other to meticulous preparation. The trio of refrigerators stood as sentinels to this mobile feast, ensuring freshness and delight with each passing mile.

A slender corridor traced along one side of the car, offering a clandestine route from one end to the other, cleverly circumventing the bustling heart of the kitchen. Sliding doors closed this passageway off at either end.

As Lyric noted, the dining car was sleek and covered in polished metal. The enemies had been able to bust through the wooden ceilings of the previous cars but they would be hard-pressed to be successful in that move with the next several. While the body of a ghoul may have been strong, it was still subject to the limits of its human frame. Bones would shatter and flesh would rip free long before they could break into these cars from the outside.

Pushing the passengers out of the previous car and into the dining car had been a wise maneuver. It was rare that the car was ever completely filled, so there would be room for the displaced passengers to take a moment of reprieve while they assessed the situation.

Lyric slid down the ladder and jumped from the passenger car platform to the dining car. She had slowed the progress of the ghouls climbing across the roof as best as she could. But she was only one person, and had limited ammunition. The dining car was their best chance.

She rapped on the rear window and one of the porters turned around. He nodded and pulled the car door open, then quickly slammed it closed and barred it shut.

The car was in chaos.

The iron clang of Jalin's voice echoed through the narrow saloon, a fistful of dread clinging to each word. "No. One. Moves."

Lyric, peered past the hulking silhouette of the porter. Inside, a nightmare unfolded. Kitchen staff, clad in stark white, stood frozen, hands trembling. Their blue-grey uniformed brethren mirrored their fear, punctuated by the crumpled form of the Assistant Conductor, kneeling on the sticky floor.

The Conductor was dead.

He lay sprawled across the cold tile, his pristine white shirt stained crimson. One look at the gaping wound in his belly, and Lyric knew they were dealing with a practiced hand.

Another assassin.

Four terrified cooks, and three equally petrified trainmen huddled in fear at the scene.

"Cortez?" Lyric said.

"The old man was dead by the time we came in. I'm guessing he saw who was out of place," he said as he scanned the faces. "Come on, you pinche bone sucker... you have nowhere to run," Jalin said as he looked at each of them.

From the corner, a voice, quiet as a tomb, broke the silence. "Inquisitor, perhaps a word of-"

"Shut the hell up Kane!" Jalin said.

Emilio pursed his lips in response to the reprimand. He straightened the collar on his oversized shirt. Ignoring the

Inquisitor, his voice tinged with practiced calm, Emilio spoke again.

"If you are a member of the Guild, please slowly reach into your shirt with your left hand and show us your chain of service."

A slow ballet of fear unfolded. Each person, with trembling fingers, produced a chain worn around their neck. A mix of copper and silver, each bearing the unmistakable emblem of the Guild - a stylized scorpion glinting in the dim light. All but one medallion rose in mute surrender.

All eyes turned to the woman, tears carving glistening tracks through the grime on her face. Her smile sent a shiver down Lyric's spine.

"May Bones Taste Flesh."

Before anyone could act, her body started to convulse, and her mouth began to foam. Panic erupted, cooks fleeing the scene like startled roaches.

"FUCK!" Jalin shouted rushing towards the body with Kane at his heels.

Lyric pushed past the porter, desperately trying to get eyes on the situation. Cooks fled through the kitchen and into the gathered group of passengers in the other saloon. A flash of saffron yellow told Lyric that Esperanza would be trying to manage the chaos in the other end of the car.

Kane quickly knelt by the fallen woman as she went through her final death throws clearly torn in his duties.

"Is there anything you can do, doctor? She may have the answers we need, and we're running out of time," Lyric said.

Kane finished his grim examination, his eyes flickering from the woman's ravaged form to the Inquisitor looming over him, then back to Lyric. "There might be a way, Ms. Wax," he said, his voice a low murmur, "but it comes with a price."

Jalin's response was immediate, the pistol a cold kiss against Kane's temple. He pulled the hammer back.

The Necromist held the gaze of the Inquisitor, the man sworn to protect the world from the vestiges of evil that haunted it from ages past. A man caught in the clutches of superstition and fear. "Do you want to know if they are causing all of this and what they are doing? I have one chance, but if I do not act now, we will never know."

The tension between the two men stretched taught, threatening to snap. Jalin's finger tightened on the trigger. The pistol clicked, sharp and final.

The chamber was empty.

Jalin smiled, his point made. "Do it."

Kane shot Cortez a withering look before turning to his bag. He rummaged inside, extracting two vials – one filled with a viscous yellow liquid, the other holding a dark, unsettling powder. With practiced ease, he spread the powder over the woman's chest, then poured the oily liquid into his palm, anointing her forehead with it as her vacant eyes stared sightlessly upwards. As he drew symbols on her forehead with oily fingers, Lyric glanced in Esperanza's direction.

The saffron-clad Voca had come forward to watch the spectacle unfold. Unlike Jalin's raw fear, Esperanza's eyes held a chilling curiosity and hunger for the forbidden knowledge Kane was about to wrest from the dead.

Finally, Emilio opened a leather pouch and retrieved a long, silvery needle. Taking the woman's hand, he pierced each fingertip, a cluster of crimson jewels blooming momentarily. He pressed her bleeding palm into the dark powder, then, with gestures that seemed born of forgotten nightmares, Kane's body pulsed with a faint blue light.

Fear coiled in Lyric's stomach. Esperanza wielded Hil's light, but this was a different magic, born from the cold embrace of the grave. It was the stuff of nightmares, of whispered legends, dark pacts and souls bartered away.

The dust stirred, coalescing into a spectral echo of the dead woman, her face a mask of terror. It seemed tethered to her lifeless hand, like a puppet on a string of death.

Kane, his eyes glowing with an unnatural blue-green fire, spoke with a voice that chilled Lyric to the bone. "The Promise is held. Ask your questions quickly, for the dead linger on borrowed time, and cannot lie."

The woman's spectral face contorted in panic, darting around the room. "What...where am I? This is...darkness..." Her voice trailed off into a whimper.

Cortez grimaced with distaste, "Are you with the Cult of the Bone?"

"Yes," the swirling visage confirmed, "But...where am I? Why is it so dark...oh gods..."

Ignoring her pleas, Cortez pressed on, "How many of your cult are on this train?"

"Four," she revealed, a tremor of fear running through the dust-formed face. "Am I dead? This wasn't supposed to happen..."

"How are you controlling the ghouls?" Jalin demanded, cutting through the woman's confusion.

"Ghouls? We didn't know about any ghouls," a moment of genuine terror replaced her earlier confusion. Then, a scream ripped through the room. "WHAT IS THAT? GODS, WHAT ARE THOSE THINGS?!"

"What is she seeing, Kane?" Jalin hissed.

"La Corrupta," Kane rasped, "They're coming. She sees them for what they truly are."

The woman's spectral form writhed in the air, "Please! They're coming closer! Let me go!"

"Why is the Cult here?" Jalin barked.

"We were sent to...cleanse someone in First Class," she stammered, her voice laced with rising panic. "Bonilla knows who..."

"Who is Bonilla? Describe him!" Jalin cut her off.

The form began to struggle, pulled by unseen forces. Kane met Jalin's gaze. "I can't hold her any longer. Her time is due."

Jalin's protest died in his throat as Kane began speaking in hushed tones. With a gentle touch, he closed the woman's eyelids. Lyric watched as the wisp of dust, tethering the woman's image to her body, rose into the air.

The woman's spectral face whipped around in a final scream, "NO! THIS WAS NOT THE PROMISE! WHERE IS OSSILARO?! WHERE IS OUR REWARD?!" The air split with her shriek as the dust dissipated, leaving only silence and the echo of terror in the room.

"What the hell was that doctor?" Lyric said, her voice trembling in both horror and anger. "What did you do to that woman's soul? What was the Promise?" The pistol, cold iron against her trembling hand, found itself aimed at Emilio Kane. This time, the gun was loaded.

Kane's gaze with its unnatural green sent shivers skittering down Lyric's spine. His focus dropped to the gun, then climbed back to the Scribe. Disappointment guttered in those emerald depths, like a dying candle flame.

"Nothing, Ms. Wax. When I severed the anchor, she saw what awaited her. Where? I can't say. What? That's a mystery even death keeps close." He rose slowly, hands outstretched in a gesture of surrender, the picture of weary compliance. "The Promise... well, it's what we call the journey a soul takes after it leaves its fleshy shell. A Necromist, you see, swears an oath. The Promise of Death. A guarantee that the soul gets where it needs to go, when it needs to be there. I... I bent the rules and stayed my Oath hoping to save some lives."

Despite the tremor in her hands, the cold fear clawing at her throat, Lyric saw a hint of something else in Kane's eyes. Not fear, but a dull, heavy shame. He wasn't enjoying this macabre performance. It twisted him inside, and made him feel... unclean.

"At what cost?" Lyric asked.

Emilio shook his head. "One only I will have to pay... eventually." Clearing his throat, he continued, "As for what she saw, I can only presume it wasn't the paradise promised by her false god, and I'm fine with that. She killed an innocent man and probably more. As far as I'm concerned, she got what she deserved."

Lyric's grip wavered on the pistol. A gentle hand settled over hers, warm and reassuring. Esperanza, the Voca, stood beside her, grim approval in her eyes.

"Doctor Kane speaks the truth, Lyric," Esperanza's voice was a soft murmur. "She saw only what awaited her. He merely gave us a glimpse into the abyss she was staring down."

A reluctant grunt rumbled from Jalin. "Boyorquez is right, Wax. She is headed to whatever she earned. And I expect Hil will have no mercy for her. Focus on the now. Focus on what she told us."

Taking a deep breath, Lyric squeezed her eyes shut and shoved all her emotions into a mental box. When she opened them again, they were clear and cold. Stepping forward, she addressed Carlos, the Assistant Conductor.

"We need to get these people moving. Get them into the next car."

"The next car's the sleeper," Carlos replied, concern etching lines on his face. "Then it's First Class, but I don't see how we can cram everyone in there. Passengers and staff – there'd be no way to move."

"How secure are the sleeping compartments?" Jalin asked, ever the strategist.

"It's a double-decker coffin car...." His eyes darted toward Emilio, suddenly self-conscious of his choice of words. He cleared his throat uncomfortably, "I mean to say ...the compartments don't have windows, meant to be kept dark," Carlos explained.

"Can you secure them from the inside?" Jalin pressed.

"I think so," Carlos said, but before he could elaborate, a shout ripped through the tense silence.

"Stay away from us, you freak!" one of the staffers bellowed at Emilio.

The Necromist raised his hands in practiced surrender. He gestured with a single raised finger, "These wounds need cleaning, or something worse might happen. And we need to make sure the Conductor's body isn't a target for possession."

One of the staffers rose, fists clenched, his intent to bring injury to the Necromist clear when a sudden burst of golden light filled the room, forcing everyone back. Esperanza stood at the epicenter, her hand outstretched, a ball of shimmering energy crackling in her palm.

"In the name of Hil's Glory, you will stand down and allow Doctor Kane to perform his duty as a sanctioned Necromist for the Realm!" Her voice boomed with divine authority. "Your complaints are noted, but you are ordered to have your wounds cleansed, if not by Doctor Kane, then by one of your own. All of you save the Assistant Conductor, leave immediately!"

Her tone brooked no argument. Slowly, reluctantly, the porters shuffled out, their faces a mixture of awe and fear at the raw power they had just witnessed. Yet despite the dazzling display, Lyric realized the truth. That wasn't the potent light of command Esperanza usually wielded, nor the cleansing fire of Hil. While the source was divine, the effect was simple – blinding, overwhelming light.

Once they were alone except for Carlos, Esperanza dropped the charade, fatigue draining the color from her face. She slumped against a nearby counter, the light dissipating in her hand.

Jalin eyed Esperanza as he re-holstered his pistol. "Wax," he started, "I take it you figured out a way to buy us some time?"

A sly smile played on Lyric's lips. "I bottlenecked them in the car behind us," she admitted. "Because the next stop is Sandoval Pass."

ESCRITORA

S andoval Pass wasn't a valley, but a natural cathedral carved by the breath of forgotten gods. Here, landbridges soared like petrified rainbows, each a testament to nature's artistry. These weren't mere spans of rock; they were the ribs of the earth itself, arched majestically across the chasm. Millennia of wind had sculpted them smooth, their surfaces catching the sunlight and erupting in a spray of colors.

The Guild meticulously wove the tracks for their railway through the valley, each curve and run was built in artistic reverence to the natural wonder of the Pass. A compliment to the artistry of the Divine. Only twice did the Guild dare pierce the landscape with tunnels for their rail, coming into the Pass and leaving it.

Now, the iron snake of the 505 approached the sacred beauty of this natural wonder. The narrow passage carved into the mountainside would surely scrape any of the remaining ghouls off the side of the train, freeing them from the undead parasites that remained outside its metal skin.

The solution was double-edged. While the 505 might be rid of its external threat, the survivors, those tenacious enough to weather the scraping, would be unleashed upon the area like a plague. Grim fodder for a realm already cursed with restless dead.

Emilio nursed a lukewarm cup of tea in the rear saloon of the dining car. His stomach roiled at the prospect of what was yet to come. A map of the Guild's sprawling rail network across the Imperium lay unfolded across the narrow table. He meticulously marked sections with the nub of a pencil, his back to the kitchen, eyes fixed on the door to the tail of the train. Half a car's length away, the remaining ghouls struggled against the trap that Escritora Wax had laid.

Clever girl, the University had honed her skills well. But fear still danced in her eyes when she had leveled her weapon at him – that was a different story. He sighed, a weary sound escaping his lips. Education could only go so far. Ultimately, she was still a pawn in the Inquisition's deadly game.

And the Inquisition, with its unwavering zealotry, craved nothing more than the eradication of those like him – those who danced with a different kind of magic, a magic the pious elite deemed heretical.

In the front saloon of the dining car, Inquisitor Cortez and his Voca counterpart argued with the Assistant Conductor and Staff about the current situation. Thankfully, convincing passengers to relocate to the cramped confines of the sleeper car hadn't been a terrible task. Ghouls, after all, weren't known for their intellectual prowess. Breaching doors held little appeal to them unless something – or someone – unwisely drew their attention. Fortunately, the narrow space of the sleeper dorms had allowed for most passengers to find refuge in the car's upper level. With the stairwell doors firmly locked and a resolute porter standing guard on the other side, a fragile sense of security had been established.

The more challenging fight had been convincing the Assistant Conductor to allow Emilio to secure the fallen Conductor's body. A swift beheading would have been the simplest solution. But Emilio knew none of the Staff would stomach such a barbaric act. Leaving the Conductor's body unattended was unthinkable. Even if a malevolent spirit didn't claim it, the inevitable ghoul horde would find it a grotesque feast.

Unacceptable.

Eventually, Emilio convinced the younger man (along with the Voca's insistence) to allow him to sanctify the body under Styx's protection. Placing two silver coins over the man's eyes, he wrapped a blindfold around the man's head to prevent them from coming free. The last of the precious juniper oil, a potent deterrent against restless spirits, was meticulously applied to the face, hands, and chest. With a murmured incantation and a prayer whispered to Styx, the body shimmered, briefly taking on an unnatural blue hue before returning to a semblance of normalcy.

It was the best he could hope for in these circumstances.

With Ms. Wax's help, they managed to clear a cold storage locker, a temporary tomb for the Conductor. Now, both physically and spiritually shielded, the body was, for the moment, out of sight and, hopefully, out of mind.

He rubbed his eyes and the bridge of his nose trying to contemplate next steps. Boot steps interrupted his musings.

Please don't be Cortez, he thought.

He opened his eyes and glanced to the side where Lyric stood. Her face was covered in grime and sweat. Her jerkin soiled with blood. She had pulled her red hair back and secured it into a knot at the nape of her neck. The red Escritora tattoo of her assignment proudly displayed for all to see.

Historian.

Servant of the Throne.

Imperial, not Inquisition.

Emilio shifted in his seat and gestured across the table for her to join him.

Lyric nodded in quiet thanks and sat. Her eyes on the group at the head of the car, while Emilio watched the tail. She glanced at the map.

"What are you working on?" she asked.

"Trying to keep track of where we may need to send people when we are done."

Her brow crinkled in confusion.

"Just because we knocked them off of the train, doesn't mean they won't become someone else's problem."

Lyric's face blanched, "What have we done?"

Emilio reached across the table and lay a warm and gentle hand on hers. It was the hand of a surgeon, a healer, warm and smooth and reassuring.

"Only what was necessary, I assure you."

Lyric slowly pulled her hand away from his touch.

Emilio nodded, accepting her response. It was one he was used to. Few people were willing to accept the touch of a man who dealt with the dead. "Once we can get word, I am certain your Manos and Voca will want to advise the Faithful of where they need to patrol."

"I didn't think you would approve of how Hil's people would handle the situation?" she asked carefully.

Emilio shrugged and leaned back a little. "I don't. These souls should be sent to their rest, not destroyed. It's not their fault they have become enslaved," he sighed deeply then. "Hopefully, we can figure out these collars and release the trapped spirits. If not... I am only one man, and the Faithful... are many."

Lyric stared at her hands a moment and then looked back up, "I'm sorry about earlier, doctor," Lyric said quietly.

"You didn't pull the trigger. It's fine," Emilio replied with practiced ease.

"No... no, it is not. I'm sorry. I just did not understand," she said.

"How could you? I doubt it's taught at University. Forbidden magic, remember?" He forced a smile.

"But what you did, for the Conductor... that was a kindness for a man who probably would have thrown you off his train if he'd known what you are," she said.

"And?" Emilio asked.

"It doesn't bother you?"

"Deeply. But I have a duty to perform," he gestured to her tattoo. "Just like you."

Lyric's fingers strayed to the red ink on her neck.

"You said that my people were responsible for how the world treats you?" she said quietly.

The Necromist pursed his lips together and tapped the blunt pencil on the table, considering his response.

"Words, perhaps spoken in haste and anger," he offered.

Lyric shook her head. "Don't do that."

"Pardon?"

"Brush off something that clearly bothers you. Avoidance of an issue rarely solves it," the young woman said.

Emilio looked down at his hands on the table, hands that had saved hundreds of lives, and sent as many souls to the afterworld. He chuckled softly, "No. But it does tend to keep me alive in a world that wants me dead." His eyes, an eerie and unnatural shade of green, slid up to meet hers. "As much as I hate to admit it, your Inquisitor and I are alike in many ways." He pressed his lips into a thin smile. "Our battlefields cross one anothers. We both must choose when to take up arms and for whom... and we will both probably die at the hands of that which we are sworn to protect".

He held her eyes then, the Necromist and the Historian. For a moment they could have been two students in a dark study room of the University Library. Comparing notes on some ancient document they had uncovered. Then he blinked, and the moment was gone.

Emilio leaned back and then resumed examining his map. "Now, Ms. Wax you should probably get up and walk away from me before Cortez decides I am trying to corrupt your soul by breathing the same air."

Lyric allowed the edges of her lips to tug upward slightly at the remark. She stood. "It's Lyric."

Emilio turned his face to look up at the young woman, a hint of curiosity in his eyes.

"I think we've been through enough that you can use my given name, Doctor."

Emilio nodded in appreciation.

She looked over to Esperanza and Jalin as they talked to the Assistant Conductor "Though you should mind who is within earshot when you do."

"Oh, I quite understand," he said.

As Lyric stepped away, she glanced back at Emilio poring over the map spread out before him. The gaslight's glow cast fleeting shadows across his furrowed brow, a silent reminder of the burdens they both carried.

Bonilla's frustration seethed. He took a deep breath, his chest heaving, and unleashed his anger on the stack of blankets. Whispers among the staffers dubbed this a runaway ghost train—no communication, no brakes, and a complete lack of understanding on how to halt it.

In another lifetime, this might have been their golden ticket. But Guild procedures—oh, those wretched, binding procedures—were nooses fashioned from red tape, threatening to choke the very life from their mission.

Bonilla was not a man given to hatred. Hate was a luxury that devoured time and energy, leaving precious little room in one's mind for the truly important things. Like survival.

But in this case, he made an exception. He despised Procedure with every fiber of his being. Procedure was a relentless taskmaster, a demon that wore a suit and tie, stamping out the twin virtues of laziness and procrastination—the very qualities that allowed an assassin to blend into the shadows of normality before striking.

This damnable train, this iron beast of constancy, had become his nemesis. It should have been a proud symbol of punctuality and order. Instead, it refused to stop, barreling through stations and expectations alike with gleeful abandon.

It was... inconsistent.

Normally, Bonilla danced with inconsistency like an old lover. It was a human foible that often played into his hands, leaving cracks in the facade of normality through which he could slip unnoticed. But this particular brand of chaos was a wild card he hadn't anticipated, a joker laughing in the face of his carefully laid plans.

He had hoped the train's erratic behavior would create fissures in the rigid procedures, allowing him to inch closer to his quarry. But the staff, bless their mortal hearts, clung to their routines like drowning men to driftwood. Their eyes might betray quiet panic, but their actions remained as predictable as the ticking of a clock in a nightmare.

Each passing moment felt like a tightrope walk over an abyss of failure. Yet Bonilla's mind, honed by years of deception, kept him balanced, a master acrobat in the circus of subterfuge.

Their mission, on its surface as simple as a child's puzzle, was in truth a labyrinth of deadly intricacy. Arrive at the station (check), procure the camouflage of staff uniforms (check), and locate the target (in progress). Then would come the holy trinity of their craft: distract, dispatch, depart. The fly in the ointment was the valise, a seemingly ordinary bag that held secrets worth killing for. Bonilla didn't know what lay within, nor did he care to. Curiosity, after all, was a luxury afforded to cats and the soon-to-be-dead.

As the hands of time spun their relentless dance, the carefully woven tapestry of their plan began to fray. Herrera and Tita had vanished into the ether, their fates unknown. Had they sent the Inquisitors to meet their makers, or had they themselves been ushered into the afterlife? Their reputations suggested they'd choose a warrior's death over capture, so at least their secrets were safe, locked behind lips stilled by death or stubbornness.

Alvarez, ever the patient spider, waited in the dining car. All that remained was for Bonilla to spy their prey, to confirm that the lamb had indeed wandered into their slaughterhouse on wheels.

Timing, that fickle mistress, now danced just out of Bonilla's reach. The plan, once a beautifully crafted timepiece, now ticked with the erratic rhythm of a broken clock. He had envisioned their macabre ballet reaching its crescendo at Truitt Lake. Deeno Flats was to have been their dress rehearsal, a chance to ensure all the players knew their parts. From there, it would have been a simple matter of orchestrating their grim performance – the cleansing, the departure, all choreographed to the train's final whistle at Truitt station.

But Truitt had come and gone like so many forgotten dreams. They were now hurtling towards an uncertain future, the landscape outside a blur of possibilities. Bonilla could still salvage this with Alvarez's help, but the final notes had to be played before they reached the Northern Gate.

Guarded by the watchful eyes of uniformed men, who saw too much and understood too little, that portal offered slim hope of escape. Their only chance now lay in a daring leap before the train could reach that destination. The route ahead whispered promises of opportunity... small lakes like black mirrors reflecting the stars, rolling hills that could cradle secrets in their folds. But each option came with its own pitfalls.

A strange popping sound interrupted Bonilla's reverie. He gazed at his fist, half-expecting to see the bones of his hand rearranged into some eldritch sign. But no, his knuckles were merely reddened. Lifting the blankets revealed a ruined landscape of flesh that had once been a face painted now in shades of crimson and purple.

With delicate fingers that belied their recent savagery, Bonilla unpinned the golden scorpion pin from the corpse's collar. The tiny arachnid gleamed in the dim light, its metallic legs seeming to twitch with phantom life as he affixed it to his own uniform. This golden seal was more than mere decoration; it was a key to unlocking doors both literal and metaphorical in the rarified air of the First-Class car. Only those who had weathered the storms of service were granted this talisman.

As he gazed down at the crumpled form of the staffer, Bonilla felt no stirring of pity. The man had been a prick, the kind of petty tyrant who derived joy from wielding the smallest morsels of power. He had taken it upon himself to escort Bonilla back to the Sleeper car, like a parent dragging a misbehaving child. The sharp chop to the throat left the man gasping. The subsequent pummeling with blankets had been... less artistic, perhaps, but satisfying.

With practiced ease, he folded the body into the cabinet. The blankets followed, covering sins both fresh and premeditated. As he closed the door, Bonilla mused that cabinets on trains were rather like secrets – best left shut, lest their contents spill out at inopportune moments.

Bonilla straightened his jacket, each movement a brushstroke in completing his disguise.

It was time to dance.

FAILSAFE

E steban urged his horse forward, each gallop bringing him closer to the station looming ahead. Behind him, the 505 had vanished into the distance. Time was running short, and he knew it.

The station buzzed with activity. Angry voices filled the air, their owners united in their frustration at a train that had failed to arrive. Amid the human chaos, large steers swayed on their tethers, adding their low bellows to the cacophony of discontent.

Esteban ignored the commotion, his eyes fixed on the stables. Two women emerged from the shadows, their riding gear marking them as fellow travelers of long roads. The Guild's sigil adorned their saddlebags, a silent marker of their allegiance.

"You the messenger from Deeno Flats?" one asked, her tone heavy with expectation.

Esteban replied cautiously, "Quick is the secret..."

The women's eyes lit up, and they finished the phrase in unison:

"To find its home, but..."

"...only by those that refuse to speak it."

The tension eased, identities confirmed. Esteban dismounted, his legs adjusting to solid ground.

"I'm Esteban Marquez," he said. "The Station Director's expecting these." He patted his satchel meaningfully.

"Emma Durango," said one sister, her voice dry. "And Mona," she added, nodding to her twin. "We'll escort you to North Gate Archive once you're done here."

Esteban raised an eyebrow but said nothing. He strode into the station, leaving the sisters to wait.

Inside, the station was a testament to Mechanist ingenuity. Whirling fans kept the air moving, their constant motion almost hypnotic. A well-stocked commissary lined one wall, its shelves filled with food and other necessities. Clocks of various sizes dotted the walls, each displaying the time in different parts of the Imperium. Pipes ran along the ceiling and baseboards, disappearing into unknown recesses of the building.

The Director's office sat at the heart of this mechanical wonder. Esteban entered to find three men absorbed in comparing notes and numbers, their murmured calculations creating a soft backdrop of sound.

"Director," Esteban said, his voice cutting through their concentration. "I bring this from Deeno Flats." He held out the leather folder, suddenly aware of its potential importance.

The youngest of the three men accepted the folder with visible reluctance. He opened it on a nearby rolling tray and pushed it towards the others. "Sir," he said, his tone laden with unspoken implications.

The eldest leaned over the open folder, his eyes narrowing as he examined the contents. "This penmanship is atrocious. Is that Olivares? By the gods, you'd think she'd have learned to write properly by now."

The three men studied the notes intently, the silence in the office broken only by the soft ticking of numerous clocks. Finally, they looked up at Esteban, acknowledging his presence with a slight nod.

"You may pass these on to your associates," the eldest said, his voice dry and disinterested. "They've been instructed to take them to the Northern Gate for archiving."

Esteban blinked, confusion evident on his face. "Is that all? Aren't you going to do anything about the situation?"

The eldest raised an eyebrow. "Do what, young man? The 505 will arrive here shortly and be assessed for repairs. Our calculations indicate it will stop in the next five minutes. You are dismissed."

"How?" Marquez asked, rooted to the spot.

"I beg your pardon?" the eldest replied, his words clipped.

"I asked how you plan to stop the train," Marquez persisted.

The youngest of the three stepped forward, his face a mask of polite disdain. "I fail to see how that's any of your concern, sir," he said, the last word tinged with false politeness. "This isn't some outdated Messenger relic. This is a Mechanist train, equipped with technological fail-safes beyond your understanding. We have the situation under control. As Director Cole has said, you are dismissed."

"That may be a Mechanist train," Esteban said firmly, "but Messenger Guild members are staffing it. That makes it my concern." He stood his ground, eyes locked with the youngest man, his thumb hooked on his belt. The gesture was clear, and the three men understood its implication without words.

"Perhaps some clarification is in order, along with introductions," the second man said smoothly. He gestured to Esteban.

"Marquez. Esteban Marquez," he offered.

"Assistant Director Lopez, at your service," the man replied with a slight nod. "This is Station Director Cole," he continued, indicating the older man. "And our colleague here is Mr. Perry, our Personnel Manager. Mr. Perry, you should get going now."

Perry bowed his head formally to Lopez and Cole, then turned to Esteban. "Happy learning, sir," he said, his tone barely concealing his disdain.

Before Esteban could respond, Lopez spoke. "Tell me, Mr. Marquez, what do you know of electro charges?"

"Next to nothing," Esteban admitted, "but you have my curiosity."

"Curiosity!" Lopez exclaimed, his face brightening. "Curiosity is essential for all Mechanists! It's what led to our early warning system for trains." His words came quickly, full of enthusiasm. "The 505 has no front windows for the engineer. That space is dedicated to a specialized engine. No need for coal, water, or steam. We've removed all unnecessary elements, leaving only power."

Director Cole interjected, his voice calmer than Lopez's. "The 505 missed two stations, likely due to faulty connection points. We can't reach the engineer or crew, but one thing remains reliable - the electro charges."

"Imagine a constant static charge running ahead of the train," Lopez continued, "about 30 yards in advance. If anything blocks the track - a tree, cattle - the charges are disrupted. This triggers a fail-safe, stopping the engine's power immediately."

"Outside," Cole added, his tone suggesting finality, "Mr. Perry is leading some borrowed cattle onto the track. In two minutes, the 505 will encounter this barrier, and Mechanist innovation will demonstrate its effectiveness."

Perry and a group of pale-faced cattlehands led the massive animals onto the track. Perry sat on his horse in the middle, clearly visible from the Station Director's window.

Esteban glanced at one of the many clocks in the room. Each second seemed to pass slowly. The rumble of the approaching train grew louder, maintaining its speed.

"Directors," Marquez said urgently, "you need to tell him to clear the track. The 505 will not stop."

"Nonsense, sir," Lopez replied, his voice strained. "This is all under control!"

But the train did not stop.

What followed was horrific. The train plowed through the animals without slowing. Screams filled the air as the 505 continued its relentless journey.

Then, as quickly as it had come, the train was gone, leaving behind a scene of devastation.

Cole and Lopez stood motionless, their faces ashen. Esteban forced himself to look away from the carnage.

"Director," he said, his voice sounding odd in the sudden quiet, "you need to send a message to the Northern Gate."

"It... it should have stopped," Cole muttered. "The science... the science..."

Esteban grabbed Lopez's shoulder, turning him around. "Lopez! Look at me," he said firmly. The sudden movement seemed to bring Lopez back to awareness.

"What... what do we do?" Lopez asked, his eyes focusing on Esteban.

Esteban looked at the map on the wall. "Send a message to your Mechanists who know about your trains," he said. "The rail goes through the valley wetlands in Carolina, then climbs to reach the Northern Gate, right?"

"Yes... that's correct," Lopez replied. "Why? Is that important?"

"Does the train slow down when it goes uphill here?" Marquez asked, his finger tracing the steep terrain on the map as if it might come to life under his touch.

Lopez blinked, his mind visibly refocusing, like a camera lens adjusting to a new, harsh reality. "Yes... yes, it does. To save fuel and avoid overheating, if the instruments detect a significant elevation change, the engineer reduces the engine's speed."

"And if the engineer is... unable to do so?" Marquez asked carefully, each word weighted with unspoken possibilities. "Or if the instruments aren't working?"

Lopez swallowed, his eyes drifting upward as if searching the ceiling for answers hidden in the plaster. "If the engineer can't manually lessen the power, the engine will automatically shut down if it nears overheating. However, there needs to be a constant release of the pressure or..." His voice trailed off, leaving the sentence dangling like a man at the end of a rope.

"Or what?" Marquez demanded, his words sharp enough to cut through the silence.

"Or the engine will superheat and explode," Lopez replied, his voice barely above a whisper, "more than likely derailing the train."

Marquez sighed, the sound heavy with the weight of lives hanging in the balance. "And the instruments?"

"They're internally built into the engine's design. The engine wouldn't work if they weren't functional and vice versa."

"Then we need to act fast." Marquez's pen scratched across paper, the sound like a mouse trying to gnaw its way out of a trap. "Tell your people to get to Plaza de Piedra as soon as possible. It's a Guild Outpost. Tell them everything and that they need to work with my Guild to find a way to stop it before that engine blows."

"Mr. Marquez, where are you going?" Lopez asked, his voice tinged with the desperation of a man watching his world unravel.

Esteban grabbed the leather folder, a talisman against the chaos unfolding around them. "There are outposts along the way. Everyone needs to know, and if we're lucky, we might find another way to slow it down. I don't have to go through the valley. I can beat the train to Piedra if I take a fresh horse."

As Marquez nudged Lopez towards the telegraph, a final, chilling thought occurred to the Assistant Director. "We thought Olivares was overreacting... but she said there was a possible ghoul infestation aboard. Do you... do you think...?"

"Type the message," Marquez cut him off, his words sharp as a knife's edge. "Alert the Outpost, Gate, and every other stop. Tell them everything."

As Marquez turned away, the air in the room grew thick, as if reality itself was condensing around the weight of their knowledge. A train full of ghouls, an overheating engine, countless lives balanced on a razor's edge – it was a nightmare conjured from the unholy union of progress and hubris, careening towards an uncertain future. And Marquez, armed with nothing but a leather folder and his wits, was about to race against the clock, the train, and perhaps fate itself.

Stepping out of the station office, Marquez found himself in a world transformed. The Durango sisters stood frozen, their faces mirrors of shock, while the remaining cattlemen scrambled among the dead and dying beasts. Perry and his horse had vanished.

A sharp whistle cut through the air, snapping the sisters to attention. Marquez's words tumbled out, urgent and heavy with purpose. "Our job's not done. Hit every post towards the Northern Gate. Any building with a telegraph, relay the message. That iron monster isn't stopping the Mechanist way, so we need another solution. We're meeting at Plaza de Piedra. Lopez is sending word, but it won't be enough. If anyone has ideas, tell them to act now, ask forgiveness later. Safety of those on board is paramount – derailing is not an option. Understood?"

The sisters nodded, their synchronicity eerie, before vanishing in a cloud of dust and urgency.

Esteban turned to the stables, a place of wood and hay that suddenly seemed as fragile as a child's drawing. He selected the healthiest-looking horse, its eyes wide and knowing, as if it understood the gravity of their mission. As he threw his saddle on, the weight of time pressed down on him. Even if he reached Plaza de Piedra before the 505, how much time would remain? How long before the engine's fury consumed itself and everything around it?

Looking up at the sky, Esteban found himself searching for... something. A sign, perhaps, or a glimmer of hope in the vast indifference of the universe. But the heavens offered no answers, only the silent watch of distant stars, unmoved by the dramas of men and machines playing out beneath them.

"Hil... for all those people's sakes, I hope you have a plan."

ESCAPE ROUTES

The train shrieked past the station, a blur of iron and steam, but the faces it left in its wake screamed silently. Lyric caught Jalin's eye, and in that glance, they shared a terrible understanding. Something – or someone – had been claimed by the relentless machine.

They'd passed Deeno Flats and Truitt Lake without incident, but Sandoval Pass told a different story. Its horror-struck witnesses offered a sliver of bitter hope. Yes, the train thundered on, perhaps leaving death in its wake. But now, at least, the stations knew. They would try to halt this iron beast and its cargo of dread.

They had to.

Lyric's gaze drifted to the map on the wall, tracing their path to the looming Vargas Mountains and the Northern

Gate. A wry smile touched her lips. The last time she'd crossed the Vargas, she'd been pursued by death. Now, she rode upon its very shoulders.

"Carolina," she murmured, the name falling like a pebble into a deep well.

Jalin grunted, setting down a now empty pitcher. The nagging words of Esperanza had forced the Inquisitor to reluctantly accept some form of nourishment from the kitchen. His wounds begged for attention, and this was all he would offer.

Carolina – the last whistle-stop before the Great Gate.

"Your optimism is truly dazzling," Jalin drawled, sarcasm dripping from each word.

Lyric arched an eyebrow at the Inquisitor. Color had crept back into his cheeks, but the pain still etched itself in the lines around his eyes. She longed to inspect his wounds, knowing full well he'd sooner kiss a viper.

"I take it you've conjured a master plan, then?" she prodded.

"Simple," he replied, voice flat as the plains they'd left behind. "We stop the train."

"Brilliant! Why didn't we think of that sooner, O Wise Inquisitor Cortez?" Lyric's words dripped with honey-coated venom. "Do enlighten me on how you plan to tame this iron monster."

"You're overthinking," Jalin said, his eyes glittering dangerously. "This is Mechanist craft. For all their vaunted genius, they build with glass bones and paper skin. I'd wager the guts of this beast are as delicate as a child's dreams. Our path is clear: find Bonilla, the shadow with the knife, and bring this metal nightmare to its knees. Simple tasks for complicated times."

"What of the ghouls?" Lyric whispered.

"Leave them to the Voca and her grave-dancing friend," Jalin replied."Should he stray, Boyorquez will ensure his dance is brief."

Lyric's next words fell like autumn leaves, fragile and brown. "She... Jalin, she's fading. I don't know how much further she can push against it all"

Jalin's gaze turned to flint. "She walks on borrowed breaths, Wax. They all do. Mortal clay was never meant to house divine fire, let alone wield it. Each sunrise she greets is Hil's twisted mercy. And with each, the danger she poses grows like a cancer in our midst."

"What are you saying?" Lyric's anger flared, a match struck in darkness.

"Imagine, if you will," Jalin leaned forward, "what happens when her fragile form can no longer contain even a whisper of Hil's might. She won't simply cease. No, she'll wither, a flower of agony blooming from within. And when at last she bursts..." His eyes glittered. "The ruin of Paraíso Verde will seem a child's sparkler by comparison. One day, she'll unmake us all – the innocent, the monstrous, and everything in between."

Lyric shook her head, denial a shield against truth. "No. She would have told me. In Biruji, facing the horde... she would have said..."

"Deny it all you wish," Jalin cut in, "but truth cares little about our desires. And the cruelest truth? It falls to us, you and I, to snuff out her candle before it becomes an inferno."

Silence fell, heavy as a burial shroud. Lyric's mind spun, replaying conversations in Biruji like faded film. Jalin's words, much as she longed to reject them, slotted into place like missing puzzle pieces. Esperanza's fear of vampyre bites... not self-preservation, but terror of what unholy power might birth from such a union.

"Why tell me this?" Lyric asked.

Jalin's finger pointed toward her holstered pistols, "When that day comes – for her, for me, for any of us... hesitation is a luxury you cannot afford."

"Why...," she began, but Jalin's wave cut through her words.

"Bad things happen, Wax," he said, "You've danced with darkness, tasted its bitter fruit. Evil doesn't discriminate; it infects with blind hunger. But should you ever need to press cold steel to my temple... make sure your aim is true." A ghost of a smile haunted his lips, grim amusement in a world gone mad.

"You must be truly unwell if you're attempting humor," Lyric said, her words a shield against the growing dread.

"I make jokes," Jalin protested, wounded pride in his voice.

"You make cutting remarks at others' expense," she countered.

"My wit isn't for the faint of heart," he conceded.

"No, Inquisitor. It's for you alone," she replied, perhaps too curtly. She considered her tone and the situation and continued. "Now, how do we drive out an assassin on this iron coffin?"

Jalin rose, pain etching lines in his face. "We need the Assistant Conductor's ear. If they seek to 'cleanse' First Class, we must know its occupants. Then, we become shadows, never leaving our quarry's side until the assassin shows their hand."

"How can we be certain they haven't already struck?" Lyric asked, doubt gnawing at her.

"We'd know," Jalin's voice hardened. "Even drenched in blood, they can't resist preaching to the masses. They spread their 'loving' message while bathed in the tears of the bereaved."

Unbidden, Gale Stonebridge's face rose in Lyric's mind. Jalin's mentor... father... consumed by the Cult's poison, his path twisting into darkness. She watched Jalin's face, his jaw clenched, a muscle twitching beneath the skin. Regardless of Gale's fate, Cortez thirsted for blood to balance the scales.

She would need to watch him carefully.

"We know there were four of them, and at least two of them are dead, so that leaves a possible pair to continue their work. The reports say that while they deal death in their false god's name, they aren't nihilists. They cannot spread their poison if they themselves are ashes. A cult cannot flourish, cannot display its trophies, if its knives are broken."

Jalin's eyebrow arched, a question unspoken.

Lyric smiled, "I asked for some books while I was in the Infirmary. What did you think I was doing? Counting ceiling tiles?"

Jalin's shrug was eloquent in its simplicity. "Fair."

"But the question remains," Lyric pressed, "How can we be certain their bloody work isn't already done?"

"Two reasons," Jalin said, his fingers dipped into a pocket and producing a small notebook. He slid it across to Lyric,"First, their displays are always... theatrical. The passengers in first class aren't known for their silence in the face of horror. Second, they're trapped in this iron beast with us."

Lyric's hand hovered over the notebook, hesitant. Its leather bore the patina of sweat and blood, but the pages within remained pristine. She snatched it quickly, before the surly Inquisitor could change his mind. As she leafed through its contents, Jalin's cramped handwriting revealed a picture of stops and landscapes. "What is this?" she breathed.

"Escape routes," he replied, the words hanging heavy in the air.

"What?"

"Always be prepared, Wax," Jalin intoned. "While you and Boyorquez gathered supplies, I read the route handbook. It was on the caboose's desk.I mapped our potential exits, should the need arise."

Lyric's eyes devoured the pages. Sandoval Pass, marked as a desperate gambit with only a whisper of hope. Carolina, promising safer harbour, with 'Wetlands, Lakes/Ponds' underlined like a prayer.

"You believe they'll make their move at Carolina?" Lyric asked, pieces falling into place.

"After," Jalin confirmed. "Carolina is built on treacherous wetlands. Beyond lie bridges spanning vast chasms. It's the last bastion before the Vargas mountains."

"And beyond... the Northern Gate," Lyric added, a shiver in her voice. She consulted her own notebook, a twin to Jalin's dark tome. "We have just over an hour. Sixty minutes to complete this task before we lose access to the optimal escape option."

Jalin nodded, his movement a whisper in the stale air. "We'll soon leave the land bridges behind. Time grows short." He rose, his eyes setting on a target. "You there!" he yelled out to the Assistant Conductor. "This car may soon fall like the others. We need to secure the sleepers. I'd rather not serve those creatures breakfast in bed."

The Assistant Conductor, caught mid-conversation with Esperanza, stiffened as if struck by lightning. "Sir, given the delicate nature of our..." he began, but Jalin's words sliced through his protest.

"Yes, yes... poor taste. Now move!" Jalin barked, his impatience a living thing. He turned, then paused as his gaze fell on Esperanza. "Boyorquez, the assassins are ours. You and the graverobber can tend to the dead. I trust you'll introduce him to the wheels should he prove... troublesome?"

Esperanza rewarded his comment with an eye-roll. "Try not to paint the walls with your insides before the job's done, Cortez. Kane and I will manage our end. You focus on not mucking up yours."

Lyric sighed, a soft exhalation of weariness. Even battered and bruised, these two couldn't resist trading barbs, each word a tiny dagger. Yet beneath the venom lay a current of grudging respect, a shared faith that when the chips fell, the other would stand tall.

Closing her eyes, Lyric sent a silent prayer spiraling into the void, beseeching any god with ears to hear. *Watch over us*, she pleaded to the indifferent cosmos. *Guide our hands, steel our hearts.*

For time, that most merciless of masters, was running out.

QUEMAR

P anic at its finest. That was how Emilio saw the dining car. All around were tables containing half-eaten meals, tipped-over glasses, and knocked-over chairs. His stomach chose that moment to voice its displeasure, a low rumble that would have surely drawn Cortez's ire had he been present. The Inquisitor's prejudices ran bone-deep; no doubt he'd have accused Emilio's very organs of dark sorcery.

But Cortez and Lyric had vanished towards the sleeper car, leaving Emilio to spy his salvation: an untouched sandwich, a lonely island in a sea of chaos. *I've eaten worse things*, he thought, snatching up the prize and devouring it with fervor.

"I never cared for cold chicken myself," a nearby voice mused, amusement flavoring its edges.

Emilio froze, heat rushing to his cheeks as he turned to find the Voca slowly rising, a study in careful motion. Instinctively, he moved to abandon his ill-gotten meal, but Esperanza's shake of the head stayed his hand. "That was not judgment, Doctor. Merely commentary on the virtues of sandwich meats."

Embarrassment still clung to him as he forced down the final morsels. A nearby decanter beckoned; he filled a glass, quenching his thirst before bringing a second to the Voca. "You three have... an interesting working relationship," he ventured, gesturing to where the others had departed.

Esperanza accepted the offering, the ghost of a smile playing at her lips. "It keeps us young and dutiful," she said, words laced with dry humor.

"You must be in a lot of pain to crack a joke," Emilio observed, his physician's eyes cataloging a thousand tiny tells.

Before Esperanza could respond, he pressed on. "A trained healer knows the signs. How bad is it, the Quemar?"

Quemar. The word hung in the air, hinting at the price all magic-users paid, even those who claimed divine favor. By rights, Emilio should have been similarly afflicted. The exorcism, the halting of the Promise... such workings should have left him hollow. Yet he felt... fine. A fact the Voca, too, should have noticed, yet left unmentioned.

Esperanza's sigh was a complex thing, equal parts defeat and relief. With careful motions, she unfastened the top buttons of her high collar. As she pulled it back, angry red tendrils stood stark against her skin, a roadmap of pain etched in her flesh.

Emilio's sympathetic hiss cut through the air. "You've been burning the candle at both ends, Voca. Dangerously so." His eyes met hers, a question unspoken but heavy between them. "Do they know?"

"Cortez, even in his state, has eyes sharp as an eagle's," the Voca murmured. "And Wax... she's seen me dance with this fire before. She understands, in her way."

"How long since your last episode?" Emilio probed, his voice gentle but insistent.

"Two months," she breathed, the words barely a whisper.

"TWO MONTHS!" Emilio's hushed exclamation was a thunderclap in the quiet car. "Madness! If it ravaged you so, you should have been resting for half a year, at least!"

Esperanza's eyes flashed defiance kindling within. "The Order deemed my respite sufficient for a simple escort. Which was all this was to have been, Doctor. I never intended to call upon Hil's blessings so soon."

"Forgive me," Emilio backpedaled, "but surely you see the peril here. It's not just your soul at stake..."

A cold fire blazed in Esperanza's gaze, her words razor-sharp. "I understand perfectly, Doctor Kane. The weight of this burden is etched into my very being... as I am sure it is yours. While I'll gladly answer my god's call when the time comes, I've no desire to hasten that journey."

Their gazes locked, a silent battle of wills stretching between them like a taut wire.

Yet it was Emilio's own traitorous body that broke the spell, his stomach growling like some hungry beast. He glanced down, sighing. "I fed you already."

"Clearly not enough, Doctor," the Voca observed, a hint of wry amusement creeping back into her voice.

"Listen, I didn't mean to... " Emilio began, but Esperanza's wave cut through his words like a knife.

"Your concern is valid," she conceded. "When... if... that dark day comes, I trust we'll all play our parts." She paused, then gestured to his arm.

"Of course," Emilio responded without hesitation, moving close to offer sturdy support. Satisfied with her grip, Esperanza leaned into him, her weight a reminder of the burdens they all carried.

Of all the strange twists fate could weave, Emilio never imagined himself playing the role of crutch to an Inquisition member, let alone a Voca blessed by Hil. This entire ordeal stretched beyond the boundaries of his wildest imaginings. What would Mari think if she could see him now? Would she be as astounded as he, or would that familiar teasing glint dance in her eyes? Given their brief but intense time together, he suspected both.

His gaze drifted to the window, half-hoping to catch a glimpse of her spectral form flickering just beyond the glass. But there was nothing... no ghostly visage, no memory of what had transpired. Was she somehow caught up in whatever had happened to him in the forest? He prayed that was not the case. She was no mere Spirit. Marisol was a unique being. A Spirit fully aware of who they had been when alive, and capable of maintaining memories and independent thought in the present.

Emilio and Esperanza were the last souls to exit the second part of the dining car. Their undead pursuers would be on the move again soon, he knew. Whoever pulled their strings was playing a careful game, conserving their ranks. Yet, fewer numbers brought a chilling benefit. The ancient texts whispered of how a Necromancer, with a smaller horde to control, could imbue their puppets with more complex actions beyond the base instincts of attack and kill. Perhaps it was better Mari wasn't here to witness this macabre dance.

His chest constricted a moment at the thought of some Necromancer binding her to their will.

Mari.

The Queen's memory, however painful, sparked an idea in Emilio's mind. "I know you have no reason to trust me, given what I am..." he began, the words hesitant on his tongue.

"I trust you more now than I did mere hours ago, Doctor," Esperanza interrupted, her voice steady. "Then, you were a suspect in some dark necromantic rite. Now, Hil has shown me you were its victim, not its architect." She paused, rolling up her sleeve to reveal a tapestry of ink etched into her skin. Emilio's trained eye recognized them not as mere artistry, but as powerful wards against the undead and the dark forces that animated them.

"Had you been truly tainted, doctor," she continued, "your arm would have erupted in Hil's holy fire the moment I grasped it as you fell through the cattle car. Had my god deemed you unclean, I would have let you fall."

"Oh," was all Emilio could manage.

"So yes, Doctor Kane, I do place some trust in you," Esperanza concluded. "Why do you ask?"

"I could help... take the edge off your pain," he offered, the words hanging in the air between them like a fragile thread.

Esperanza froze, her gaze piercing. "You know Equilibrio?"

"Necromancy is but one face on Styx's coin," Emilio explained, his words measured. "I was schooled in the sanctioned Necromist rites, yes, but I also delved into Equilibrio. While no master, I'm proficient enough for emergencies. This, I believe, qualifies. It's not a cure, mind you, but a bandage for your wounded soul."

"And what of you?" she probed. "A transference demands a source. If you give of yourself, it may leave you vulnerable. Even your... extraordinary stamina has its limits."

Emilio sighed inwardly; she had noticed. And how could she not? He should have been stumbling around and unable to function from the head injury alone. But here he was finding his way through an unimaginable scenario, with little more than indigestion and a headache.

The stamina and power gifted to him from his encounter in The Barrows had been more than he could have imagined. The more complex questions were inevitable, lurking just beyond the horizon. He would have to answer them, eventually.

"If you believe it won't drain you excessively..." Esperanza continued, "I'll accept Your Lady's Blessing. Hil has allowed such before, in dire straits. I doubt they'd object now."

"The Order has an Equilibrio practitioner?" Emilio couldn't mask his curiosity.

"A tale for calmer times, Doctor," she deflected. "What do you require of me?"

They moved to the last table, a precaution against prying eyes. Emilio produced a stubby candle from his bag, its flame dancing to life. With a blackened beeswax pastel, he began inscribing arcane runes on his left palm, the wax softening in the candlelight.

"Your left hand, palm up," he instructed.

As Esperanza complied, Emilio began the quiet incantation. His mind drifted to months past when he'd performed the Wrixlian Rite on Marisol, stabilizing her ethereal form. That had drained him utterly. Yet Wrixlian was but a whisper compared to the full symphony of Equilibrio. Where Wrixlian merely brushed the power of the Alma... the true soul within all living things... what he attempted now was a far deeper communion.

Drawing upon his own Alma, Emilio siphoned away the pain of the Quemar. In peak condition, he might have attempted more, but here, on a train besieged by ghouls and assassins, this would have to suffice. His eyes opened, revealing the familiar blue aura pulsing around him. Focusing on the Voca's neck, he drew the Quemar into himself.

Pain seared through him, white-hot in a place beyond sight. The air shimmered with released power as he made one final pull. The angry red tendrils on Esperanza's neck faded to a pale pink, and she drew a deep, relieved breath.

Releasing her hand, Emilio sagged against the table, feeling as if he'd run a marathon. Esperanza examined her arms, the evidence of their arcane exchange clear to see.

"Another satisfied patient?" he quipped between labored breaths.

A sharp bang echoed from the far end of the car, shattering the moment. The enemy was coming.

Esperanza rose unaided, offering her hand to Emilio. "I believe that's our cue to depart, Doctor," she said, a new strength in her voice. "And yes, thank you. Most sincerely."

BACK ROOM DEALS

Gods, did everything hurt? Esteban mused, his body a collection of aches and pains from his journey. He doubted his ability to sit comfortably for a fortnight, let alone a week. The journey from Sandoval Pass to the Plaza outpost had been brutal.

The horse, a creature of flesh and thundering hooves had become an extension of Esteban's will. They galloped when the horizon permitted and trotted when the earth rose to challenge them. The foothills of the Vargas mountain range were not an easy terrain to cross. It wasn't kind to the beast, this relentless pace, but kindness was a luxury they couldn't afford. Lives hung in the balance, ethereal weights that spurred them onward.

The hills, those earthen waves frozen in time, were both a curse and a blessing. While they tortured rider and mount alike, their very existence forced the 505 to slither through the flats just outside the wetlands instead of striking true for Northern Gate. Time, that most fickle of currencies, had been bought with sweat and strain.

"By the Giver of Names, you'll have no more running this week," Esteban promised his mount, sliding from the saddle with a grateful pat. The invocation of Geekind, the whimsical deity of naming, hung heavy in the air, a pledge as binding as any oath.

Both man and beast plunged their faces into a cool, inviting trough, a reckless indulgence born of desperation. The corral beckoned, a haven for weary limbs and spirits. As Esteban secured his horse, he noted the burgeoning crowd of carriages. It seemed the message had reached its intended audience.

"Looks like the party's started," he muttered to the horse, who merely snorted in reply.

A cacophony of accusation and defiance met him as he entered. The Messengers, weathered and worn by the road, stood in stark contrast to the sleek, supercilious Mechanists. A storm was brewing, a clash of iron and flesh, and Esteban, the diplomat, was caught in the eye of it.

Two factions faced off in the hall's center, their stances rigid, their eyes flashing. A physical confrontation seemed imminent. The Messengers, their rough-hewn faces etched with lines of fatigue, bore the marks of countless journeys. Across from them, the Mechanists, immaculate and arrogant, exuded an air of superiority.

"WELL, MAYBE YOU SHOULD GET THAT ROAD DUST OUT OF YOUR BRAIN IF YOU WANT TO UNDERSTAND HOW A SIMPLE GEAR SYSTEM WORKS!"

"YOUR GEAR SYSTEMS ARE WHAT CAUSED THIS MESS IN THE FIRST PLACE!"

"OUR SYSTEMS ARE PERFECT! YOUR HAMHANDED PEOPLE ARE THE TRUE CAUSE OF THIS TRAGEDY!"

Before the insults could escalate further, a ratcheting sound of a racked shotgun echoed through the hall. All eyes snapped to the doorway where Esteban stood, a shotgun held loosely at his side. His voice, when he spoke, was a whip cracking through the storm. "Thank you all for coming," he said, his words carrying over the din.

A Mechanist, face flushed with anger, demanded, "Who the hell are you?"

"Esteban Marquez, Guildsman from Deeno Flats," he replied, the shotgun lowering slowly. "Lopez sent word when the 505 broke through. Your name?"

"Armando Ruiz," the Mechanist replied, his tone dripping with contempt. "Why couldn't they stop it?"

Esteban met his gaze, his expression a mask. "That's the question, isn't it? A failed safeguard costs one of your own. We need to understand why."

The mention of the safeguards failing caused a few snickers from the Messengers and looks of irritation from the Mechanists.

Ruiz's eyes narrowed. "Did they even try to communicate with the train?"

"They did. No response."

"Our machines are flawless!" Ruiz retorted, his voice rising.

Refusing to be drawn into an argument of design application, Esteban took a step closer, his smile tight.

"Tell me, Mr. Ruiz, how often should the pressure valves on a Railed Gear Car be released?"

The question surprised Ruiz, who stumbled over his response. "Valves? How do you? Wait…" he said as he looked back at the group and then back at Esteban. "What are you getting on at?"

"Lopez said that if the pressure valves were not released on time…" Esteban said.

"The engine would superheat, triggering an explosion with enough power to…" said a younger Mechanist as he was jotting down the math, "…to take out the engine and the rails it's riding on. While not explosive, the fuel would get a back flush of superheated liquid that would expand the fuel container, blowing it out and sending shrapnel everywhere."

"I'm guessing it would include the First-Class car, a heavy casualty," Esteban added grimly.

Ruiz bristled. "That's all speculation! You're assuming the engineer isn't in control!"

Esteban's voice was steady. "What if the engineer is incapacitated? What then?"

The Mechanist sputtered for an answer.

An older woman, her face etched with concern, broke the tension. "Mr. Marquez, what happened at Sandoval Pass?"

"Lopez tried electro charges," Esteban explained. "Steers were used to trigger them. It failed."

A heavy silence fell over the room as the gravity of the situation sank in.

"You witnessed this?" the woman asked.

Esteban nodded, his eyes hard.

The woman turned to Ruiz; her hand a comforting touch on his shoulder. "Any casualties?"

Esteban closed his eyes in a moment of silent prayer. "Mr. Perry was lost," he said simply.

The bravado that had fueled Ruiz's defiance was extinguished. Esteban turned back to the woman.

"I'm sorry, I didn't catch your name..."

"Lino, Gloria Lino. I am a local Foreman for the Mechanist."

"Thank you, Foreman Lino. I've called you all here to find a solution, not to assign blame," he said, his voice cutting through the tension. "Derailing isn't an option. We have lives at stake. Ideas, people. We need them now."

"To be honest, a downed Engineer had factored into our list, but with very few solutions," Gloria said. "Tomas and Armando have been puzzling over design complications. Ms. Diaz has several ideas for stopping a high-speed vehicle," she said as she motioned to a younger woman, "but they require supplies and creation time that we don't have. Mr. Borromeo has reviewed the physical build to see what was exploitable; however…"

"You built too grand of a beast that would never fail," said an unfamiliar voice.

The voice drew the attention to the back of the room. A well-dressed man walked into the main hall, and behind him were two equally imposing figures of physical means. Both mountains wore more practical garb, but no less respectable. It was obvious that the trio were neither of the Messenger nor the Mechanists.

"I'm sorry, sir, this is a closed meeting of the Guilds… but you look familiar. Do I know you from somewhere?" Esteban asked.

"Apologies, I am Adrián Ernesto Ortega. I was informed that the Guilds required assistance," he said relaxedly.

The man's manicured features clicked with the name Ortega! Publically, La Familia Ortega owned several mining operations within the Imperium, producing ore for metal and other resources. Considered respectable by many, they were also one of the significant criminal enterprises that plagued the Messengers Guild. Thieves, highwaymen, and hired killers. Over the years, many of the Guild fell to Ortega's blades and bullets. While there was never enough evidence to convict the Ortegas of wrongdoing, many knew they were dangerous. It was rumored that Imperium had a formal agreement with the Ortegas, but that was a rumor that was never spoken aloud. So while Adrián Ortega was not on a wanted poster, he was undoubtedly a dangerous individual to be in their midst.

The realization of who was standing in their midst was not lost on the assembled Messengers. The room grew in sound as bodies shuffled with the sounds of pistols being cocked. A low growl rippled through the group, a collective expression of anger and fear.

For his part, Ortega made no move, nor did the two mountains that stood calmly behind him. Their impassivity seemed to amplify the tension, casting an eerie calm over the brewing storm.

The tension seemed to rise steadily, and at that moment, Esteban wondered if he should attempt to do something. His hand hovered near the hilt of his sword, a silent question hanging in the air.

"Now, I may not have all the details, but ultimately, I think that the solution may simply be getting an Engineer on to the train to cease its movement, correct?" Ortega asked, his voice cutting through the charged atmosphere.

Eyes narrowed, but the tension did not lessen. Esteban silently reminded himself of the lives at stake and, for a moment, weighed it against the Guild's need for vengeance. The decision was a bitter pill to swallow, but he nodded slowly.

Thankfully, Gloria answered, "Correct, Mr. Ortega. However, as simple as the solution is, getting an Engineer onto the train is a larger issue. A team of two horses might catch up with the train, but based on its current route, that is not feasible because of the landscape. A single horse, while quick, might catch up just as well. However, those trained to operate a Railcar are not horsemen and not exactly the most athletically inclined to board a train in such a way."

"Humor me, Foreman Lino." Ortega nodded with a slight smile. "If we could get someone who understood the machine's workings to the lead car, they should be able to stop the train, correct?"

Gloria did not mask her surprise but looked at Esteban. For his part, the Guildsman gave her a simple nod. She turned back to Ortega, "Yes, Mr. Ortega. There are several means to stop the train. Even in a full system failure, there is a way to stop it safely from inside the engine. If you don't mind me asking, what resources does a mining operation have to perform such a complex and dangerous feat?"

Ortega smiled. "We are a very diverse organization with dozens of talented individuals with very forward-thinking ideas. We even employ a few former members of the Mechanist to hash out our more complicated issues."

"You have an Engineer on staff?" Gloria said with surprise.

"Of a sort. Ms. Ivette Ramirez has already volunteered to assist us in this dangerous endeavor," Ortega said.

A collective gasp rippled through the room. Ivette Ramirez was a name whispered in hushed tones among the Mechanists. Once a promising young engineer, she'd betrayed the Guild for personal gain, her actions resulting in the deaths of countless workers. Her name was synonymous with treachery.

Gloria Lino's face turned ashen. "I see...," she choked out. "And I suppose Ms. Ramirez is asking for reinstatement to reward her efforts?"

Ortega shook his head. "Oh no, Ms. Ramirez is quite happy with her current employment. She only wishes to help out those poor people in need."

Esteban's eyes narrowed. He could feel the anger and disbelief radiating from the Mechanists. This was a dangerous game Ortega was playing. "And what do you require for this feat, Mr. Ortega?" Esteban asked.

For his part, Adrián Ortega gave a practiced smile. "If this train derails or worse... that would look badly for both of your Guilds. I would hate to see the Imperium place further restrictions or limitations on either of your groups' services, even worse if this ends in tragedy." Looking around the room, he took a few practiced steps with open arms akin to a politically minded noble. Motioning to the assembled, "I want everyone to succeed, Mr. Marquez, Messenger and Mechanist alike. All I am asking for is a simple favor from each of your respectable organizations: nothing dangerous or illegal, just a favor from one friend to another. I know Foreman Lino here has the authority to accept this offer. Given the situation, I am sure you can convince Guild Officer Botero of the same."

Gloria looked at Esteban; her face was a mask of anger and defeat. Clearing her throat, she walked toward Ortega and held out her hand. "The Mechanist Guild accepts your offer of assistance, Mr. Ortega."

Ortega gently took Gloria's offered hand in both of his. "Thank you for your friendship and confidence, Foreman Lino."

Esteban felt the weight of every eye in the room on him. He could feel the tension, the anger, the fear, and the desperation. But most of all, he felt the weight of responsibility. No Messenger could cease the train's operation, nor could the Mechanist get an Engineer aboard in time. They had no choice. It could be their only shot to save everyone on the runaway train.

With a heavy heart, Esteban stepped forward and offered his hand to Ortega. "The Messengers will assist in any way possible, Mr. Ortega," he said, his voice firm.

Ortega took his hand, a satisfied smirk playing on his lips. "You see, it is the duty of every citizen of the Imperium to do what is necessary and right. I am simply a man doing my part." Releasing Esteban's hand, Ortega nodded to the group. "Thank you all for your hospitality," he said, turning towards the door.

"If I might, Mr. Ortega," Gloria asked, "Do your people require support?"

Ortega gave that practiced smile again. "Oh no, Foreman, my people are already on the way to meet the 505," he said, pulling out a pocket watch. "We'll talk again after it stops."

THE SWITCH

Lyric chewed on her lip as they entered the sleeper car. Where the luggage car had been a sprawling catacomb of forgotten treasures, this new space was a gleaming casket. Its polished wood and metal surfaces reflected distorted images of those who dared enter. As soon as they had entered, she spied a thin staircase going up a level. At the top, she could see a closed door.

"Two ways of getting in," Jalin said as he continued looking around the area. He still leaned heavily on the wall for support as he walked.

"Three," Lyric corrected. "There is an entryway for staff to use in the center." She turned to look at the Inquisitor, taking note of his posture. "Head for the center of the car. I want to check that door to make sure it's secured."

Jalin's nod was a barely perceptible thing, more felt than seen. His uncharacteristic silence gnawed at Lyric's resolve. He was never a man of many words, but it was clear his injuries were taking up most of his energy as he moved forward. She couldn't allow herself to linger on it.

Be careful with his kind. Those had been the words that Voca Lupe Casteneda had shared with Lyric the night of her Volver. When they had all recovered enough from the incident in Paraiso Verde. *Don't give too much of your heart, or you may lose it all when they are gone.*

She steeled herself against the nagging urge to offer him aid and instead turned toward the staircase. She ascended the half-flight and got to the door. With a rapt knock, she asked, "Is this door secure?"

She could hear voices, and a partially muffled voice called out, "Yes! Locked and building a barrier!"

They must be using mattresses and bed frames, she thought. It would undoubtedly halt the first point of entrance. The door appeared solid, but enough blows would cause it to splinter. After that, it would be layers of mattress fabric. Even if the ghouls began to claw their way through, it would still take time.

"This is the best we have," she said quietly and headed back down. Despite the shuffle of feet and the natural sound of wheels running on the rail, she could hear raised voices.

What fresh hell has Jalin unleashed now?

Rushing toward the center, she saw Cortez leaning against the wall, observing a small group of people. In the mix was Carlos Monterro, the Assistant Conductor, trying to control the would-be argument. Moving to the Inquisitor's side, she saw the Monterro, a staffer, and a dozen people lined against the wall. Before them, a red-faced staffer jabbed an accusing finger towards the upper level, his voice a shrill harbinger of panic.

"He's barring entry, sir!" the staffer cried,

From above, a familiar voice carried down, tinged with steel and weariness. "We're packed to the gills! Women and children crammed four to a bay!"

"You see, sir! There is still plenty of standing room up there, and this man thinks he has authority on a Guild train!"

Monterro, desperation etched in every line of his face, called up, "How many people are up there right now?"

"Except for those below, everyone that was in the passenger car. Look, I do not want to stay here, but someone has to remain here, watch the blockades, and keep everyone calm," the man's voice said.

"Coward!" the staffer spat, his accusation hanging in the air like a curse.

In that instant, the atmosphere shifted. The staffer's bravado evaporated like mist before a rising sun, his spine turning to water as he stumbled back. Even Monterro retreated, as if sensing an approaching storm.

From the stairwell, an imposing figure came into view, one that Lyric instantly recognized. Finn Carstein emerged, his massive frame stooping in the confined space. Simple clothes belied his formidable presence, blue-gray eyes as sharp as winter frost sweeping over the assembled crowd.

The staffer's gaze dropped to the crowbar in Carstein's hand, the tool's presence a silent threat more potent than any spoken word.

Carstein's voice cut through the tension, cold and measured. "My nieces and their mother are up there – children with special needs. Their calm is our silence, our shield against that rolling mass. I've faced these horrors before. Can you say the same?"

Before the challenge could be met, Lyric's voice rang out, clear and certain. "I can vouch for Mr. Carstein's prowess against the undead."

All eyes turned to Lyric and Jalin, but none wider than Finn's. "Ms... Wax?" he breathed, disbelief coloring his words. "What are you doing here?"

Lyric nodded to the large man. "Same as you, trying to stay alive." Turning to the Assistant Conductor, she said, "Sir, Mr. Carstein was instrumental in protecting a mining town from a ghoul infestation. If there is anyone you want to help protect your passengers, that is your man. If he says adding more people into an already crowded space will hinder their safety, you should consider his words. I know I would."

Monterro looked at the imposing man and then back at Lyric. With a resigned sigh, he spoke, his words heavy with responsibility. "By Guild law, only a member can be authorized to protect passengers." His hand moved to his lapel, unpinning a golden scorpion - a symbol laden with meaning. "As the ranking Guild member present, I, Carlos Monterro, hereby invoke the right to temporarily induct a civilian into our ranks, solely for the protection of those under our charge." He fixed Carstein with a penetrating stare. "By accepting this, Mr. Carstein, do you swear to shield these souls above us, even at the cost of your own life?"

A collective breath was held, the air thick with anticipation. Finn's response was swift and unwavering. "Yes! Without hesitation."

The scorpion pin glinted in the dim light as Monterro affixed it to Finn's suspender. "Then it is done. Guard them well, Mr. Carstein. When this nightmare ends, I'll need that token returned." Turning to the people in the hall, "You heard the man, Nico. Take these people to the next car and get them situated."

As Nico herded the remaining passengers forward, Lyric observed the weight of responsibility settling on Finn's broad shoulders. For a moment, it seemed to bow him, but he shook it off like water from a bear's coat.

"I assume both doors are blocked off accordingly, Mr. Carstein?" the Assistant Conductor asked.

"Finn, please," the large man insisted, running a hand through his hair. "And yes, we've fortified both doors with bed frames and mattresses. If they breach the outer defenses, they'll face layers of obstacles. We've arranged the remaining mattresses for comfort, but space remains at a premium. That extra dozen would have tipped us from crowded to dangerous, especially if we have to fight."

Monterro nodded and turned to Lyric and Jalin. "How much time do we have before they head this way?"

Jalin's response sent a chill through the air. "Ten minutes, maybe, but we are running out of time for another matter. "He nodded toward the head of the train, "There are a pair of assassins in the First Class car. We need to find and stop them before they can take another life."

Finn's gaze swept over Jalin's battered form, concern etching lines in his weathered face. "With all due respect, Inquisitor, you're in no condition to confront anyone."

Jalin's eyes locked onto Finn, a fire burning within them that belied his physical state. "Tend to your charges, Carstein. We know our duty." He turned to Monterro, his words clipped and precise. "The assassins' target is in First Class, but they'll aim to disembark after Carolina station if they hope to survive their mission."

Monterro's brow furrowed. "Why after?"

"The wetlands offer the only viable escape route," Jalin explained, his tone dark with knowledge. "Beyond lies the ascent to the Northern Gate - a death trap for would-be jumpers. These killers serve a false god; they can't fulfill their unholy duty if they're dead."

Lyric's voice cut through the tension, pragmatic and sharp. "The real challenge is covering all four exits with just the two of us. If we could funnel them to one side, our odds would improve dramatically."

A flicker of something - memory, perhaps, or inspiration - crossed Monterro's face. "If we were on the old route, that might be possible."

Jalin's eyebrow arched, a silent demand for elaboration.

"The original Guild track skirted the valley," Monterro explained, his words painting a picture of forgotten paths. "It's still there, unused since we built the bridge across the great lake that feeds the wetlands. Longer route, but..."

"Is there a way to switch the tracks?" Lyric asked.

Monterro's reply was tinged with regret. "There's a manual switch near Carolina station. But someone would need to be there and flip it before we pass. With communications down, it's impossible to coordinate."

Jalin's eyes narrowed in thought. "What does this switch look like?"

The Assistant Conductor quickly sketched the mechanism, pointing out the crucial lever. "Push this forward, and we're on the old track."

"What are you thinking, Cortez?" Lyric asked.

"Nothing yet. Give me time," Jalin said as he ripped the sketched image from Monterro's book.

The relative silence of the car was broken as the rear door pulled open, filling the area with the roar of the tracks. Esperanza walked in with Emilio Kane in tow. The Voca no longer relied on the doctor as a crutch and had a bit of color back on her face.

"They're breaching the passenger car," she announced, her words a grim portent of the approaching storm.

Kane, though winded, secured the door with newly learned efficiency. Jalin's gaze flicked between the doctor and Esperanza, suspicion etched in every line of his face.

"Equilibrio," Esperanza offered, the single word heavy with meaning.

The term ignited a spark of recognition in Lyric's mind, conjuring images of Voca Lupe and whispered tales of mystical healing. Had Kane tapped into this arcane art? Whatever the case, its effects on Esperanza were undeniable.

Jalin's lips moved in a silent curse, his distrust of Kane evident in every taut line of his body.

Esperanza's gaze settled on Finn, memory dawning. "Mathis," she said simply.

Finn nodded, a rueful smile touching his lips. "It's been a while, Voca. We boarded at 'Cruces, bound for the Truitt ferry. Fate, it seems, had other plans," he added, gesturing to their dire surroundings.

"The plans of the Gods are an infinite mystery," Esperanza said, "Though I'm glad Hil has blessed us with your presence."

"Hate to be the harbinger of doom, but we've got maybe five minutes before our unwelcome guests come knocking. What's the plan?" Kane interjected.

Lyric turned to Jalin, half-expecting a caustic suggestion involving Kane as ghoul bait. Instead, the Inquisitor's eyes remained fixed on the switch sketch, a fierce intensity burning in their depths.

"Carstein," he barked, "fortify this central entrance. Hold the line. Failure is not an option." His gaze swept to Lyric and Kane. "You two, to First Class. Cover the nearest doors." Finally, he addressed Esperanza and Monterro. "You're with me."

"And where exactly are we going?" Monterro asked, trepidation coloring his words.

Jalin's reply was laced with grim determination. "Above First Class. With Hil's grace, I'll force a track switch. If we succeed, we'll enter from the opposite side. Monterro, you'll identify our interlopers. Then, we end this. Simple."

The tension in the cramped train car crackled like electricity as Jalin's words hung in the air. Lyric felt anger rising within her. The Inquisitor's plan, born of desperation and stubbornness, seemed a fool's errand given his battered state.

"Inquisitor," she began, her voice tight with barely contained frustration, "wouldn't it be wiser for you to take the rear doors with Dr. Kane and Mr. Monterro? The Voca and I can handle the other side without putting you at unnecessary risk."

Jalin's eyes narrowed to slits,fury in his dark eyes. For the first time, Lyric saw the full force of his anger directed at her. His words, when they came, were sharp enough to draw blood.

"Mind your place, Escritora Wax," he hissed, each word dripping with venom. "I know my duties, my capabilities. We're out of time and luxuries. Carolina approaches, and lives hang in the balance. You'll follow orders or join the civilians upstairs. There's no room for your misplaced concern."

Lyric felt her face flush hot with indignation, her own rage rising to meet Jalin's. Their gazes locked in a silent battle of wills, neither willing to back down.

The tense standoff was broken by an unexpected sound – the rustle of fabric and clink of glass. Kane was rummaging through his bag, seemingly oblivious to the powder keg of emotions around him.

"What in Hil's name are you doing, Kane?" Jalin snapped, his voice razor-sharp.

The doctor withdrew a small glass jar, its contents resembling tea bags. With deliberate calm that stood in stark contrast to the charged atmosphere, he opened the container and extended one of the bags towards Jalin.

Disgust and suspicion warred on Jalin's face. "What bullshit is this?"

"Hígadolina, Inquisitor," Kane replied, his tone unnervingly severe. "You'll need it for what you're planning."

Jalin's anger faltered momentarily. "And you are just mentioning this now?"

Kane's response was chillingly pragmatic. "It's a dangerous stimulant that will override your body's limits. You'll ignore fatigue and pain, but risk further injury. I won't question your orders, but time is running out. This will help you do what's necessary.." He paused. Then, "I cannot promise you will survive."

After a tense moment, Jalin took the packet and shoved it into his mouth.

Lyric rounded on Kane, her fury exploding. "You're a doctor! How can you let him endanger himself like this? Do you hate him enough to watch him die?"

Kane's expression remained impassive. "Ms. Wax, we're out of time. If he fails, we're all in greater danger."

"Explain," Jalin demanded.

Kane's words fell like lead weights. "If we don't change course, we cross Lago Azul – once Pueblo Medina, now a watery grave for hundreds. El Lago de Dolor."

"The Lake of Sorrow," Jalin spat.

Hundreds of years ago Pueblo Medina was a thriving trade hub at the foot of the Vargas Mountain Range. It was now buried beneath tons of silt, rocks and water, a victim of the Corpse Wars. Some claimed that on clear nights tiny balls of light bobbed above the surface of the lake. How many souls were still bound here?

Kane turned to Lyric, his eyes grave. "We're hauling a train of ghouls infused with La Corrupta. Crossing those waters will draw more restless dead like a foul magnet and engulf every village, township and City from here to Valentina with the souls of the dead. I'm doing what's necessary to save us all."

Jalin fixed Lyric with a challenging stare. "What'll it be, Wax?"

Rage still churned in Lyric's gut, but the dire picture Kane painted was impossible to ignore. She strode past Jalin, her voice steely with resolve. "The Voca may be fine, but for whatever madness you're planning, I'm the next best shot if you miss." She turned, meeting the Inquisitor's gaze. "If you insist on this insanity, I'm going with you. Whatever you're planning, *we're* seeing it through to the end."

ECHOES

Despite his outward clinical demeanor, pain gnawed at Emilio's core. He could not remember if had ever felt this way. Thinking on his situation, he realized had been pushing his limits since the experience in the Barrows. Simple uses of power that once taxed him now barely registered. Major rites and even drawing down Styx's gifts once demanded a week's bed rest. Now they felt more like a mild workout.

Equilibrio had changed that. Everything felt raw. A nagging doubt plagued him—was this solely the cost of art he wielded? Necromancy was its own beast, but fear stayed his hand from chancing anything unless absolutely necessary.

When Lyric and Jalin's emotions had erupted, Emilio felt the recoil of their fury like a physical blow, too much for his frayed senses to process. He watched as the Escritora, the Inquisitor, and the Assistant Conductor exited the Sleeper car, their departure leaving a vacuum of tension in their wake.

Meeting the Voca's eyes, Esperanza merely shrugged. "You heard Cortez, Doctor. We have a job to do."

Slowly through the noise of the train's motion and the aching protests of wood above, other sounds began to filter through Emilio's consciousness. He paused, closing his eyes in concentration. Where were these voices coming from?

Why did she leave me? All I ever did was love her!

Emilio's eyes snapped open as he whirled around, searching for the source. But there was no one. The voice hadn't been close but it felt as if someone were whispering directly into his ear. He was about to dismiss it when an unearthly chill slithered up his arms, raising gooseflesh in its wake.

He pulled his attention back to the Voca, who was clasping hands with the large man. "Mr. Carst... Finn. Those things back there are clever. Not like Mathis, but clever nonetheless. May Hil protect you."

"Thank you, Voca Boyorquez," Finn replied, his voice steady despite the tension evident in his posture. He paused, nostrils flaring as he glanced towards the exit leading to the First Class car. "Do you smell that?"

Before Emilio could process the question, another spectral voice assaulted him.

LEAVE ME ALOOOOOOOOOOOONE!!!!!

The scream was shrill and ear-piercing, seeming to vibrate through Emilio's very bones. His ears rang from the shock, and he found himself leaning against the wall as his legs threatened to give way. Something felt terribly wrong, not just with the situation, but with him.

Shadows flickered in and out of his vision, and a horrible realization dawned on him: Children! There were children up there! The thought sent a wave of nausea through him. Gods, no!

"Doctor? Is everything alright?" Esperanza's voice cut through his panic, her face etched with concern.

Fighting to maintain his composure, Emilio reached into his medical bag and produced a small leather pouch, about the size of a fist. The stakes were too high; he had to risk it. Opening the bag, he called upon the Grace of Styx to bless its contents.

Familiar power coursed through his body, but this time it felt different—like a drop of water on a searing pan. It burned and cooled simultaneously, as if his body couldn't decide on a temperature. After a moment that felt like an eternity, the contents gave one final bluish pulse of power.

Satisfied, he closed the bag and weakly tossed it to Finn, who caught it deftly. "Doctor?" the large man queried, confusion in his voice.

"Salt," Emilio explained, his voice strained. "Salt imbued with Styx's grace. Spread it along the floor, especially under the children. Tell them they must close their eyes or make blindfolds for them quickly." A violent chill racked his body as he turned towards the Voca. "I can hear them now... I can't stop hearing them. It's bad. I can see their shadows moving fast, like a feeding swarm."

I WILL NEVER HURT YOU, I SWEAR! I SWEAAAAAAAAAAAAAAAAAAAAAAAARE!!!!

The spectral scream drove Emilio to his knees. He clutched at his ears, but it did nothing to block out the onslaught of voices. Sweat poured down his face as his mind swam in a sea of fear and confusion. Dozens of voices, thick with anger, regret, and terror, flooded his senses. It had never been like this before. This influx of sensations and sounds was overwhelming. Something within him had opened up, and he couldn't control it.

Through blurred vision, he saw the Voca looking down at him, then pointing to Finn. She reached for something around her neck, and suddenly the room blazed with a reddish-golden light.

Esperanza knelt beside him and placed something around his neck. In an instant, silence fell, accompanied by a comforting warmth. Emilio looked down to see Hil's sigil glowing brightly from a simple leather string.

"Can you hear me, Doctor?" the Voca asked, her voice steady and calm.

Emilio nodded slowly, his thoughts gradually clearing. "Yes... I'm sorry. I'm not sure what happened." He glanced back at Finn, who stood ready with his crowbar, prepared to defend against an unseen threat. Turning back to the Voca, Emilio saw a mixture of concern and understanding in her eyes.

"Why children, doctor?" Esperanza asked as she helped Emilio to his feet, her touch steady and reassuring.

Emilio's voice was strained, each word an effort. "Some children can see the dead. Most lose the ability as they grow into teenagers. The ones that continue to see the dead are blessed by Styx." He paused, his eyes distant. "Regardless... these voices are not the ghost of Abuelo or a tía. They are not friends or family. These things... are angry. Sprinkling blessed salt will deter most of them and offer a type of invisibility to the children. It will help keep them safe." His gaze fell on the glowing sigil around his neck. "What did you do to this?"

"Something similar, I suppose," she replied, guiding him to lean against the metal rail. Her voice low. "However, I need to stay focused on the object. If I don't, the charm fades, and you'll experience whatever you're going through again." She studied his face intently. "At first, I thought it was the Quemar, but I've seen those effects on both Necromist and Necro—"

"You're nothing but a HORRIBLE WIFE! I GAVE YOU EVERYTHING, AND THIS IS WHAT I GET AS THANKS!" The disembodied voice sliced through the air for all to hear, each word dripping with venom. The temperature plummeted, frost crystallizing on the windows.

As one, the trio turned towards the source of the otherworldly shriek. A cabinet door creaked open, spilling bloodied blankets onto the floor. From within, a figure emerged, moving with unnatural, jerky motions. A man, or what remained of one, crawled out of the bundle with disjointed limbs. His face was a ruined mess of pulped flesh, one eye dangling grotesquely from a shattered socket. The stained uniform of a train staffer clung to his broken form.

"How?" Esperanza breathed, her composure cracking for the first time.

Emilio's voice was grim. "Mad spirits are drawn to corpses. This man must have been killed and stuffed into the cabinet recently." His eyes darted around the car. "That means they're around us, and the ghouls aren't far behind. We need to get past him if we're going to get out."

The Voca's grip on Emilio's arm tightened. "Remember when I said I needed to concentrate, doctor? If we're going to get out, brace yourself."

In an instant, the protective warmth vanished. A bone-deep chill settled over Emilio as a clamour of spectral voices assaulted his senses. The world tilted precariously.

Esperanza's eyes scanned their surroundings. "Finn, I need this rail. Can you do it?"

The large man nodded. He drew back his foot and delivered a powerful kick to the decorative wooden brackets holding the metal safety rails. There was a satisfying crack as the wood splintered under Finn's strength.

Seizing the shattered end, Esperanza wrenched the metal rod free. She gripped it like a sword, both hands wrapped around the makeshift weapon. Emilio felt a shimmer of power radiating from her, waves of heat pulsing outward. The metal began to glow with Hil's light, casting dancing shadows across the walls.

With purposeful strides, Esperanza advanced on the reanimated corpse. She thrust the glowing end of the rail against the dead man's chest, pinning him to the hallway wall. A gurgling scream of rage and agony tore from the creature's ruined throat.

"Doctor, the door!" Esperanza shouted, her voice strained with effort as she held the thrashing corpse at bay.

The world spun around Emilio, a maelstrom of spectral voices and encroaching darkness threatening to overwhelm him. But Esperanza's voice cut through the chaos like a lifeline. He stumbled towards the door, every step a battle against the supernatural forces pressing in on all sides. Time seemed to stretch, each moment an eternity, as he reached for the handle.

The thunderous roar of the open tracks competed with the furor of spectral voices assaulting Emilio's senses. He stumbled out onto the platform, grasping the metal railings for support, his knuckles white with the effort of staying upright.

With a primal roar that seemed to shake the very air, Esperanza Boyorquez drove the dead man out of the sleeper car and onto the platform. The reanimated corpse, still struggling for control over its uncooperative limbs, lurched awkwardly. The Voca, her face filled with determination, seized upon this weakness. In one fluid motion, she thrust the glowing metal rod hard against the creature's chest.

The dead man teetered on the edge of the platform. For a heartbeat, he hung suspended between the train and the rushing ground below. Then, with no sense of balance to save him, he tumbled backward over the railing, disappearing into the blur of the passing landscape.

"Of course Cortez isn't here!" Esperanza spat, her chest heaving as she fought to catch her breath. The exertion had taken its toll, but the fire in her eyes remained undiminished. She lunged for the door, her movements precise despite her fatigue. "Seal yourself upstairs!" she shouted into the car. "Do as the Doctor says with the salt immediately!"

The door slammed shut with a resounding clang. In one smooth motion, Esperanza slid the metal rod through the door's latches, creating an improvised barricade. "If someone's still using them as puppets, they'll be hard-pressed to get in now." She turned to Emilio, her gaze searching. "Are you ready, Doctor?"

Emilio closed his eyes, reaching out to the familiar power of Styx. The response was immediate, a cool burn that flowed through his veins. Instead of allowing the energy to flow outward as he usually did, he concentrated on pulling it around himself, like a refreshing dip in a mountain pool on a sweltering day.

The effort was taxing, sweat beading on his brow, but the result was instantaneous. The voices fell silent, leaving only the rhythmic clatter of the train on the tracks. Like the Voca's charm, this shield required constant concentration to maintain, but the respite it provided was worth the strain.

Emilio opened his eyes, a wry smile tugging at the corners of his mouth despite the situation. "If we live through this, I'd like to sleep for the rest of the trip, please."

"You and I both, Doctor," Esperanza replied. "You and I both." With a determined set to her shoulders, she pushed forward toward the next platform, the glow of Hil's power still emanating from her impromptu weapon.

As they moved, Emilio couldn't shake the feeling that the two divinely touched souls were walking a tightrope between two worlds. On one side, the physical dangers of a train hurtling through the night. On the other, the supernatural horrors that seemed to press in from all sides. Their path forward was narrow and treacherous, with no guarantee of safety at the end.

The wind whipped around them, carrying with it the faint, distant screams of the angry dead. Ahead loomed the unknown of the first-class car and the innocent lives they were racing to save.

THE IMPOSSIBLE SHOT

The wind howled, a furious banshee determined to rip them from the train's roof. Lyric's hair whipped about her face, a copper storm that stung her eyes and blurred her vision. Each gust was a physical blow, threatening to send them tumbling into the abyss that rushed by on either side.

Beside her, Jalin moved with the practiced grace of a man accustomed to dancing with death, but even he couldn't fully hide the toll this ordeal was taking. The stimulant Emilio had given him coursed through his veins, a fire that kept him on his feet but couldn't completely mask the tremors of exhaustion that wracked his frame. His eyes were too bright, his movements a touch too jerky - a man running on borrowed time and borrowed strength.

They crawled forward on hands and knees, the metal of the train's roof burning cold beneath their palms. Every few seconds, the train would lurch or sway, sending them scrambling for purchase. Traversing across the First Class car had been easy. The water tender car was taking its toll on them, but they needed a better vantage point. Lyric's fingers were numb, her knuckles bloody from scraping against rivets and seams in the metal.

"There!" Jalin's voice barely carried over the gusts of wind and grinding steel. His arm extended, pointing towards a distant glint of metal. The switch.

Lyric squinted, her eyes watering. It was so far, a fool's errand to even consider hitting it. But they were out of options, out of time. Unholstering the pistol, she handed it to the Inquisitor.

Jalin pulled out a strange-looking stock extension from his jacket. She had noticed the item earlier while they dressed his wounds. Unlike a heavy wooden stock, it was lightweight, with a thin metal frame encompassing a wooden core. She watched as he snapped the extension onto place. For all his disparaging talk about the Mechanists, Jalin Cortez certainly loved their inventions. Here, on the top of a train car, hurtling down a track, Jalin worked with the same calm precision she saw in Emilio Kane when he was stitching up the wounded Inquisitor.

With a careful twist, Jalin removed the pistol's barrel and pulled a second one from an internal pocket. He glanced through the longer barrel and then quickly locked it into place. It was a thing of beauty, and a testament to the tradecraft. The weapon became extended a sleeker instrument of death that seemed an extension of the Inquisitor himself. He lowered himself to a prone position, using a ventilation duct for cover and support. The metal groaned ominously under their combined weight.

As he tried to steady the composite gun, a hiss of pain escaped through clenched teeth. The wounds from his earlier fight, exacerbated by their perilous climb, were taking their toll. The stimulant might have dulled the pain, but it couldn't erase it entirely. The barrel of the composite gun wavered, unable to find a fixed point as the train rocked beneath them.

"Cortez," Lyric called out, her voice nearly lost in the maelstrom. "Let me help steady your aim."

His head snapped towards her, eyes blazing with indignation. "I don't need your help, Wax. I've made shots twice this distance with a crossbow in a sandstorm."

"This isn't a sandstorm, and you weren't bleeding half to death then," she countered, already moving to his side. The wind caught her jacket, nearly pulling her off balance. She grabbed a nearby pipe, her fingers screaming in protest. "Stop being stubborn and let me help."

Jalin's face darkened, pride and anger warring across his features. A bead of sweat rolled down his temple despite the biting cold - another sign of the stimulant's effects. "I am the Manos of Hil, girl. This is my duty, my burden to bear."

"And I'm your partner," Lyric shot back, refusing to be cowed. She pressed herself flat against the roof as another violent gust threatened to send them both flying. "Let me do my job and support you."

For a long moment, Jalin didn't move. Then, with a grunt that might have been assent, he shifted slightly, allowing Lyric to brace his shoulder and help steady the gun.

"On my mark," Jalin growled, squinting down the sight. His breathing was ragged, each exhale forming a small cloud in the frigid air.

Lyric held her breath, feeling the tremors running through Jalin's body. The switch seemed to dance in the distance, a mocking reminder of their desperation. The train hit a rough patch of track, jostling them both. Jalin gritted his teeth, fighting to maintain his aim.

"Now!" Jalin squeezed the trigger.

The gun's report was swallowed by the wind. They waited, tense, hoping against hope.

Nothing. The switch remained unmoved.

He tried to line up another shot, but his arms were shaking visibly now, the strain evident in every line of his body. The stimulant was wearing off, leaving him pale and clammy.

Jalin swore, "Pinche grave-robber. I knew I shouldn't have trusted his medicine!"

"Cortez," Lyric said softly, "let me take the shot."

"Absolutely not," he snarled, but the effect was somewhat diminished by the tremor in his voice. "I can do this. I have to do this."

Lyric took a deep breath, steeling herself for what she knew would be a difficult conversation. "Jalin," she said, using his first name deliberately, "look at me."

Reluctantly, he tore his gaze from the distant switch, meeting her eyes. The raw determination she saw there was tinged with something else – fear, perhaps, or the first flickers of doubt.

"You've already given everything to this mission," Lyric continued. "You've fought assassins, endured injuries that would have laid most men low, and you're still here, still fighting. That's not nothing."

Jalin's jaw clenched, but he didn't interrupt. Encouraged, Lyric pressed on.

"This isn't a failure on your part. You've pushed yourself beyond any reasonable limit. But now? Now it's time to let me step up. To trust me, as your partner, to carry this burden with you."

"I am the Manos of Hil," Jalin growled, but the words lacked their usual fire. "It's my duty-"

"Your duty is to see this mission through," Lyric cut him off. "To protect the innocent lives on this train. And right now, the best way to do that is to let me take this shot."

She could see the conflict raging behind his eyes. Pride warred with pragmatism, duty with reality. The train lurched beneath them, as if to emphasize the urgency of their situation.

"You trained me, Cortez," Lyric said, softening her tone. "You've seen what I can do. Trust in that. Trust in me. This isn't about you failing – it's about us succeeding, together."

For a long moment, Jalin was silent, the only sound the howling wind and the rhythmic clatter of the train. Then, slowly, painfully, he lowered the composite gun.

"If you miss, Wax," he said, his voice rough with emotion, "I'll never let you forget it."

Lyric allowed herself a small smile. "If I miss, I don't think any of us will be around long enough for you to remind me."

Jalin snorted, a sound that might have been a laugh under different circumstances. "One shot," he said, holding out the weapon. His eyes met hers, and in them, she saw not just resignation, but a flicker of something else. Trust. "Make it count."

Lyric took the strange gun, its weight a stark reminder of the responsibility she'd just assumed. "I won't let you down."

As she took position, Jalin moved beside her. "Remember your training," he said gruffly. "Account for wind speed, train movement. You'll need to lead the target."

Lyric nodded, not trusting herself to speak. She braced the composite, using every technique she'd been taught to steady her aim. Time seemed to slow as she peered down the sight. The train's movement, the howling wind, even her own heartbeat - all faded away. There was only the gun, her finger on the trigger, and that distant glint of metal that held their fate.

Breathe in. Aim. Breathe out. Squeeze.

The composite kicked hard against her shoulder, the report once again lost in the wind's scream. For an agonizing moment, the world held its breath.

Then, impossibly, miraculously, the switch moved.

The change in the train's trajectory was subtle at first, then violently apparent as it swung onto the old track. Lyric and Jalin were nearly thrown from their positions, clinging to whatever handholds they could find as the train realigned itself. Metal screamed against metal, the entire world tilting on its axis.

As the chaos subsided, Lyric found herself laughing, the sound bordering on hysterical. They'd done it. They'd actually done it.

She turned to Jalin, expecting to see his usual stoic expression, or perhaps lingering anger at her usurping his role. Instead, she was met with something she'd never seen before - a hint of grudging respect, maybe even admiration.

"Well done, Wax," he said, the words clearly costing him. "Come on, we need to get to the engine, and stop this pinché train!"

"Wait! What about the Cult ... the ghouls?" Lyric said.

Jalin turned to face her. His eyes were wide and glassy.

She hesitated to reach out to him when he closed his eyes and began violently shaking his head, "Damn graverobber drugs! GHAAAAAA!"

Quickly reeling back, Lyric slapped Jalin hard across the face, "FOCUS CORTEZ! You're needed HERE and NOW!"

Jalin's eyes snapped open, seething.

"We have people to save, Inquisitor," Lyric said.

Jalin's fury cooled. Reason returned to him. He nodded his head. "Priorities. We've switched tracks to corral them to one side. We can access the engine, but we need to stop them from exiting."

She couldn't tell if he was telling her or himself, but she watched him take a few practiced breaths before looking up at her.

"Gracias, Senorita," he said. His eyes slowly awakened from the fog and focused on her.

"It was nothing. I had a good teacher." Lyric nodded at him and handed the gun back.

Their fingers brushed momentarily as Jalin took the weapon, and Lyric felt an unexpected jolt of... something. She quickly withdrew her hand, unsure of how to process the moment.

Jalin cleared his throat, looking suddenly uncomfortable. He opened his mouth to speak, but before he could, a voice called out from behind them.

"Inquisitor! Ms. Wax! We need to get inside, now!"

They both turned, startled, to see Carlos Monterro, the Assistant Conductor, clinging desperately to the edge of the hatch of the water tender. His face was pale, eyes wide with fear and urgency.

"Dios mío," Jalin muttered. "I'd forgotten he was with us."

Lyric felt a flush creep up her neck, embarrassed at how easily she'd lost track of their surroundings. "Right," she said. "We should go."

They cast a quick look toward the engine as they made their way back past the hatch. They were so close. There was no sign of another person in the Engine compartment. Perhaps it was just a bad angle? Maybe they were seated and not visible. The questions gnawed at her as she followed him. Something had shifted between them. A respect, hard-earned and fragile, but real.

And perhaps something more, something neither of them was quite ready to acknowledge.

Going from tender to First Class, they entered into the train's interior, the wind's howl faded, replaced by the urgent murmur of passengers and the distant, chilling moans of the ghouls. Monterro quickly secured the door behind them, his hands shaking slightly.

"The assassins," Jalin said, his voice rough with exhaustion but still commanding. "They'll be making their move soon. We need to know who your First Class passengers are."

Monterro balked at the question, "Guild regulations..."

"Can be damned, Monterro." Jalin swore. "We need to know who they might be targeting."

"Do any of them stand out for any particular reason?" Lyric added.

Monterro paused and then took out a folded piece of paper and opened it. "Most of them are merchant travelers." He held out the notepad to the pair, who began scanning the printed names.

Jalin's eyes scanned the list quickly, then he handed it to Lyric. "There are just under a dozen names, but no one of real note," Jalin said and looked to Lyric, who nodded in agreement. "No one's name stands out."

"We also have a military clerk, a pair of unrelated nobles, and a retired Peacekeeper," Monterro added.

"Why aren't they on this list?" Jalin demanded.

"The Merchants travelers are consistent, and the businesses they represent provide all the travel arrangements ahead of time, so we have a printed list of when they are coming," he said as he folded up the list and pulled out his notepad. "The Nobility rarely announce when they will be traveling. For the sake of personal security. The Conductor is made aware, so they can make arrangements. Then they advise me and the other need-to-know-staff on the day of the arrival."

"Who are the nobles?" Lyric asked.

Flipping through the pad, Monterro read, "We have Joseph Raymond Casteneda, heir to La Familia Casteneda, his exit is the Northern Gate. The other is Anna Marie Aguirre, of La Familia Aguirre; she exits at the Northern Gate as well."

"Was the military clerk traveling with an escort?" Jalin asked.

"No, he's listed by himself. A Corporal Ernesto Ayala. He also exits the Northern Gate," Monterro replied.

"And the Peacekeeper?" Jalin continued.

"He was supposed to get off at Truitt; his name is Erasmo Trujillo."

Lyric considered the names offered. "Casteneda could be a target if they were looking to cause issues with the House, especially if he is their only heir. They are a well connected House, but I cannot recall why off hand. I want to say agriculture, but I can't be sure. However, La Familia Aguirre holds significant sway in the Imperium as they oversee the minting houses. What would they gain in killing her if another family member could easily replace her?" Lyric said.

"If the clerk were traveling with an escort, they might be of some value or someone vital. If he's alone, it would not be out of place..." Jalin said, "Although, he normally wouldn't be riding in First Class. The military is efficient to the point of threadbare at times. He might be someone to consider."

"What about the Peacekeeper?" Lyric asked."This could be a vengeance thing from when he was active."

Jalin nodded. "That is sound reasoning."

"Do you have any other information about him?" Lyric asked the Assistant Conductor.

Monterro shook his head, "No, the Conductor only gave me the additions. All that other information would be in his office."

Jalin glanced down train,"Which is full of ghouls and barricaded luggage." He pursed his lips. "Do the nobles have people accompanying them?"

Monterro nodded. "Casteneda has a man with him, but I think he's more of an assistant, maybe his Steward or Mayordomo? Aguirre has an obvious bodyguard with her."

Jalin sucked on his tooth and then nodded to himself. "The three of us should be able to cover the individuals. I want Boyorquez to handle Casteneda, and I'll watch Aguirre." His eyes landed on Lyric, "I want you to cover the Clerk."

"What about Doctor Kane?" Lyric asked.

Jalin squinted momentarily as if to start on another insult, but he instead said, "We'll put him on him, Peacekeeper. If they go after the lawman, he could use Kane as a shield."

Lyric scowled at the response.

"Ah, true. We still need him for the ghouls. Maybe the Peacekeeper will be kind, and let him live."

"What should I do?" asked Monterro.

"Give us five minutes to get into place," Cortez said. "After that, simply walk the car as you normally would and assess the passengers and staff. The second they see you, they will know their ruse is at an end. From there, we will put them down."

"Five minutes? Shouldn't we alert the people that they are being targeted?" Lyric asked.

Jalin shook his head, "Why? It will give away that we know there is a killer among them. Their ignorance is for their own protection. This is my job remember? Trust me to do this thing."

She wanted to argue back, but the look in his eyes was different. She could not tell if it was a plea or something else. Regardless, she kept silent and just nodded.

"It will be crowded in there, Inquisitor," Monterro added, "What about the dead? Eventually, they will head this way."

Before Jalin could answer, Lyric said, "One problem at a time, Mr. Monterro."

BEACON

*C*omfort cushions for a nominal fee.

That was a sign that hung on the wall in the passenger car. Emilio remembered it. He'd ridden the rail sparingly. It was expensive, and he was not a wealthy man. His parents had some small holdings when he was younger. They'd given up the comfort of their titles and their land when Emilio came into his Gift. *Blessed by Styx* was not often seen as a blessing in the Imperium. He'd learned to be thrifty from them. It was necessary.

He remembered how it made him feel seeing that sign for the first time. Asking passengers who were already paying what they could afford to dig a little deeper into their pockets for something as simple as a cushion to sit on. It did not seem right.

The passenger car had racks on the walls above the wooden bench seats, which left just enough room for one's legs, and a lone, narrow service vestibule. The benches ran on both sides of the car and had enough room to seat two people. Three, if one was a child. Wooden floors ran the length of the car with widows that only opened partially. Every inch of space was put to use. Crowded. Efficient.

Then there was First Class.

Emilio peered quietly through a set of burgundy red velvet curtains that separated the rear service vestibule from the main car.

If there was a statement about the division in social classes within the Imperium, this was it.

The dark, natural wood tones in the passenger car, were replaced with warm cream and gold wallpaper and paint. The wooden floors replaced with deep burgundy, almost brown carpet. Velvet curtains in a shade that complemented the carpet covered the elegantly crafted windows. The carpet and curtains muffled the sounds of the car and the rail.

Overstuffed chairs sat facing one another. Each chair was upholstered in a floral pattern of soft creams and buff tans, and decorated with ornamental gold fringe and tassels. Tables were built into the walls that could be folded out and used for dining or card games if the passenger wished so.

At the far end of the car was a low pony wall, roughly three feet high, with a pass through built in. It separated the main car from another, smaller section beyond. This smaller area featured a pair of chairs on one side, and a pair of comfortable couches on the other.

Beyond this section was another pair of heavy velvet curtains, like the ones Emilio peered out from now. He assumed they hid another service vestibule dedicated to the service of the passengers in that exclusive section.

The ceiling of the entire car had been painted with a mural of a serene landscape.

It was peaceful.

And its decadence was appalling.

One of the train staff had walked three passengers to the other end of the car and into that service vestibule after sealing Finn Carstein into the sleeper car with his charges. Esperanza assured Emilio that the burly man was more than capable of protecting the group and holding the barricade.

"He's familiar with life outside the walls, Doctor. He knows what he's doing."

He hoped she was right. He couldn't bear the idea of what would happen if she was wrong.

There had been some small uproar from a group of merchants when the passengers were brought through. Their great displeasure at having to share space with "others" had been very evident.

Three additional passengers crowded around in the vestibule that Emilio occupied. They'd had to find space for them when the sleeper car reached capacity. They huddled in a corner, as far away from Emilio as possible. Their hushed whispers burned his ears with their fear and hatred.

It was always the same.

Behind him, Esperanza comforted one of the remaining staff members. What was her name? Ginny. She'd come forward with their group and had maintained her composure for quite some time. Given the circumstances, Emilio was impressed she had held things together as long as she had. Guild staffers were trained to deal with the dangers of the road, but for train staff, that usually meant robbers, not a cadre of the dead rushing the cars.

The Voca was a credit to her calling. He could hear her offering words of comfort and inspiration to the broken soul behind him. Sharing the beauty and light of Hil's message of love and protection. For a moment, he almost believed.

This is what they should be, he thought to himself.

He peered out once more, trying to size up the occupants of the car. Somewhere in this collection of persons was an assassin.

A warm hand gently rested on his shoulder and he jerked out of instinct, then realized it was Esperanza.

"Anyone of note?" she asked quietly.

He shook his head. "I can't tell from here. But no one stands out. It doesn't appear they have enacted their plan yet. We should be approaching Carolina station soon, though."

"MMMhrm...where are the other staff for the car?" she asked.

"Some are with the passengers in the head vestibule. There are three just outside the doorway here, along the wall. I can't see them very well." He paused. "How is Ginny?"

"She is a strong woman, and she will be fine. She was involved with someone downtrain who did not make it this far."

Emilio's heart ached for a moment. "I see," he said a quick and quiet prayer to Styx to welcome the soul of the departed.

"And the general mood of the room?" Esperanza asked.

"Cranky? The group from the Merchant's Guild here in this front section of chairs has been very vocal about questioning why the staff were visible, and who dared bring common passengers to the front," he replied.

"Well, they are about to become more so. Come along, Doctor."

Esperanza straightened her shoulders and with a practiced move that spoke of power that demanded respect, she flung the velvet drapes aside and stepped into the car.

All eyes turned to look at the Voca.

Her normally pristine saffron robes were stained with blood, grease, and dirt. Her gentle countenance was stern, as her gaze fell on the occupants of the car.

Two of the merchants scowled disapprovingly at her appearance. One leaned in to the other, "By the Gods, is this what our Temple has become? She looks like she's been drug behind a horse."

The conspirator nodded, their disgust evident, "No respect for station, clearly."

Esperanza's eyes slid over to land on the two merchants. Her glare was ice cold as she tugged at the hem of her sleeves.

"Hrmph" she scoffed. "Hil reminds you gentlemen that is the the place of the Heavens to judge, not mortal man."

Both men blanched and sat up in their chairs, a pair of naughty school boys caught by the teacher.

Esperanza glanced over her shoulder. "Doctor, please join me."

"Of course..." came Emilio's hesitant reply. The doctor gingerly stepped out of the vestibule and to the side of the Voca.

If there had been disgust at seeing the condition of Voca Boyorquez, there was an almost primal fear in the eyes of the onlookers when the Necromist came into view.

Emilio had managed to pull his unnaturally white hair back and knotted a piece of twine there to hold it into place. His bloodied sleeves were rolled up to the elbows. Dark pants, borrowed from the dead, bloused into the tops of his worn boots. A pair of suspenders held them in place. Over his shoulder he carried his leather medical satchel. Esperanza's sigil of Hil hung around his neck still, continuing to boost the buffer to the voices of the dead that surrounded them.

He reached up and gently pushed his dark glasses up to the bridge of his nose, covering is ethereally green eyes.

"Dios mio," the whispered words danced across the room.

From the back of the car, two men seated in the comfortable chairs looked in Emilio's direction.

One appeared to be dressed in the formal military uniform of The Reach. A simple leather valise occupied his lap. Across from him him sat an older man, in worn attire. Threadbare in places,his clothing was clean and pressed, and his mustache trimmed impeccably. The glint of a Peacekeeper's badge peeked out from under his jacket.

Both men met the eyes of Esperanza. The older man quirked an eyebrow upward slightly. She nodded simply and the men returned to their conversation, unconcerned by the Voca or her strange companion.

Satisfied with the exchange, Esperanza approached the disapproving merchants who sat in a pair of chairs to the left side of the car.

She offered them a thin smile, "We require your seats, please join the rest of your Guild." It was a statement, not a request.

One of the merchants attempted a blustered objection, but his companion reached out and slapped his arm with a newspaper.

"Move!" he hissed, his eyes fixed on Emilio. He stumbled over himself gathering his belongings and nodded at Esperanza. "Voca."

Chairs vacated, the two merchants moved to join another group of similarly dressed individuals. They exchanged hushed comments, watching the pair carefully.

Esperanza gestured to Emilio to take the seat that allowed him to watch the majority of the car. She settled into the one opposite him, her entire frame relaxing noticeably as she sank into the chair.

"Tell me what you see," she whispered.

"Pair in the front chairs... military?" he asked.

She nodded. "And a Peacekeeper. Could be useful if things get bad."

Emilio glanced to the other side of the car. Two men and two women sat on the couches opposite the PeaceKeeper and the Military Officer. Perhaps it was the cut of their clothing, or the way they carried themselves, but they had the feel of nobility about them.

One of the nobles was a young man. *Perhaps returning from his Prueba? He looked about the right age.*

With him was a stern looking man with chiseled features. A chaperone?

Across them were a pair of women. One, a warm and inviting-looking matron. The other was a tall and stern-faced woman, leaning against the doorframe. A bodyguard?

She reminded him of Kalidah, Captain of the Gran Salón. He felt an ache in his chest. It had been months since he had seen his friend. The thought of her and strictness to duty kept his head moving, avoiding the other woman's direct gaze.

"Group of nobles," Emilio offered. "Could be a single family, traveling together, or two groups. One with a young man that could be old enough for his Volver."

Esperanza nodded once again. "Bodyguards?"

"One...that I can see."

As if on cue, the curtains opened behind Emilio, and Ginny appeared with a tray of water glasses for the assembled. Turning to Esperanza and Emilio, Ginny gave them a small smile despite the pain in her eyes as she handed them glasses. "Thank you, Voca."

Esperanza accepted the glass with a nod, "No thanks is necessary. Trust me when I say I understand."

Ginny nodded again and began handing out the glasses to those who needed them, filling the water glasses for the pair.

"How long do we have?" Esperanza asked Emilio. "The sleeper car is reinforced, but they will get through eventually." Her eyes lifted toward the heavy drapes of the vestibule.

This was the last car. They would have to make a stand here.

"A good question that I don't have a hard answer to. Not long," Emilio answered.

"A better question is, what do we do when they get here?" the Voca asked.

Emilio chewed on the inside of his cheek in contemplation, "Trying to destroy them in mass is a no-go. You tried it, and they didn't stop coming."

"Would be easier if you could just tell them to halt," Esperanza said.

"Commanding the dead is not exactly something the Academy likes to teach us. It treads into some dark, if not questionable, waters."

"Waters you have some experience swimming in..." the Voca replied factually.

Emilio paled, his mouth suddenly dry. He met the Voca's penetrating gaze and slowly nodded in agreement. Like the dead, he had no reason to lie.

Esperanza's eyes slid to the vestibule. "Cortez and his ilk are taught that all who wield the power of Styx are Necromancers, born of evil, and fated to bring about a second Corpse Wars." Her eyes returned to his. "Any mask of innocence you wear is false, and you all must be destroyed. Thus is the way of the Manos." her finger gently traced the path of a droplet of condensation that trailed down the water glass that Ginny left.

"Those of us touched by the Divine know better, don't we?" she asked.

Emilio looked down at his hands a moment. They were the hands of a surgeon, trained to save lives. But they were also the hands of a mortician, and one who dealt with the dead.

He nodded silently.

"Tell me about the Ghost Light above your house," Esperanza asked as she lifted the cool water to her lips.

Emilio's face reddened, and he swallowed involuntarily. If she was going to have him killed, she would have done so while he was bound earlier. "Members of the Divinity rarely travel to my area of the Reach," he said softly and then looked up at her slowly, "The Manos are the ones that usually inspect my offices, if they remember me. They rarely have the ability to look into the beyond." He fidgeted with his hands. "I altered a ritual and hoped no one would notice."

Esperanza nodded. "The original rite is meant to draw spirits and shades to be placed under the yoke of control, if I recall."

Another silent nod.

"Beacons should be green, Doctor. Why is yours blue?"

Emilio pursed his lips and glanced around furtively. This was not a dialog for open conversation.

"A Beacon that uses the original rite would call the dead and weaken their will. It makes them easier to bind and control. That has never been my desire, Voca. I want to send them on their way. My Beacon merely calls to them, offering them the safety and surety of Styx's Promise. Once in my presence, I can talk to them and determine how to grant them their Promise." His palms were sweating. "Its range is very limited, I promise... and I don't use any of the... unsavory... ingredients required in the original spell. It's not about binding them, it's about helping them..." He paused a moment, his voice trailing off.

Esperaza looked back at Emilio, noting the curious look of thought on his face. "Doctor?"

"Spirits and Shades ultimately desire to move on. They don't WANT to stay here. La Corrupta and ghouls are driven mad by their insatiable need to STAY in this world. Their refusal of the Promise makes them what they are."

"Yes."

"What if I altered the ritual again... and we masked this car to appear like the Beacon? Except not for luring or a promise of safety... but a threat of...destruction and ending?"

"We?" she said, suddenly apprehensive. "My gifts are not like yours, it..."

"Light, your divine light!" he said excitedly, then quickly covered his mouth and lowered his voice. "I do not possess the materials to create the candle that I would place in a Beacon... and this car is much larger... but...I still know the rite itself!" He patted his pockets and pulled out a worn down nub of a pencil, he glanced around quickly, then shrugged and began drawing on the table between them. "If I can create... sigils... instead of candles... and place them around the room, altering the appearance of intent..." He looked at the strange glyph drawn on the table before him. Then he licked his thumb and removed a line and nodded. "Yes. That should do it." He looked at Esperanza, "Voca, together, we could empower the rite ourselves with minimal effort. It would allow us to create a simple light that threatens destruction for the restless."

"But we cannot destroy them."

Emilio held up a finger. "But the dead... and whoever is controlling them... does not know that." He lowered his voice once more and leaned forward. "Whoever is doing this, has to control a dozen mad souls, who have no desire to leave this existence. Easy enough to do when the targets ahead are a promise of food. But when it threatens to remove them from this plane?"

Esperanza's eyes widened with realization. "Even the thought of being ended would cause them to fight against their master. It would be a contest they are not prepared for."

"Precisely."

"What about the drain this will be on us? Considering the past few hours, you and I are not exactly in the best shape," Esperanza cautioned. "Won't the Quemar be an issue?"

Emilio shook his head. "Carving and blessing the sigil will be the heavy lifting, Voca. We just have to keep a candle lit."

She smiled then and nodded.

Emilio looked at her, suddenly suspicious. "Did you know I was going to suggest this?"

She shook her head. "Oh no, Doctor. Your knowledge of such things far surpasses my own." She pointed at the sigil of Hil that hung around his neck. "I merely hoped that Hil's divine light might lend you some inspiration for our salvation."

Emilio smirked slightly and lightly wagged a finger at her. "Oh, you're good. Inspiring indeed! We should get to work, though we probably should alert the staff so they don't try to kill me when I start carving into their walls."

"Allow me," she said.

At that moment, the sound of a shot drove everyone to silence. Both Emilio and Esperanza exchanged glances and quietly said, "Cortez."

Emilio quickly began digging through his bag and Esperanzas stood. She smoothed her wrinkled and dirty robes and made her way toward the center of the car.

"Good people, my name is Esperanza Boyorquez, Voca of the Divinity of Hil. As you are aware, the train is currently experiencing some issues with adherence to its established schedule."

Everyone in the car focused their attention on her.

"The shot you just heard was Inquisitor Jalin Cortez attempting to re-route the path of the train, to aid in that issue."

Several murmured voices could be heard to whisper, *Thank the Inquisition.*

Esperanza continued, "Some time ago, as we traveled through these territories, a group of willful dead managed to board the train. We have slowed them as best as we can thusfar..."

"Blame the freak you brought in here with you, Voca!" one of the staff called. Esperanza remembered them from the Dining Car. "We saw what he did. Corpse Caller."

The room exploded in commentary, and stares of curiosity morphed into ones of fear and hatred.

Esperanza sighed. That sigh became a prayer, as she lay her right hand over a tattooed sigil on her left arm.

Suddenly the room blazed with a powerful reddish-golden light. Its sudden appearance instantly cowed many, but those who willfully refused the display of power soon found themselves thinking otherwise as Esperanza spoke. Her presence rippled with unyielding power, and the sound of her voice heeded command.

"This man is Doctor Emilio Kane, the Authorized Necromist for The Reach. He is working with the most Holy Order of Hil! If it were not for his knowledge and talents, many of you would be dead already. What he has done here today, and what he is about to do, is authorized by the Inquisition. You. Will. Not. Question. Him." The Voca dropped the light and another shot rang out in the distance.

The train suddenly lurched to the left as it made a wide turn.

"Now then. Doctor Kane will be carving sigils of protection into the walls. Once completed, he and I will keep us all safe. Please do not interfere with his work ... unless you wish to meet your chosen gods through the uncaring hands of ghouls."

Fearful, angry silence was the only reply.

Emilio pulled his head out of his satchel, an irritated look on his face. His carving knife and scalpels were gone. He knew Cortez had no doubt seized them under the auspice of contraband. He stood, setting the satchel on the table top and glanced around the room quickly.

Ah ha!

Carefully dodging past the group of irritated merchants he approached the soldier and the Peacekeeper, whom Esperanza had made eye contact with earlier.

He gave the man in uniform a semi-embarrassed smile. "Excuse me sir, one of my companions took my knife. You wouldn't happen to have one, would you?"

Surprised, the soldier quickly nodded and started to reach for his belt, only to pause and say, "I'm sorry, sir, but I'm not carrying anything on me, dress uniform and all."

Holding out a well-worn handle, the older man said, "Will this do?"

Carefully accepting the sheathed weapon, Emilio removed it and examined the blade. It was sharp and bore a well-honed point. " It's perfect, mister..."

"Mo. Mo Trujillo," said the older man. "Reachers have to help one another, right?"

Emilio gave a dutiful nod. "Always, sir, and thank you. I will have this back in a few minutes." Making a beeline toward the nearest wall, he began to carve into cream-colored paint. He could feel the eyes set upon him, watching his every move. Yet, none of them existed at this moment. His focus was on the sigil, and every second counted.

BONES TASTE FLESH

Lyric's fingers curled around the edge of the heavy curtains, the plush fabric a stark contrast to the tension that hung in the air. She paused, steeling herself before drawing them aside. The buzz of anxiety that greeted her was almost palpable, a living thing that writhed through the First Class car.

The opulence of her surroundings struck her anew. Cream and gold wallpaper gleamed in the muted light, a far cry from the utilitarian passenger car she'd left behind. But Lyric's gaze focused instead on the faces of those within. They were huddled in clusters, some sitting on plush carpet that had never been meant for such indignities, others trying to maintain a semblance of normalcy in their overstuffed chairs.

Kitchen staff and porters acknowledged her with subtle nods, a silent communication born of shared purpose. Lyric returned their greeting, her smile tight but genuine. These were her people, after all, even if they didn't know it.

She stepped fully into the car, letting the curtain fall closed behind her. The rumble of discontented merchants reached her ears as she passed, but she paid them no mind. Her eyes were fixed on the center of the room, where Esperanza stood like an island of calm in a stormy sea.

As she moved, Lyric's gaze darted to the side, cataloging faces and positions, pulling up in her mind, the notes that Monterro had shared earlier. The nobles were easy to spot, creatures of habit that they were. Aguirre and Casteneda sat facing the lake, their profile outlined against the window. It was the only 'safe' point of exit for their quarry, a fact that twisted Lyric's gut with frustration. Too late to change it now, she thought, forcing her attention to the other side of the car.

There sat Corporal Ayala, his military bearing evident even in repose. Beside him, the weathered face of the retired Peacekeeper, a man who'd seen his share of trouble if Lyric was any judge. And there, kneeling on the floor, was Doctor Kane. His hands moved with practiced precision, carving symbols into the wall that Lyric couldn't begin to comprehend.

She reached Esperanza, leaning in close to murmur, "Is everything okay with Doctor Kane?"

The Voca's eyes never left the Necromist as she replied, "Yes, he's come up with a tool to halt the dead until we can find a way to stop this train." Her gaze flicked to Lyric. "I assume the shooting we heard meant you were successful?"

Lyric nodded, her eyes scanning the room once more. The other passengers seemed more interested in Doctor Kane's arcane workings than in their whispered conversation. Still, she leaned closer, pitching her voice low. "We forced a track change. It'll take us longer to reach the Northern Gate, but it limits the escape options for our... friends."

"So what is Cortez's plan?" Esperanza asked, a note of wariness in her voice.

"Monterro will emerge from behind the curtains in a few minutes," Lyric explained. "He'll look around, trying to spot who doesn't belong. We think it'll force their hand once they see the Assistant Conductor."

Esperanza's face twisted into a grimace, an expression Lyric recognized all too well. It spoke of anger, worry, and a hint of resignation. "That isn't enough time to warn the targets," the Voca hissed. "And it puts Monterro at considerable risk. Cortez's impatience is gambling with their lives."

"I know," Lyric admitted, the words tasting bitter on her tongue. "But I couldn't sway him. He wouldn't listen. He wants to end this quickly, thinks that alerting them would only tip off our friends and endanger everyone here."

Esperanza's eyes narrowed, pinning Lyric with an intense stare. "Is he well? Give me an honest assessment, Lyric Wax."

Lyric held the Voca's gaze for a long moment before shaking her head slightly. "I'm not sure," she confessed. "But we can't turn back now. Monterro's already agreed to play his part."

Esperanza closed her eyes, a deep sigh escaping her. When she opened them again, worry and regret played across her usually stoic features.

"Cortez wants you near Casteneda over there," Lyric continued, motioning towards the nobles. "He'll be watching Aguirre."

"Wait." Esperanza's brow furrowed. "Did you say Casteneda?"

"Yes," Lyric confirmed, her gaze drifting back to the group of nobles. "Oh." She whispered, taken aback. "He's just a boy." She shook her head, refocusing. "Yes, the boy with the older man is Joseph Raymond Casteneda, heir to La Familia Casteneda. You know him?"

"If I'm correct, that's Lupe Casteneda's younger brother," Esperanza said, a note of surprise in her voice.

"Lupe?" Lyric blinked. "Wait, Voca Lupe? She's nobility?"

"A story for another time," Esperanza said, her tone brooking no argument. "What about you?"

"I'm watching the Corporal and the former Peacekeeper next to Doctor Kane," Lyric explained. "We're not sure who the target is, but you and Cortez are lakeside. If our 'friends' try to act, they'll have to go through you." She paused, meeting Esperanza's eyes. "Please, please be careful."

The weight of what was to come settled over them both, as heavy and suffocating as the tension that filled the car. In the background, Doctor Kane continued his work, his knife scraping against the wall in a rhythm that sounded eerily like a countdown.

At that moment, the heavy curtains parted once more, and Cortez emerged. The usual bluster of the merchant travelers died in their throats as the Inquisitor's stern gaze swept over them. His presence seemed to suck the air from the room, leaving behind a vacuum of tense silence.

Lyric watched as Cortez's attention fixed on the corner where Aguirre sat. The tall woman beside him met the Inquisitor's cold look with one of her own. For several heartbeats, they held each other's gaze as an unspoken challenge passed between them. Finally, almost grudgingly, they exchanged respectful nods. Cortez took up his position against the back wall, his eyes never ceasing their restless scan of the room.

His expression soured visibly as he caught sight of Doctor Kane, still etching his arcane symbols into the wall. Cortez's glare snapped to Esperanza, a question and an accusation in his eyes. The Voca met his look unflinchingly, her lips forming silent words: *Our plan.*

"Stay vigilant, Lyric," Esperanza murmured, giving the young Escritora's shoulder a gentle squeeze. Her eyes remained fixed on Cortez's angry visage as she moved quietly toward her assigned place near the young noble.

Lyric drew in a deep breath, letting it out slowly. Her gaze drifted to the curtain Cortez had emerged from. She knew Monterro would follow in less than a minute. In that brief span of time, a whirlwind of violence would erupt and end just as quickly. The question that hung in the air was: who would not be getting off the train when it finally stopped?

Refusing to give in to such dark thoughts, Lyric made her way toward the Corporal and the Peacekeeper. She leaned down, pitching her voice low. "Excuse me, gentlemen. Are either of you armed?"

Both men turned to face her. Corporal Ayala shook his head, a flicker of regret crossing his features. The Peacekeeper, however, gave a simple nod. "Is something else going on, miss?" he asked, his voice gruff but not unkind.

Lyric had hoped they'd both be armed, but one was better than nothing. She leaned closer, words tumbling out in a hushed rush. "There is, sir. In a moment, the Assistant Conductor is going to come out. We believe there is a pair—"

"Would any of you care for some refreshments?"

The question, so mundane in its politeness, cut through Lyric's whispered warning like a knife. She straightened, turning to face the staffer who'd appeared at her elbow. He was an older man, his face creased with laugh lines, holding a tray of water glasses. For a moment she became acutely aware of her parched throat.

She looked up, a polite smile forming on her lips. The staffer's own smile was warm, his eyes twinkling with a kindness that reminded Lyric of every old uncle she'd ever met. It was a face that spoke of shared jokes and smuggled sweets.

But as his gaze fell to her neck, that warmth vanished. Fear blossomed in his eyes, quickly hardening into something colder, more dangerous. "An Escritora," he hissed, the words dripping with venom. "Hil's Messenger Killers. Ossilaro will not be cheated out of his prize today."

"Wait, what?" The words had barely left Lyric's lips before the old man exploded into motion. The kindly uncle was gone, replaced by something far more deadly. The water glasses on his tray glinted in the light, suddenly looking less like vessels for refreshment and more like potential weapons.

The world exploded into chaos before Lyric could process the staffer's words. The metallic tray, moments ago a mundane object, became a weapon of brutal efficiency. It slammed into her face with a force that sent her reeling backwards, crashing into Trujillo. The clash of metal on flesh was drowned out by the of shattering glass and splashing water.

But the staffer—no, the assassin—wasn't done. With a grace that belied his earlier grandfatherly appearance, he pivoted. The tray whistled through the air once more, connecting with a sickening thud against the side of the

Corporal's head. The young soldier crumpled, unconscious before he hit the ground.

As if on cue, Monterro stepped out from behind the curtains. His appearance was the match that lit the powder keg. The car erupted into pandemonium. Screams of panic mingled with shouts for order. Bodies scrambled in every direction, a chaotic mass of fear and confusion.

Above it all, Inquisitor Cortez's voice boomed, a furious tide fighting against the wave of fleeing merchants. "MOVE, YOU ASSHOLES!" His words were punctuated by the sound of bodies being shoved aside.

The assassin—Bonilla, Lyric's mind supplied through the haze of pain—used the chaos like a master painter uses a brush. He spun, his arm describing a perfect arc as he launched the heavy tray. It cut through the air, finding its mark with unerring precision. The Voca's throat.

"No Gods for you, bruja!" The words were spat with venom, barely audible over the din.

Bonilla turned back to the fallen Corporal, his movements economical and purposeful. He snatched the leather bag from the unconscious soldier's lap, ready to make his escape. But fate, it seemed, had other plans.

A cry of pain erupted from Bonilla's lips as fire laced upward along the back of his leg. He stumbled, caught off guard by the sudden agony. His eyes, wide with shock and fury, found the source of his misery.

The Necromist knelt on the floor, his strange eyes boring into Bonilla with an intensity that seemed almost supernatural. For a heart-stopping moment, Bonilla could have sworn those eyes glowed. Then he saw the blade in the doctor's hand, its edge painted with a thin line of red. Another step back, and the pain intensified, shooting through his leg like lightning. Bonilla fell, his grand escape thwarted by a most unexpected adversary.

Meanwhile, Lyric's world had become a muffled haze of sound and motion. Everything seemed to move in slow motion, voices distorted as if she were underwater. Hands at her back pushed her upright, and she turned to see the Peacekeeper steadying her. The old man's face filled with determination, a rock in the storm of chaos around them.

Lyric shook her head, trying to clear the fog that clouded her senses. Instinct took over where conscious thought failed. Her hand moved of its own accord, drawing her pistol with practiced ease. Lessons from Inquisitor Cortez taking control of her motions. The weight of the weapon was comforting, an anchor in the sea of madness that the car had become.

She fought against her swimming vision, desperately trying to aim at the fallen assassin. Bodies continued to move around her, a living obstacle course that threatened to foil her every attempt to line up a shot.

And then, cutting through the din like a knife, came a sound that seemed to freeze time itself. A loud crack split the air, the unmistakable report of a firearm.

The world held its breath, waiting to see where the bullet would land, and whose fate it would seal.

The world had barely registered the first gunshot when another crack split the air. Behind Lyric, Trujillo had drawn his weapon. The report of his gun was deafening in the enclosed space, worsening Lyric's already fragile focus. The sound seemed to reverberate through her skull, compounding her disorientation.

Bonilla, his movements hampered by the severed tendon, rolled forward on his good foot. Fortune, it seemed, still smiled on the assassin as Trujillo's shot hit the ground, missing its mark. Bonilla's eyes locked onto the double doors, where the Voca had fallen. Esperanza lay on the ground, clutching at her throat and gagging. Her eyes blazed with an otherworldly power. Undaunted by the display, Bonilla charged forward, his hand reaching into his jacket for a concealed weapon.

Another thunderous crack rent the air.

The enclosed space amplified the sound, sending more waves of panic through the crowd. But this time, the bullet found its mark. It tore into Bonilla's shoulder, throwing him off balance. Instinctively, he tried to compensate with his injured foot. The attempt failed as pain lanced through his body and sent him crashing to the ground.

By the time Bonilla rolled over, Jalin Cortez loomed over him. With a motion born of years of practice, the Inquisitor's scoring blade snapped free from its bay. "May Hil grant you the suffering your kind deserve," Jalin intoned, his voice cold as he raised his arm to strike.

"Ossilaro will get his due!" Bonilla snarled. His hand flew to his forearm, yanking back to reveal a hidden arm bow.

Jalin's eyes widened, fury and surprise warring on his face. He lunged forward, driving his blade deep into the assassin's chest. But he was too late. The bolt launched, whistling past the Inquisitor's unarmored chest by mere inches.

"Your aim is as weak as your false god, murderer!" Jalin spat, grim satisfaction coloring his words.

Blood bubbled from Bonilla's mouth as he choked out his final words. "Di...did I? ...may bones taste..." The light faded from his eyes, life ebbing away with each labored breath.

Jalin took a step back, pulling his bloodied blade free with a sickening sound. Behind him, a chorus of gasps rose. He whirled around, dread settling in the pit of his stomach.

Lyric blinked slowly. A curious warmth spread through her body, contrasting sharply with the pain that seemed to radiate from everywhere at once. Her gaze drifted downward, settling on her chest with a detached sort of interest.

The sight before her was strange, almost amusing in its surreality. As she stared, the pain intensified, all sensations narrowing to a singular point: the metal bolt embedded in her chest.

She lifted her eyes, meeting Jalin's shocked gaze. "I..." The word died on her lips as darkness rushed in, swallowing her whole.

The last thing Lyric saw was the horror dawning on the Inquisitor's face as the world faded to black.

LA CORRUPTA

The moment Lyric Wax hit the ground, an eerie silence descended upon the car. It was as if the world itself held its breath, suspended in disbelief. But like the calm before a storm, it was short-lived.

The silence shattered, giving way to a tempest of rage and fury. At its epicenter stood Jalin Cortez.

Emilio, being the closest, instinctively reached for Lyric's fallen form. His movement sparked an immediate reaction from Cortez.

"GET AWAY FROM HER!" The Inquisitor's voice cracked like a whip, raw with emotion.

Emilio's response was equally sharp, tinged with urgency. "Do you want her to DIE, Cortez?!"

The words struck Cortez like a physical blow. He faltered, then thrust his blade toward Emilio, desperation evident in every line of his body. "If she dies, so do you."

"Then shut up and let me save her," Emilio retorted, his voice steady despite the threat. He closed his eyes, ancient words forming in his mind and spilling from his lips. One hand rested on Lyric's head, the other over her punctured heart. A bluish-green haze coalesced around the Necromist, soon enveloping Lyric's unconscious form.

The train fell silent once more, the rhythmic clacking of rails on tracks the only sound. Emilio felt the weight of every gaze in the car. It was a palpable mix of fear, horror, and perhaps—if there was any kindness left in the world—a glimmer of hope. With a final prayer, he sealed the rite.

Cortez's voice broke the silence, trembling with barely suppressed emotion. "What did you do, Kane? Why... why does she look dead?" The heavy pistol in his hand began to rise.

Emilio looked up, meeting the Inquisitor's tortured gaze. "El Reposo—the Healer's Blessing. It is the last gift that Styx can give to the dying. It stops the final breath, suspending her between life and death. Her body and all its processes are frozen in place. Nothing will rot or waste away. This will allow us to try to save her without losing time. It will also prevent anything else from barging their way into her body." He paused, studying Cortez's face. "Does this satisfy you, Inquisitor?"

Words failed Cortez. His body sagged, the toil of the last few hours finally catching up to his mortal frame. Pain etched across his visage, emotions raw and frayed. Whatever relationship he shared with Lyric, it was evident that Jalin Cortez cared for her.

Turning from the broken Inquisitor, Emilio's gaze fell on Trujillo. The Peacekeeper's face was a filled with both concern and fascination, though he seemed more intrigued by witnessing a Necromist's work firsthand. Inwardly relieved, Emilio addressed him. "Mo, can you pass me one of those glasses?"

Trujillo quickly complied, scooping up an empty glass and passing it to the Necromist.

Emilio nodded his thanks, setting the glass beside Lyric's head. But before he could explain its purpose, an unearthly stirring drew everyone's attention.

The assassin's corpse twitched, and an otherworldly voice emanated from its lifeless mouth. "We... we were supposed to be a FAMILY..."

The unnatural sound sent a fresh wave of terror through the car's passengers, eliciting gasps and cries of fear.

Emilio's head snapped toward Cortez. "Inquisitor, keep that body from moving, but do not dispatch it. If you do, that spirit will get loose and become something far worse!" His eyes bore into Cortez's, urgency clear in his tone.

For once, the Inquisitor offered no argument or biting retort. He simply turned and strode toward the dead man. With trained detachment, he began to systematically dismember the corpse, slamming his blade into its struggling joints. The gruesome spectacle drew horrified gasps and caused more than a few passengers to faint, but Cortez paid them no mind.

The corpse's reaction was as unnatural as its animation. The creature hissed and continued its awkward struggle. With a powerful kick, Cortez flipped it onto its stomach and drove his scoring blade through its back, pinning it to the floor. Only then did the creature's hissing transform into howls of pain. The blade, a Mechanist invention by design was also blessed and silvered by the Order. It proved particularly effective against the undead.

Cortez unlatched the scoring blade, leaving it embedded in the corpse. He moved to the window, yanking down one of the heavy curtains. He wrapped the corpse's head and upper body, binding it like a grotesque parcel of butchered meat. As he tied off the rough knot, the full weight of the situation hit him. He sagged against the wall, his usually imperious demeanor crumbling under the strain of the day's events.

The car fell into an uneasy quiet, the air thick with the mingled scents of blood, fear, and the acrid tang of gunpowder. The passengers, having witnessed horrors beyond their imagining, huddled in shocked silence. And at the center of it all lay Lyric, suspended between life and death, her fate hanging by the slenderest of threads.

Cortez leaned against the wall, his breath coming in short, ragged gasps. His eyes remained fixed on the Necromist, and watched his every move.

Ignoring Jalin, Emilio began the second, more perilous part of his task. More whispered words fell from his lips, prayers to powers beyond mortal ken. With agonizing slowness, he eased the bloodied bolt from Lyric's chest. In defiance of nature, no blood flowed from the wound—a testament to the otherworldly state in which Lyric now existed.

Emilio examined the bolt's tip, its surface slick with Lyric's lifeblood, before carefully placing it in the empty glass. Closing his eyes once more, he murmured a prayer to Styx and ran his fingers across his eyelids. As he opened them again, the world changed.

The car was now awash in ethereal light. Each person appeared as a brilliant candle, their life forces burning with varying intensities. Esperanza Boyorquez blazed like a miniature sun, her divine connection evident in the intensity of her flame. Jalin Cortez's light flickered dimly. Without proper medical attention, that guttering flame would soon extinguish.

But these living lights were not alone in the car. Dark shadows flitted about the edges of Emilio's vision, their presence marked by whispered voices that seemed to come from everywhere and nowhere at once. La Corrupta, drawn by the scent of death emanating from the assassin's corpse, now coveted the rich flames of life surrounding them.

Emilio watched, helpless, as formless shadows reached out to caress the brightest lights in the room. Though the passengers remained oblivious to the unseen dead, their bodies reacted. Shivers ran through the crowd as an unnatural chill permeated the air. What had started as a mere coolness quickly intensified, the temperature plummeting until Emilio could see his breath frosting in the air.

He turned to Esperanza, urgency clear in his voice. "Voca, I need you to power the sigil. They are coming, and I have to concentrate on the girl."

Esperanza's response was strained. "This is not my magic," she protested, fighting back a cough. "I cannot do this. It is not within my god's acceptance. I cannot do this without you, Doctor."

"Look around us, Voca," Emilio pleaded. "You can feel it in the air, just like in the sleeper car. The spirits are already coveting and tasting the life here. If they are here, then the others are not far behind."

Esperanza met the kneeling Necromist's gaze, the internal struggle evident in her eyes. What he asked of her went beyond the sacred teachings of her faith. Hil and Styx were opposing forces, two sides of a divine coin. To use Hil's power to fuel a rite of Styx was akin to handing an enemy the bullet with which to shoot you. It was anathema.

Yet, there was no other way. To fight the restless dead as Hil would have her do, she needed to wield Styx's tools.

"If Hil allows me, Doctor, I will do it," she said at last. She reached down, gently removing the symbol of Hil from around Emilio's neck. "I will need this for a start."

Voices rushed back into Emilio's ears as the talisman left his body. He closed his eyes and gathered the cool blanket of Styx's powers tighter around his narrow frame.

"Silence!" he hissed.

And the voices became but a murmur.

Esperanza wrapped her finger around the symbol, the air thickening with tension. The fate of everyone in the car now rested on this unholy alliance between the powers of life and death. Emilio turned his attention back to Lyric's motionless form, acutely aware that time was running out. The shadows grew bolder, pressing closer, their whispers growing louder with each passing moment.

Esperanza lowered herself beside the carved sigil, her movements deliberate and reverent. Following Emilio's instructions, she traced her fingers along the complex patterns, each touch accompanied by a softly spoken word of the rite. As she progressed, the symbols came alive, glowing with a rich, warm light.

When the final symbol was activated, Esperanza placed her palm flat against the sigil. The effect was immediate and dramatic. The temperature in the car began to rise, pushing back the supernatural chill. Invisible to her eyes, the mad spirits fled the train car, cowering from the promise of final rest that the sigil offered.

Emilio had assured the power drain on her form would be minimal, but the pull she felt was far stronger than anticipated. Then came a burning sensation. Esperanza's eyes flew open. The wood beneath the sigil blackened and charred.

Clutching Hil's symbol tightly, Esperanza reached out to her god. Her prayer was not for forgiveness of this transgression, but for the strength to endure, to save the lives that hung in the balance. Whether through divine intervention or her own iron will, the draw of power lessened.

"Please hurry, Doctor."

"I will," Emilio replied, his focus returning to Lyric's motionless form.

With practiced breaths, he centered himself and stretched out his hands. Through the eyes granted by Styx, he peered into Lyric's chest. A web of dark malevolence radiated outward from her heart. Carasin. The poison's design was both beautiful and terrible in its efficiency. Only the stasis granted by of El Reposo halted its lethal progress.

What came next was dangerous and any misstep could prove fatal. Exerting his will over Lyric's suspended form, Emilio reached outward and tugged at the tiny invisible threads that surrounded them all. Threads of Life and threads of Death. Death was the foundation of Carasin, nurtured by disease and plague. To turn from Life and control Death was to take the first step towards true Necromancy.

It must be done.

The aura that surrounded them shimmered, from a tranquil blue to a brilliant green. It wavered and returned to blue. Emilio grasped at the air, pulling an invisible rope. Sweat beaded on his brow. Slowly, inexorably, the first tendrils of poison emerged from the puncture wound. The greenish-milky fluid hung in the air. With a careful motion, Emilio guided the poison into the waiting glass.

Exhaling deeply, he turned to Trujillo. "Mo, please toss this out the window... carefully?"

The Peacekeeper nodded and tugged on a pair of weathered gloves. He accepted the glass gingerly, moving towards a nearby window. The military officer rose to assist, opening the window to allow Trujillo to dispose of the lethal liquid.

Emilio returned his attention to Lyric, assessing the damage wrought by the poison. Death would claim her in seconds if he released his hold on her form. Where there should have been healthy flesh, only rotted remains persisted. What was meant to be whole was now broken and destroyed.

He eyed the threads that only he could see.

Perhaps.

"Inquisitor Cortez, will you join me?" Emilio asked, his tone carefully controlled.

"Why?" Cortez's reply was terse.

"Because I prefer not to yell across the car about the chances of your teammate's life." Emilio responded, a hint of impatience coloring his words.

Cortez struggled to his feet, pushing himself away from the wall. His usually feline grace had abandoned him, leaving his movements clumsy and uncertain.

"Well?" He asked. A single word, wrapped in uncertainly.

Emilio met the Inquisitor's gaze. "The damage is severe. It has eaten through the interior walls of her heart and spread to her lungs. If I were to release my hold on her now, she would die. It will not be painless." He paused, letting the gravity of the situation sink in. "I'm sorry, but this is beyond the skill of any mortal healer. As a physician, there's nothing I can do."

Cortez's hand shook visibly as it gripped the pistol, his knuckles white with tension.

"However," Emilio continued, his words measured, "As you have pointed out, I am more than a mortal healer. If you are willing—" The sight of the raised pistol cut him short. He pushed onward. "If you're willing to sacrifice some of your life for hers, she may live."

The ominous click of the pistol's hammer being cocked drew Esperanza's attention. "For the sake of Hil and all that is Holy, Cortez, listen to the man before you execute him," she snapped. He voice raw and bruised. "If you kill that man, she dies. Lyric will die a painful death—a death YOU will have caused."

Rage twisted Jalin's features as he turned to face the Voca, her hand still pressed firmly against the glowing sigil. As her words sank in, the fury in his eyes began to dim.

"How?" The question was barely more than a whisper.

Emilio spoke quickly, sensing the fragility of the moment. "I can rebuild her flesh, but I need a source of living tissue. It would have to be someone like her—untouched by the divine. I can draw from you to rebuild what was damaged, but it's not without risk. Your muscles will atrophy, and you'll be weaker than you are now. There's even a chance the process could kill you—"

"Do it," Cortez interrupted, his abruptness catching Emilio off guard.

"Inquisitor, I need to make sure you understand—"

"Are you deaf and stupid?" Cortez snarled. "I said do it now!" With that, he lowered himself to sit beside Lyric's motionless form.

Emilio glanced at Esperanza, noting with alarm how the Voca's condition worsened with every passing second. She gave him a simple nod before closing her eyes in silent prayer.

"Doctor Kane," the Peacekeeper interjected, concern etched on his weathered face, "that man isn't in any condition to give to this young woman. If you take anything more from him, he'll be as good as dead."

Emilio offered a sad smile in return. "You're not wrong, Mo. But for this to work, there needs to be a sympathetic relationship between the parties involved. It creates the bridge for the transference." His expression grew distant. "It was said that the Necromancers of old could rip out whatever life force they needed. I am not them, nor would I ever want to be. But this," he gestured to the Inquisitor and the Escritora, "this is the only way I know."

"Get on with it, Kane, before you kill me with your prattle!" Cortez snapped.

"Give me your hand, Inquisitor," Emilio said, placing his left hand over Lyric's wound.

As Cortez extended his hand, Emilio grasped it and prayed to Styx for her divine aid. The bluish glow surrounding them faded once more, overwhelmed by a brilliant green light that enveloped both Cortez and Lyric.

The car fell into a horrified silence as the onlookers watched the Inquisitor's features and frame wither. Lyric showed no visible change, but beneath her skin, a miraculous transformation was taking place. Brackish flesh reshaped and reformed. Veins and arteries opened and took shape. The valves and ventricles of her heart became whole once more.

She would have a weak but functional heart, enough for a few more years of quiet life. He turned his gaze to the withered figure of Jalin Cortez. He saw a man transformed. The Inquisitor's hand now resembled that of a venerated elder rather than a champion of Hil. And the guttering light within him had dwindled to barely an ember.

Esperanza slumped suddenly against the wall. Violent red tendrils crept up her neck and covered her face. The once-blazing torch of her soul now a mere spark.

Suddenly, the sound of shattering glass pierced the air, eliciting screams from the service vestibule. Several staff members scrambled out in terror.

The dead had arrived, and they would not be denied.

TETHER

The rising tide of panic was palpable, fear and terror spreading through the car's occupants like wildfire. Under Monterro's direction, passengers frantically jammed chairs and small benches into the vestibule, a futile attempt to halt the inevitable breach of the dead. Emilio knew that it was no longer a question of if, but when the horde would break through.

Where chaos had reigned during the assassin's attack, now a different kind of madness took hold—one of despair and heartbreak. In one corner, a cluster of passengers huddled together, their fervent prayers a collection of pleas to any deity who might listen. Others sat in stunned silence, their minds unable to process the horror unfolding around them. The scene was one of true desolation.

Glancing back, Emilio saw the merchants had forced their way through the far vestibule, a few desperate passengers shoving and clawing to follow. But escape was an illusion. With Styx's gift, Emilio gazed beyond the material world. Heavy footfalls on the roof above. It would be minutes before the dead descended upon those cowering on the outside platform.

The nobles, the lone Peacekeeper, and the Officer had taken up positions in the far corner. Couches were upended as servants and others scrambled to create a makeshift fortress for a final stand.

Emilio's gaze fell upon the dying forms of Jalin Cortez and Lyric Wax, the weight of despair growing heavier. To take any more life force from Cortez would kill him, and would only restore Wax enough for her to die in agony.

It's not enough.

Nearby lay the Voca's unconscious form, the Quemar threatening to end them all with its finality. Emilio considered briefly preparing their bodies for death, hoping to spare them the horrors to come. He could at least ensure their souls' painless release.

"This is all my fault," he whispered, the words barely audible even to himself.

His eyes focused once more on the unnatural figures surrounding them, a dark red tendril of power connecting them all. The same tendril stretched off into the distance, yet also anchored to him. He had considered himself a tether, binding the creatures and leading them to fresh meat and new host bodies. But their attempt to attack him as well had changed that thought.

This magic was beyond him, the work of a true necromancer. It wasn't the lack of power that galled him, but the absence of knowledge. The Inquisition of Hil had placed a sanction on such lore, and with good reason—that knowledge had cost thousands of lives three centuries ago. Yet it was that very knowledge Emilio now needed to save those around him, to save the lives of those sworn to the Order.

Frustration welled up as he stared at the cord. He was impotent to act. He bellowed out then. Anguish and tears streaming down his face. He was helplessness to lend aid. He was helpless to heal. He had failed, monumentally.

"I'm sorry."

The dark red tendril anchored to him was the manifestation of that failure. To this team. To his God. To his parents.

To Marisol.

She was gone. He had lost her, and now, he was about to lose everything. In a surge of anger, he channeled the power of Styx into his hand and attempted to rip the cord away.

A sharp, physical pain tugged at his abdomen.

Shocked, he tugged again, watching his skin respond—or rather, something beneath his skin. His fingertips probed the area, feeling not smooth flesh but rough bumpy flesh akin to a scab. Another tug sent pain shooting through him, but he could sense something there, something small.

His eyes fell on Mo's knife. With trembling hands, he picked it up.

Taking a deep breath, Emilio steeled himself and plunged the sharpened tip into his flesh. He cut, a growl of pain escaping through gritted teeth as he dug deeper. His other hand continued to pull, two arcs of agony competing for dominance. But he denied their demands, pushing through the pain. He had to see this through.

With the blade nearly two inches deep, he gave one final, desperate tug. Something emerged—a glass marble, small and innocuous, yet pulsing with dark energy.

As Emilio stared at the blood-slicked orb in his palm, the implications of its presence began to unfold in his mind. It was no simple marble. The surface was painstakingly etched with tiny sigils and marks of power, pulsing with an eerie greenish hue. More curious still was the fluid within—a deep, viscous red.

This tiny object, somehow embedded in his flesh, was the key to everything. It was the source of his connection to the dead, the reason for the horrors that had befallen them all.

"A Blood Token!" he exclaimed, his voice lost in the chaos surrounding him. All around, panic and fear consumed the car's occupants as unrelenting hands beat down on the ceiling, and screams and hisses erupted from the engine-side vestibule.

That's how you're doing it!

A flicker of understanding crossed Emilio's face. A Blood Token was a tool to send orders and extend one's reach of control. Burdened with this horrid tool, Emilio had unwittingly served as a transmitter for the puppet master, extending the necromancer's reach over their minions.

Relief washed over him as he realized he hadn't been leading the ghouls and spirits on this hellish ride of his own volition.

The token alone couldn't account for the extraordinary resilience displayed by the undead. Something else was amiss. Blood dripped from Emilio's fingers onto the carpet. His eyes were drawn to the color and stain.

The blessing he'd received in the Barrows! It was through him that the dead had become resilient, granted Styx's protection to ensure their master's will be done.

The Death Mage on the other end was stealing the Blessing of Styx from him!

Instinctively, Emilio reached back, nearly hurling the token out the nearby window when a crucial thought stopped him: *Blood.* They had used his blood to empower the token.

"In blood, there is life, knowledge, and power," Emilio thought as he pulled from his memories, an incantation, ancient and forbidden.

Forgive me

Closing his eyes, he focused, channeling his power into the token.

"Show me your mind."

Memories assaulted him—dozens of them, screaming, wailing, mad with insanity. The experiences of every ghoul and spirit became a whirlwind of thought. Undaunted, Emilio dug deeper into the main cord of power, a single question driving him: *How?*

No face appeared in his mind's eye, but he could feel the knowledge of the Blood Token's creation unfurling before him. He pulled hard on the thread within, ripping out the knowledge of its construction, creation, where and when it was made.

He did not stop there. He pulled more and more, absorbing rites so horrible and unholy they defied belief. Teachings, taboo beyond imagination, now flooded his consciousness. His need to know, his hunger for understanding, made him blind and deaf to the chaos erupting around him.

Gunshots rang out, glass shattered, and wood splintered. The dead had breached the ceiling and the engine-side entrance. People were dying, spirits seizing new bodies in a macabre dance of death and rebirth.

Suddenly, a surge of power pushed back, halting Emilio's knowledge feed. Within the mindscape, he found himself standing in a dark gray void. Opposite him loomed a shadowy figure, their body stretched like a dozen cobwebs.

You! The voice hissed, red eyes flaring from the darkness.

"Who are you?" Emilio's voice boomed across the psychic plane as he pulled at his opponent's memories. "Tell me who you are!"

GET OUT OF MY MIND!! They howled, their will flailing as they struggled to maintain control over the myriad minds under their dominion.

There were too many.

Emilio dug his feet deeply into the mindscape that surrounded him. Within his soul, he called upon the power that had touched him in The Barrows.

"Tell me everything!" Emilio demanded. Power, raw and unfiltered washed across the scene. Images flooded his mind—dozens of places and faces flashing by as he tore into the Necromancer's psyche.

STOP IT! They screamed.

Emilio watched as the cobwebs began to release from the shadowy form. The psychic pull intensified as the Necromancer relinquished control of their puppets to focus on him. As the final cord was released, the shadowy form transformed into an abyss of power, terrible and immense.

Emilio simply smiled. "Thank you."

His opponent's eyes widened in horrified realization. In their desperation to protect themselves from Emilio's intrusion, they had ceased their control over the undead horde.

Emilio's eyes snapped open, the contest of wills ended. The Blood Token pulsed in his hand as he allowed Styx's power to fill him more completely than ever before. His body glowed like a brilliant green candle, illuminating the car with an otherworldly light.

In that moment, as chaos reigned and death pressed in from all sides, Emilio stood transformed. The knowledge he had gained, the power he now wielded, set him apart from the man he had been mere moments ago. The air around him crackled with potential, with the promise of a turning tide.

The undead creatures suddenly halted, their soulless eyes fixed upon Emilio. Even those separated from him by walls and steel roofs stood motionless, awaiting command. Emilio's gaze swept the room, aware of all facets of life and death—dozens of candles, bonfires, shadowy flames, and flares of necromantic power. He could feel their potential, their life, and their unlife pulsing through him like a single, unified heartbeat.

I can accomplish so much with this...

His eyes fell upon the servants of Hil, their broken bodies lying on the floor.

I can save you. Yes.

They were worthy of this gift, unlike the people he'd encountered in the past few hours—those who squandered the precious gift of life that Styx and Hil had breathed into their crude bodies at the beginning of time.

Not all deserve the sacred Gift of Life.

Now he could right that wrong.

His gaze settled on the kitchen staffer who had called him a freak. The man's life force glowed whole and vibrant. Emilio stretched out his hand, fingers splayed wide, ready to grasp that light. With a single gesture, he could—

Emilio.

He paused, head whipping around. "Marisol?" The name escaped his lips in a desperate whisper.

Panic seized him as he searched frantically for her. Where was Marisol? Suddenly, a memory flooded his mind—but it was not his own.

He saw himself with Marisol, walking through a sparse forest. But they were someone else's eyes who watched the scene. Someone else's memories in his mind. He felt their glee and anticipation as Marisol and his past self approached a clearing. The two shadowy figures nodded to each other, and darkness fell as an eldritch trap sprung.

Amusement coursed through him—no, through the Necromancer—as Marisol screamed for Emilio to help her. The glee intensified as they invoked Styx's name, drawing Marisol into an emerald the size of a fist. The dead queen could not deny the power of Styx as she was trapped within.

The other figure dispelled the darkness, revealing Emilio's unconscious body in the center of a strange binding circle. He watched as the Necromancer attempted to destroy Emilio's body with disintegrating power. But the power reflected back in a surge of eldritch fire, obliterating the clearing.

Then he was looking through the other's eyes as he stood over Emilio's unconscious body. A knife in one hand. A blood token in the other.

EMILIO!

The voice shattered the vision. It wasn't Marisol calling him, but Esperanza. Her face, contorted with pain and fear, looked up at him, one hand outstretched in desperate supplication.

"Doctor Kane... Emilio... please..." The Voca's weak voice cut through his inner turmoil.

Realization struck him. The power, the greed, the hunger for knowledge... was that truly him, or the influence of the Necromancer?

"Help...us," Esperanza pleaded.

"I know what I have to do," Emilio said, his gaze sweeping over the undead surrounding them. "Your Lady calls you to the next; be not afraid."

Using the Blood Token as a focus, he sapped the necromantic energies from the ghouls, extending his reach even to those unreleased in the other cattle car. One by one, the dead crumbled to ash and dust, fading into nothingness as if they had never existed. All that remained were rotted scraps of clothing and leather collar bands.

Taking a breath, he drew in the savage energies of the mad specters. Temptation whispered in his ear and across his soul.

Command us. We can be yours.

It was the fear in Esperanza's eyes that anchored him, keeping him from losing himself to the intoxicating power.

No!

With outstretched hands, Emilio channeled energy into Lyric and Jalin's bodies. From Death, he wove Life anew. Lyric's form became whole once more, her heart strong, her lungs restored. Jalin's atrophied muscles filled with blood and tissue, color flooding back into his ashen face.

As Emilio released them from the spell, their fading embers of life erupted into a brilliant flame.

Throughout the train, Emilio transformed the madness of the dead into the vitality of the living. For those already passed, he eased their transition to the next realm.

Finally, he turned to Esperanza. With gentle resolve, he drew out the Quemar, soothing her divine soul with his own. The angry red scarring faded, not to a pink reminder, but to unblemished skin. He watched in awe as her essence, visible only to those touched by the Divine, burned with renewed radiance.

As the last of the power flowed through him, Emilio drew the burn into himself as penance. The temptation he had nearly succumbed to was a sin, even if unacted upon. He needed his patron to know he understood this folly, hoping Styx would accept his offering.

The world faded around him, and darkness encroached. As pain and exhaustion overwhelmed him, Emilio's last conscious thought was a prayer—not for himself, but for those he had saved, and for forgiveness for the power he had wielded, however briefly.

Then, mercifully, oblivion claimed him.

LA FAMILIA ORTEGA

"**I** am NOT getting on that damn train!" Jose's voice cracked with fear and determination. "I don't care about the pinché money. Those things are monsters! This is suicide, and I want no part of this!"

Caldera Canyon loomed before them, a rising edifice opening up to the wetlands beyond. What was once a river decades ago now stood as a dry, gaping maw—the entrance to the final leg toward the Northern Gate. Atop the cliffsides, Lago Azul shimmered like a blue jewel encircled by a verdant ring. The vista stretched for miles to the south and west, the ocean a mere suggestion on the distant horizon. It was a view to steal one's breath, yet the assembled group atop the cliffs had eyes only for the tracks below and the approaching train.

Carmen snatched the spyglass from Jose's trembling hands, bringing the train into sharp focus. "You must be seeing things! Why would—" She leaned further over the precipice, her words dying in her throat. "No... no, those can't be people. They look like corpses!"

"It doesn't matter if they're people or not. Everyone, get into place!" The sharp command cut through the air, silencing further debate.

Ivette Ramirez's focus was sharp, her mission deceptively simple: stop the train. A former Visionary of the Mechanist Guild, she secured the last strap on her strange-looking harness. Her body moved through a series of stretches, as she anticipated the intense physical demands to come. In this gamble, every detail had to be accounted for.

Satisfied with her own preparations, Ramirez turned her critical eye to the two men, inspecting their rigging. The design was a marvel of engineering. It was similar to standard climbing gear but with several crucial modifications. Thick leather encased the upper and lower torsos, connected by thin metal boning. A trio of round pulleys sat on the abdomen, interspersed with gears, rope, and a complex device whose purpose remained obscure.

Ramirez's motivation went beyond the substantial payment promised. Her true reward would be undeniable success in the eyes of her former guild. The Mechanists would be forced to swallow the bitter draught of her victory, a thought that brought a cold smile to her lips. Monsters or not, she would not be denied this opportunity.

"We have only one shot at this," Ramirez's voice was as cold and unyielding as steel. "And I, for one, do not want Mr. Ortega to think his trust misplaced."

The mention of Ortega's name silenced any lingering complaints. Jose and his companion secured their harnesses under Ramirez's watchful gaze. Satisfied, the trio began jogging to their mark.

Carmen and the other two men inspected the ropes. Measured lengths of solid cordage stretched from Ramirez's team to additional pulleys anchored to massive boulders and sturdy trees. The cliff face where Carmen's team stood hung precariously over the distant tracks below. For any average person, this would be insanity. For this group of skilled thieves, it was still insane—but with a veneer of plausibility.

The plan, in its audacious simplicity, was this: At the precise moment, Ramirez's trio would leap from the cliff's edge, tethered securely. Their freefall would transform into a controlled swing, bringing them parallel with the speeding train. At the apex of their arc, they would activate the device on their chests, releasing a powerful magnet to latch onto the train's metal surface. Once connected, they would be anchored to the moving behemoth. From there, they'd need to release their tethers and move swiftly to complete their task.

Failure at any point carried dire consequences. If one failed to connect, Carmen's team would need to haul them back up. If they anchored but failed to disconnect their rope in time, Carmen's team would need to cut it loose. Failure to cut the rope could prove fatal—but everyone present knew that failing the mission would lead to a death far more painful and certain.

Ramirez felt a surge of confidence. Initially, they had set up anticipating the train would cross the valley directly, their chances of success slim but acceptable. The train's unexpected detour, now rounding the back end of the valley, had shifted the odds in their favor. It allowed for better positioning and, crucially, more time.

Time was the lynchpin of the entire operation.

If the train reached the mouth of Caldera Canyon, the engine would succumb to the stress of the incline. Ramirez silently thanked Mr. Ortega's extensive network for providing the data needed to calculate their timetable precisely. The course change had expanded their window of opportunity from mere minutes to a more comfortable buffer.

While a secondary team waited further up the canyon, Ramirez allowed no room for failure in her mind. She had personally promised success to Adrian Ortega. The harnesses her team wore were based on her designs. Though she hadn't dreamed them up herself,it was her brilliance that had sold Ortega on their utility for endeavors such as this.

Gazing down at the approaching train, Ramirez counted eight scattered bodies atop the car behind the water tender. Where fear might have made a normal person reconsider, it only steeled her resolve. There was no time for second-guessing, no room for a proof of concept or a pilot run. The lives of her team were a secondary concern to the mission at hand.

With a deep, steadying breath, Ramirez gripped her rope. The moment of truth had arrived. It was now or never.

The train's whistle echoed through the canyon, a mournful cry that seemed to herald the approach of doom. But for Ivette Ramirez, it was the starting gun of the most daring feat of her career. As the locomotive rounded the bend, steam billowing from its stack, she allowed herself one last thought:

Success here would rewrite her legacy. Failure... well, failure simply wasn't an option.

"Ready!" Her voice rang out, clear and commanding. The others tensed, ready to leap into the void. The train drew closer, its rhythmic chugging a countdown to destiny.

"Now!"

And with that, they stepped off the cliff's edge, plunging towards either glory or oblivion.

Lyric's eyes snapped open, her body jerking upright as if pulled by invisible strings. A massive weight lifted from her chest. She gasped, drawing in great lungfuls of air. The world around her slowly came into focus—faces stared at her in shock and surprise, their owners moving in a daze, huddling in small groups.

Her hands flew to her chest, fingers probing for a wound that should have been there. The bloodied spot on her shirt and the small hole just above her vest's neckline were the only evidence of her brush with death. No bolt, no wound—nothing but smooth, unbroken skin beneath the stained fabric. If not for the drying blood, she might have dismissed it all as a terrible dream.

A sense of vitality coursed through her veins, as if she'd just woken from the most restful sleep of her life. It was a stark contrast to the chaos surrounding her, a dissonance that left her feeling unmoored.

Across from her Jalin Cortez, leaned back against an overturned chair. His face, so recently filled with pain and exhaustion, now looked peaceful. Color had returned to his cheeks, his breathing was even and deep. Gone was the injured shell of a dying man—in his place lay the robust figure who had boarded the train that morning, whole and impossibly healthy.

Movement caught Lyric's eye, her attention drawn to a cluster of people gathered around Esperanza. The Voca sat with her back against the wall near a charred wood panel. Her gentle eyes were filled with sorrow as she looked down at the figure cradled in her lap.

Lyric's breath caught as she recognized Emilio Kane.

The Doctor's face was far from peaceful. Angry red streaks marred his features, reminiscent of the Quemar that had afflicted Esperanza earlier. His chest rose and fell in a ragged pattern, each breath seeming to cause him pain.

Lyric turned back to Jalin. She reached toward him wake him, then stopped. Instead, she called softly, "Inquisitor Cortez."

Jalin's eyes snapped open, wide and unsteady. He turned to Lyric, disbelief etched across his face as he took in her appearance. A single word escaped his lips: "How?"

Lyric shook her head softly, then pointed towards the fallen Necromist.

The Inquisitor surged to his feet. His undeterred movements surprising him. He tore at the bloodied bandage on his arm, revealing unblemished skin beneath. Panic flooded his eyes as he searched his body for wounds and stitches that were no longer there.

Where others might have felt relief or joy, Jalin's face contorted with rage.

"WHAT DID YOU DO TO ME!" he roared, charging forward. He shoved people aside, drawing a knife from his belt as he bore down on the unconscious Emilio.

Before Lyric or Esperanza could react, several passengers grabbed Jalin's arms and legs, restraining him and dragging him away from the Necromist.

"Let me go!" Jalin shouted, his voice edged with hysteria. "This monster must die for what he is!" Despite his renewed strength and training, the collective force of several arms held him fast. "LET ME GO, YOU STUPID COWARDS! THAT MONSTER NEEDS TO DIE!"

Lyric watched, her mind reeling. The Inquisitor's reaction was extreme, even for him. Was it possible that being brought back from the brink of death—had unhinged him even more somehow? Was this the raw, unfiltered Jalin Cortez, stripped of his usual control by the shock of what had transpired?

"WHY?" The shout cut through the chaos, silencing the crowd momentarily.

Lyric's gaze snapped to the source—the kitchen staffer who had earlier branded the doctor a freak. Now, he stood defiantly on the other side of Emilio's prone form. Others quickly rallied to his side, forming a protective barrier around the fallen Necromist and the Voca.

"This man saved our lives!" the staffer continued, his voice gaining strength with each word. "He saved your life and that woman's. He's not a monster, he's a hero!" His eyes swept the car, challenging anyone to disagree. "When ghouls broke in, he reached out! He showed me it would be alright! He stopped and destroyed them all, and now you want to kill him?"

The man's voice cracked with emotion as he continued, "Hil may have been with you, but Styx gave us a chance to live... through him. Through Doctor Kane's sacrifice!" With a final, defiant step, he placed himself squarely between Emilio and Jalin. "So if you want to kill him, you have to kill me first."

A crowd formed, as if summoned by his words. Guild members and regular passengers alike, some wielding makeshift weapons fashioned from broken furniture, others standing with fists clenched and jaws set. Their message was clear: the Guild would not allow harm to befall the Necromist.

Lyric rose to her feet, her mind racing. The situation was spiraling out of control. She approached Jalin, her hands raised in a placating gesture. "Inquisitor Cortez," she called, her voice steady and commanding.

The Inquisitor turned, his face flushed with barely contained rage.

"We still have a job to finish," Lyric continued, her tone brooking no argument. "There was only one assassin. However, we still have to stop this train. This was your plan, and we need to finish it." Her eyes met his, not with pleading or sympathy, but with the only thing Jalin Cortez truly respected: Imperial authority.

Jalin's face twitched, his gaze darting between Lyric and Esperanza. The Voca's expression remained cold and unyielding, offering no support for his murderous intentions. Finally, his eyes locked back onto Lyric. "Tell them to release me, Wax," he growled.

Lyric strode towards the scoring blade still embedded in the floor. She grasped the arm latch and freed the weapon. The assembled crowd watched her with a mixture of apprehension and fear, while Cortez's eyes gleamed with anticipation.

"You asked me to trust you, Inquisitor," Lyric said, her voice carrying clearly through the tense silence. "You asked me to trust you to finish this." She turned to address the Guild members holding Jalin. "Release him. He has a job to finish... and a duty to uphold."

Hesitation flickered across their faces, but after a heartbeat, they loosened their grip and stepped away, moving to join the protective circle around Emilio. Lyric waited until they were safely behind her before extending the scoring blade towards Jalin, handle first.

"Let's go, Cortez," she said, her voice low but firm.

The moment hung in the air, pregnant with possibility. Jalin's hand hovered near the weapon, his eyes darting between it and Lyric's resolute face. The entire car seemed to hold its breath, waiting to see which way the scales would tip.

Jalin's fingers closed around the handle of the scoring blade, the tension in the air palpable as he accepted the weapon. He strapped the device back onto his arm, the weapon familiar and calming.

Lyric's gaze swept across the assembled crowd. All eyes were fixed on the Inquisitor. Fear, anger, and hatred danced across their faces. These were the same looks they had directed at Emilio Kane earlier. In a twist of fate, the perceived monster among them was no longer their newfound savior, but the very man charged with protecting them from the darkness.

The irony was not lost on her.

As Cortez secured the final strap, his eyes met the crowd's, disgust evident in his features.

"None of you," he spat, locking the blade back into place with a decisive click, "will ever learn." He turned his back on them and stride towards the heavy curtains that separated them from the next phase of their mission.

Lyric fell into step behind him. Practiced. Familiar. As they moved, she caught sight of the nobles, still seated and watching the scene unfold with carefully crafted indifference. Their faces gave no hint of approval or disapproval. Even their servants mirrored their practiced blank expressions. It was to be expected, she mused. The nobility would never publicly endorse or decry the

Inquisition. They were a needed tool to manage the faith of people. The role of nobility was governance over the physical bodies of people and industry for the benefit of the Imperium—nothing more, nothing less.

Her eyes fell upon the old Peacekeeper and the Corporal. The contrast was stark. Ayala's face was etched with disapproval as he watched Cortez, the leather case once again firmly tucked under his arm. Trujillo's expression was one of weary resignation. It was what was in the window's reflection that gave Lyric pause. The older man's hand was behind his back, gripping his pistol.

Lyric hesitated for a half-second, her eyes meeting Trujillo's. His gaze flicked from her to the Inquisitor and back again, accompanied by a slight shake of his head. The message was clear: had Jalin made a move against the crowd, Trujillo would have acted in defense of the people.

As the crowd began to disperse, Lyric's glanced to Esperanza. The Voca's body seemed to deflate with a deep sigh, the weight of recent events visible in the slump of her shoulders. With a subtle nod, she motioned for Lyric to go.

"ANY DAY NOW, WAX!" Jalin's impatient bellow echoed from behind the curtains.

Lyric offered Esperanza a tight smile. With a deep breath, she steeled herself and headed towards the heavy curtains.

Jalin's silence was a palpable thing as they stepped off the platform onto the water tender. Lyric braced herself for a tirade, but the Inquisitor moved with wordless purpose.

Halfway across the tender, Jalin's raised fist brought them to an abrupt halt. Lyric's eyes followed his gaze, settling on two metal objects attached to the tender's surface. Each as thick as a fist, they bore lengths of rope stretching towards the engine. The implication was clear and unsettling: someone else had boarded the train.

Lyric looked behind them, scanning the roof of the car they'd just left. "Clear behind us," she reported, her voice low and tense.

"Reload," Jalin commanded. In perfect sync, Inquisitor and Escritora drew their pistols, the familiar weight of the weapons a cold comfort in the face of this new mystery.

They inched forward across the narrow footholds, the wind whipping at their clothes as they approached the open door of the engine car. The scene that greeted them was far from what they'd anticipated.

A man in a strange harness was doubled over the edge of the platform, retching violently. Jalin's voice cut through the air like a whip: "IDENTIFY YOURSELF IN THE NAME OF THE INQUISITION!"

Despite his obvious distress, the pale-faced man managed to raise his hands, showing he was unarmed, before another wave of nausea overtook him.

In that moment, the smell hit them—a nauseating mixture of burnt flesh, acrid exhaust, and oil. Lyric fought the urge to gag as the stench assaulted her senses.

"JOSE GET YOUR ASS IN HERE!" A woman's voice, sharp and commanding, echoed from within the car.

Lyric and Jalin exchanged bewildered glances.

Jalin gave a careful nod toward the engine. They moved forward, stepping onto the engine's platform and through the door.

The engine room was a dizzying circus of motion and heat. Pistons pumped, boilers hissed, and gears interlocked in a harmonic dance of industry. The heat was oppressive, instantly drawing beads of sweat from Lyric's brow. Above, a gas light cast everything in an eerie orange glow, illuminating dozens of gauges and meters that measured countless unknown functions.

But it was what lay on the floor that seized their attention.

The charred remains of half a body sprawled across the metal grating, a grisly testament to the dangers that lurked within this mechanical heart. The other half, Lyric realized with a wave of nausea, had been ground into the red-slicked gears. Blood spatter had dried on instruments and dials, a macabre decoration in this temple of steam and steel.

At the center of this chaos lay a lone woman on her back, working beneath a dangerous set of pistons. Her voice, the same that called out earlier, rang with impatience and a hint of desperation.

"Don't just stand there and puke, Jose! It's just a dead body! Get over yourself and turn that red valve next to you, or we will join him shortly!"

Jalin's voice cut through the noise of machinery, sharp and demanding: "Who the hell are you?!"

The woman's head snapped to the side, her eyes narrowing as she took in the armed intruders. "Ivette Ramirez, Mechanist Consultant for La Familia Ortega," she barked, her voice carrying an edge of irritation and urgency. "Who the hell are you, sir, and where the hell is Jose?!"

Lyric stepped forward, her voice steady despite the chaos surrounding them. "My name is Escritora Wax, and this is Inquisitor Cortez. I believe Jose is currently... indisposed on the outside platform." Her eyes darted to the grisly remains on the floor. "What happened here?"

Ramirez's face tightened, frustration and determination fleeting across her features. "What the hell is the Inquisition... screw it! Nevermind!" She shook her head, refocusing on the immediate crisis. "If you two don't want to die, start turning that red release valve now!"

Without hesitation, Jalin holstered his gun and grasped the valve, muscles straining as he began to turn it. The air filled with a chorus of deep hisses, and Lyric felt a shift in the oppressive temperature.

"GOOD!" Ramirez shouted over the cacophony of escaping steam and grinding gears. "You! Wax Girl! Start pulling those levers down as soon as the hissing stops! Cortez, start turning those smaller valves, starting with the one closest to you. With any luck, we'll live another day to complain."

Lyric positioned herself by the levers, every muscle taut as she waited for her cue. Jalin moved quickly into position and began turning valve after valve. The moment the last hiss faded, Lyric sprang into action, throwing the levers down in rapid succession.

As the temperature continued to drop, a niggling worry wormed its way into Lyric's mind. "Why aren't we stopping, Ms. Ramirez?" she called out, her voice tinged with concern.

Sliding out from beneath the pistons, Ramirez's grime-covered face split into an almost smug smile. "Simple, Ms. Wax," she replied, a hint of triumph in her voice. "With the pressure under control and the brakes activated, our next stop is the Northern Gate, courtesy of La Familia Ortega."

DUTY

The pulse in Emilio's ears was a dull roar, soft hands ghosting over his face as consciousness slowly returned. His body ached with soreness and pain. Somehow it seemed less intense than he'd anticipated. As his eyes fluttered open, a strange and beautiful sight greeted him.

Dark eyes gazed down at him, framed by a brilliant smile. The face was unlike any he'd seen before. The left side was covered in an intricate tattoo—a skull mask of exquisite detail. He felt as if he were looking upon their Alma.

"Am... Am I dead?" The words escaped his lips in a weak whisper.

"He speaks!" The woman's voice was filled with genuine delight as she withdrew her hands. "Welcome back, Doctor

Kane. While I have been told I'm a heavenly sight," she tossed her raven black hair for effect, "No, you are not dead."

Emilio's head swam as he forced himself upright. "Who are you?"

"May I introduce Voca Guadalupe Teresa Casteneda," Esperanza's familiar voice came from beside him.

He could feel her hands steadying him as he sat up. The room came into focus—a small office. He was no longer on the train.

The tattooed woman winked at him. "Lupe or if you wish to be formal Voca Casteneda, but you can just call me Lupe."

A half-smile tugged at Emilio's lips before panic seized him. He turned to Esperanza, questions tumbling out in a rush. "Are you okay? What happened? Where are Wax and Cortez? What about the passengers?" His eyes darted around the unfamiliar surroundings. "Where are we? How long have I been out?"

Lupe's laugh was musical. "Are you okay, Voca? How are the people? This one asks the good questions. I like him."

Esperanza rolled her eyes, a hint of fondness in her exasperation. "You've been out for two hours. We are in a guest office at the Northern Gate. Everyone is fine... for the most. The sleeper car was not breached. Mr. Carstein did his job admirably. We did lose a few when they breached our car." Her voice softened."You did well, Doctor Kane. Cortez and Wax are with the authorities. Voca Casteneda and I have been tending to your Quemar."

Lupe made a disgruntled sound. "We aren't at the Shrine, Anza! Save the titles for the masses. We are all friends here, right?"

Emilio considered again if he had indeed passed on. To be in the presence of not one, but two Vocas of Hil—and one so unlike any he had encountered before—seemed almost too extraordinary to be real.

"Además de mi hermana," Lupe continued, her tone shifting, "you need to get going soon. It will be a long ride for you and your people."

Emilio glanced up. Fleeting emotions crossed Esperanza's face—her cheeks reddening slightly. "This is highly unorthodox, Lupe. We are under orders."

"Based on what you told me, hermana, perhaps you need to shake things up and see what falls loose so you can find the truth?" Lupe cautioned. "I promise to deliver Doctor Kane to the Academy. I just need to ensure my little brother gets home."

Esperanza's brow furrowed. "What is going on, Lupe?"

Lupe's smile was enigmatic. "I am going to take Joseph home. It is on the way to the Academy, so it is really no inconvenience."

The two women held each other's gazes, a silent conversation passing between them. Finally, Esperanza relented. "Fine, but you be careful."

"Careful! Bah, you are the one always running into danger, Anza!" She leaned in with a conspiratorial smile. "I am

jealous of your freedom, hermana. You be careful yourself."
Lupe's smile faltered for a moment. "Watch Cortez. He is..."
She shook her head, "He is not well."

Esperanza's eyebrow arched as she glanced at Emilio.
"Why do you say that?" Esperanza asked, her voice carefully
neutral.

Lupe shot Emilio a curious look before answering. "He
asked me about Judex Stonebridge and whether I was
involved in his surgeries. I told him I was never brought in.
I didn't even know he was hurt until after..." She left the
sentence unfinished.

Emilio shifted uncomfortably. "Should I go take a walk?
This seems private." He started to rise, but Esperanza's hand
on his shoulder stopped him.

"I am certain you and Lupe will have some exciting stories
to tell each other," Esperanza said. "You will be going with
her to her family's estate. After that, she will escort you to the
Academy as initially requested. In the interim, I ask that you
look out for each other. Things are becoming... complicated."

Emilio nodded, reading the hesitation in her face. "You
have my word, Voca."

Esperanza rewarded him with a gentle smile."After this
ordeal, Emilio... I believe you can call me Anza. May Hil watch
over you both."

Lupe stood and embraced Esperanza tightly. She
whispered something in Esperanza's ear, too low for Emilio

to catch, before planting a kiss on her cheek. "Now get going before I decide we need to go exploring on our own!"

"Gods above, Lupe," Esperanza sighed.

"They all love me," Lupe grinned. "And I love you, hermana. We will see each other soon."

Esperanza nodded, turning to Emilio one last time. "I would caution you about my sister, Emilio, but I am sure seeing is believing."

"Oh shoo, Mamacita! He will be fine," Lupe called after her.

As the door closed behind Esperanza, Lupe's expression shifted. Her friendly demeanor remained, but a new focus sharpened her gaze. "Tell me, Doctor Emilio Kane, why has Lady Styx taken such a deep an interest in you?"

"I... I am not sure what—" Emilio stammered. Lupe cut him off with a shake of her head.

"Don't worry, we'll have plenty of time to discuss your Bendición."

Emilio returned a nervous smile, his mind suddenly flooded with flashes of memories that were not his own: strange places, stranger faces, and Marisol trapped within a gem.

As he met Lupe's knowing gaze, he realized that the journey ahead would be longer—and far more revealing than anticipated.

Lyric stood in the shade of the overhang outside the Guild Office, a sheaf of papers in her hands. She flipped through them quickly, searching their contents. Heavy booted footfalls sounded beside her as someone approached.

"Where the hell is Kane?!" Jalin's voice cracked like a whip, his eyes blazing once more.

She rolled her eyes internally in response. "Ask Esperanza."

Across from them both, Voca Esperanza Boyorquez stood. Her ragged and blood stained robes replaced with new vestments. She tugged gently at the hem along the left wrist.

"With Voca Casteneda."

Jalin scowled. "Why?"

She gestured to Lyric and the papers in her hands, "New orders."

Lyric's gaze flickered between the Inquisitor and the papers in her hand, a frown creasing her brow. "These orders seem strange, Esperanza," she mused, her voice low and cautious. "Are you certain of their origin?"

Esperanza straightened her shoulders and turned to face Lyric, "She came directly from Sanctuary to deliver them. You may not be familiar with official..."

"Give me those!" Jalin snatched the papers from Lyric. His eyes scanned the papers quickly. His brows furrowed and the corners of his mouth turned down.

"Fine!" he replied and shoved the papers back at Lyric. "Where is that bruja? I want to ask who gave these to her!" He spun on his heel, eyes darting around as if expecting to find Lupe hiding in the shadows.

"Cortez," Esperanza's voice cut through his agitation like a blade, "These orders are time sensitive. You can join us now or contact Sanctuary for a new assignment; the choice is yours. I no longer want to waste my time here."

Jalin halted mid-step, turning slowly to face them. Lyric watched him intently, noting the almost manic energy radiating from him. His eyes were alight with an inner fire, as his lips curved into a half-smile that didn't reach those burning eyes. "Reassignment? Like you would survive without us, right Wax?"

Lyric felt her chest tighten at his odd smile. Something was deeply wrong with Jalin Cortez, and she could see that Esperanza knew it too. The air between them crackled with unspoken tension.

"Cortez is right, Voca, you need us." Lyric said, addressing Esperanza but keeping her eyes fixed on the Inquisitor. "We have a duty, Cortez, do we not?"

For less than a heartbeat, Jalin's smile froze, a mask slipping ever so slightly before snapping back into place. He nodded, his voice a low growl. "We have a duty to perform."

Without another word, he turned and strode towards the stables, his movements tight and controlled.

As the Inquisitor strode away Esperanza and Lyric exchanged a loaded glance. The unspoken message was clear: they needed to rely on each other. Not just against the horrors that lurked in the realm, but against whatever darkness was consuming Jalin Cortez.

Lyric's hand drifted to the pistol at her hip, her fingers tracing its familiar contours. Jalin's words from the train echoed in her mind, a terrible reminder of the oath they'd all sworn:

When that day comes – for her, me, or any of us – hesitation is a luxury you cannot afford.

With a deep breath, she buckled her pistol back into place. Her jaw set with determination as she watched Jalin's retreating form. One thought crystallized in her mind, a solemn promise to herself and to those she swore to protect:

I'll only do what is necessary.

SHADOWS

The hanging candelabra cast a pool of warm light over the desk, its flames dancing softly in the otherwise shadowy room. A figure sat hunched over a small stack of files, fingers tracing lines of text as if to divine hidden meanings from the words.

"So the Ortegas got involved," the seated figure mused, voice low and thoughtful. "Interesting. They may be an issue in the future, so we should start doing our part to aid the authorities in enlightening them about La Familia Ortega's... other... endeavors."

Across the desk stood another man, his posture rigid and formal. "While our third party could not retrieve the files from the Salon Officer, I have been assured we will have them in the next two days." A hint of dark amusement colored his next words. "Accidents happen on the road, even on this side of the Vargas."

The seated figure nodded, satisfaction evident in their tone. "Very good. While that information is not an immediate need, it is still crucial for the long game." A pause, then, "I assume our train saboteurs have been properly rewarded?"

"Yes," the standing man replied, his voice devoid of emotion. "Unmarked graves somewhere. Thankfully, Fire Singers are easy to come by if we need those talents further."

A soft sigh escaped the seated figure. "Hrmm, yes. The train was stopped. The mission failed. An opportunity to rid ourselves of a possible annoyance and another Necromist." They leaned back, shadows playing across their features. "They are resuming the trek to Fugue Academy to drop off their charge?"

"Yes, sir, but I still think Cortez would be—"

"Cortez is no longer viable after Paraíso Verde," the seated figure cut in sharply, turning a page with more force than necessary. "Do we have a report on Torres and her hunt?"

The standing man consulted his notes. "Last contact was in Wolfram. She has verified that the target is heading south and feels confident it will be captured soon." He hesitated, then added, "However, I received a secondary report from her Acolyte. They say she sought council from a Silba. He has petitioned for her removal."

A low chuckle emanated from the shadows behind the desk. "That is why I like Torres. Her ideas are not constrained.

I am curious how she got an answer on the target's location. Our previous tries in doing the same were not as... fruitful."

"I will send an inquiry and have it sent to you as soon as it is vetted and confirmed," the standing figure assured. After a beat, he added, "Also, Valle de Espinas turned up nothing as well. The colony is still unaccounted for."

The seated figure's sigh was heavy with frustration. "Find another one, and this time, I want you to do the questioning, Tomas. We need that information. They cannot stay hidden for long."

Escritor Tomas nodded. "It will be done, sir. You have my word."

As Tomas turned to leave, the seated figure called out once more, their voice barely above a whisper. "And Tomas? Remember, discretion is paramount. We cannot afford another... incident."

The unspoken threat hung in the air, as tangible as the shadows that cloaked the room. Tomas nodded once more, a sharp, precise movement, before slipping out the door and into the night beyond.

Left alone, the seated figure returned to the files, fingers tracing the names that had become so familiar: Emilio Kane, Jalin Cortez, Lyric Wax, Esperanza Boyorquez. Pieces on a board, moving to an unseen hand. A smile, cold and calculating, curved their lips.

The game was far from over. It had only just begun.

~FIN~

THE MESSENGERS GUILD

IN COLLABORATION WITH
THE GUILD OF MECHANISTS

RAILWAY CAR

Carver's Town to Sierra Daily!

Luxury First Class ~Available~

Sleeper Car & Dining Options!

Depart...Carver's Town......7.30 AM
Arrive....Outpost Janus......9.00 AM
Depart...Outpost Janus......9.30 AM
Arrive....Cruce del Águila...10.30 AM
Depart...Cruce del Águila...11.00 AM
Arrive....Deeno Flats.........1.30 PM
Depart...Deeno Flats.........2.00 PM
Arrive....Truitt Lake.........2.45 PM
Depart...Truitt Lake.........3.15 PM
Arrive....Sandoval Pass......4.45 PM
Depart...Sandoval Pass......5.15 PM
Arrive....Carolina...........6.15 PM
Depart...Carolina...........6.45 PM
Arrive....Northern Gate......7.15 PM
Depart...Norther Gate.......7.45 PM
Arrive....Sierra.............8.45 PM

Travel in the Finest of Comfort!

SAFE Affordable Family Travel!

THE UNDEAD

&

YOU

A MESSENGERS GUILD
SURVIVAL GUIDE

A REQUIRED Reading for ALL Membes ofthe
Messengers Guild

Foreward by
F.M. Hinds

Created by
J.J. Hinds

GHOULS - ORIGINS (CONT)

Historically, Ghouls were the foot soldiers of the corpse wars. A necromancer would take a single ghoul and run it through a graveyard. This act would awaken and infect any wayward Ghosts with a hurried sense of madness. This madness would cause them to seek out the nearest body to inhabit and rise again. Those who cannot find a body will follow the herd in hopes of finding a corpse of their own. This is why ghouls are often seen running in packs.

NOTE: A strongly-willed necromancer can control several ghouls to lead packs, but to do so is trying so many employ a magical necromantic focus to augment their power and enforce their will upon many. This is what allowed them to control vast armies with little effort. Destruction of a focus does not ensure survival, but will better your odds!

Strangely, these diseased creatures do not become Spectres if dispatched. Rather, the madness of trying to become part of the world of flesh is too strong, and consumes them into nothingness.

Necromists theorized that fresh blood and

AFTERWORD

This is what you get when you love old train movies, new train movies, and spaghetti Westerns (and zombies).

Honestly, we didn't start out planning to study steam locomotives when we began this book.

In fact, the original story didn't even -involve- a train. What started out as an adventure in the forest, and along a coastline suddenly became ... WHAT IF...

And this is how inspiration happens, my friends.

Thanks to everyone for your continued support. We couldn't do this without you.

We truly hope you enjoyed this little romp as you got to see some of the inner workings of the world of Gothika. We have much more in store for our characters in the future, and hope you continue to follow along.

Who belongs to the voice in the shadows?!

Keep reading to find out!

~Tony & Charm

About Us

SandDancer Publications

C.S. Kading and Tony Fuentes have been working together and crafting stories for over two decades. Partners in both mischief and memories, this dynamic duo combines real-world experience with formal education, to bring you stories to tickle your imagination and delight your hearts.

SandDancer was born out of the pandemic and a need to stay sane. We could not enjoy the company of others beyond the safety of our bubble, so we came to you the only other way we could - through books and storytelling.

<u>*Tony Fuentes*</u>

Literary Titan Gold Award-Winning Author

Tony Fuentes is a California Born Mexican American writer now living in Arizona. Considered a Renaissance Man in Geek's clothing; he is not only an author with a weird imagination, but also a painter, gamer, and part-time occultist. With his writing, he tries to spin both Mexican folklore and sardonic humor into his work. At the same, he tries to inspire the audience to look into the stars and dream further beyond. In short, he strives to give the weird and the wondrous things a place in the world for all to enjoy.

B.S. COMM

Member: IASFA

indie B.R.A.G. Medallion recipient

<u>*C.S. Kading*</u>

Literary Titan Gold Award-Winning Author

A poet, playwright, and lover of the fantastical. Charm has been telling stories since the 3rd grade. She adores studying myths and legends from around the world and has a special love for legends from non-European origins. She is also an educator, specializing in storytelling for educators, as well as a Corporate Storyteller.

MAED

Member: IASFA, IAN

indie B.R.A.G. Medallion recipient

ALSO BY

Check out our works on our website:

SandDancer Publications

https://sanddancer.pub/

The Realm of Gothika

(Dark Fantasy)
Raise the Dead (a love story)
The Heart of Hanwi
Blood Tithe

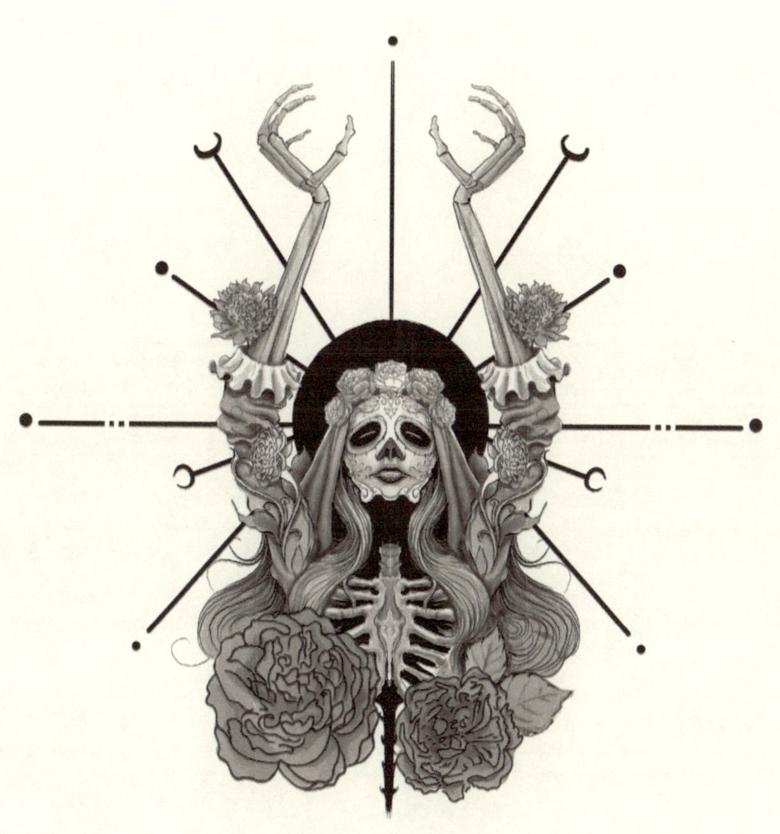